Sherwood Monastery Press Edition
Copyright © 2025
All rights reserved.

Sherwood Monastery Press
An imprint of Sageline Publishing

502 Oella Avenue
Oella, Maryland 21043

sherwoodmonastery@sageline.com

First U.S. Printing: October 2025

ISBN 978-1-931936-08-8

Book design and composition by William Meisheid

Cover art and Illustrations by Anna Marie Meisheid

Small illustrations, maps, and timelines by William Meisheid

The Chronicles of Moses the Lawgiver:

Book One: Beginnings

Book Two: A Warrior's Heart

Book Three: Remembrance (Moses, his sons, and the burning bush)

Planned:

Book Four: Exodus (Crossing the Red Sea)

Book Five: Law and Rebellion (Ten Commandments and a Rebellious People)

Book Six: Passing (Giving of the Pentateuch, death of Moses, and Joshua crossing the Jordan)

Dedication

This book is dedicated to those who encouraged me to continue writing the story of Moses' life, especially Keith Valentine and Pamela Johnson, my primary editor for the first book. I also thank my wife, Anna Marie, for her beautiful illustrations. She is a real gem.

This book has been a true labor of love, as I have come to appreciate the many trials Moses endured in his life. While Moses' time in Egypt before his exile is largely speculative, I have attempted to remain consistent with the demands Egyptian culture would place on him as a Prince of Egypt and a hero of Kadesh. He also struggled to maintain his Hebrew heritage as he navigated the events set in motion in the first two books. The relentless opposition from the priesthood of Amun-Ra continued to threaten his life. The threats were forced underground, but never disappeared.

I hope you find this story both compelling and a plausible exploration of how those forty years in Egypt might have transpired and how they set the stage for what comes next.

Prologue

There is a quiet, enduring power in the Hebrew concept of remembrance, zikaron (זִ.כָּ.רוֹן), that goes beyond the limits of mere memory. This power is profoundly spiritual, uniting the one who remembers with what is remembered, whether an event, a person, a place, or an action, especially those rooted in duty or honor. It can make the past present again, and when it touches the deep things of life, such as love, covenant, and sacrifice, it can transcend time and place, bridging what has long been divided by what seems like an impassable gulf. It can even join new participants to the significance of what it touches. It means, in a way difficult to fully grasp, that you are there, a living participant in what is unfolding, not merely remembering or memorializing something that occurred in the past.

At the core of the Hebrew experience as God's chosen people lie sacred acts of remembrance, each one a thread woven into the tapestry of their covenant, passed from generation to generation like the hallowed fire of God himself: the event of creation, Adam and Eve in the garden, Noah, the ark, and the flood, Abraham and Isaac on Mount Moriah, Jacob wrestling with God and meeting Esau on the plain of Hebron, Joseph before his brothers in the court of Pharaoh, and, at the center of our story, Moses and God's call on his life from his birth onward.

On the last day of the final season Moses would spend in the high summer pasture, as the day approached its midpoint and the sheep rested in whatever shade they could find, he felt his age. He was now eighty, and it felt as though the end of his life was approaching. Yet he could not know that another forty years, more arduous than anything that had gone before, lay ahead of him, years that would transform not just his own destiny but the destiny of nations.

Moses begins to ponder who he is, who he was, what he has done, and what he has failed to do, all of which weigh heavily on him. These are questions that have shadowed him through four decades of Midian sunrises, growing heavier with each passing season. Seated beneath the ancient terebinth tree that anchors their camp, he comes to a moment of final reckoning with the passage of his life.

To help give shape to that sense of closure, he resolves to offer his sons the gift of his remembrance, an inheritance more precious than flocks or gold, more lasting than any earthly possession. It is something so personal that he has never spoken of it, even to their mother. For the first time, he will take Gershom and Eliezer into the previously hidden part of his life. He will take them into the years before Midian, before their mother, before the quiet rhythms of shepherding. He will show them the man he was before he became their father. He will lift the veil on his past and recall for them, and for himself, the man he was: how God used him, and how he failed to live up to the call he believed was his. The call still haunts him as he listens to the bleating of sheep, punctuating the vast silence of the mountain pasture. Each bleat echoes the cries of the Hebrews he left behind, cries that remain unanswered.

Moses hopes that by sharing the hidden events of his early life with his sons, by speaking aloud what he has carried in silence for forty years, he can finally be at peace with who he is as he approaches what he believes to be the end of his life. This is both an act of penance and an act of reconciliation. In saying this aloud, he speaks not just to his sons and to himself, but also to the God he once tried to serve, the God whose Voice he has not heard since his exile from Egypt, whose silence has been as vast as the mountainous expanse before him, and as deep as the valley between the man he believed he was called to be and the old man he has become.

Midday

Using his staff for balance, Moses eased himself down onto the well-worn rug he had placed in the shade of his tent, each movement deliberate and measured despite the protest of his aging joints. The days had begun to cool, but today the midday sun burned hotter than it had in some time, pressing down on his shoulders like an unseen weight, draining what remained of his strength. Even the faint breeze that stirred the edge of his robe carried no relief, only the scent of dust and the dry tang of parched grass. He no longer tolerated the heat the way he used to. Instead of quickening his body with strength, it leached away the little vigor he still possessed.

Moses' knees ached with a dull persistence that had become his constant companion, worse in the mornings when he first rose, but present always, a reminder written in bone and sinew.

There had been a time, he could not remember how many years ago, when he could walk the mountain trails from dawn until dusk without pause, when his legs carried him wherever the flocks wandered without complaint. Now, even the short walk from the sheep to his tent left him aware of every step, every uneven stone beneath his sandals.

He flexed his fingers around the staff, feeling the familiar grooves worn smooth by decades of use. These hands had once wielded a khopesh in battle, had guided a chariot team through the chaos of Kadesh, and signed documents as a Prince of Egypt. Now they were a shepherd's hands, gnarled and weathered, the knuckles swollen some mornings until he could barely grip anything at all. But they still worked. They could still hold a staff, still guide a lamb, still do what needed to be done. For now.

How much longer? The question rose unbidden, as it had with increasing frequency this summer. How many more seasons did he have? One? Two? He suspected the answer was none. At least not in these high pastures. His body had served him well, carried him through eighty years of a life that should have ended in the Nile as an infant or later, in his exile in the desert. But everything ends, even the strongest body. Even his.

His two sons were out gathering the flocks. They would leave the high pasture in the morning and make their way down the mountain to journey to their family compound. They would return to their waiting families in the lowlands of Midian.

For many years Moses had enjoyed the summer pasture and the time he spent with his sons as they grazed their combined flocks on the high plateau. The rhythm of those seasons had become as steady and familiar as breathing. Each year was a measured inhale and exhale of life on the mountain, marked by the same paths trodden by sheep and shepherd alike, the same springs flowing in their appointed places.

But this summer, Moses finally felt his body was telling him his time in the highlands was over. He could no longer journey up the mountain next spring. He was now in his eightieth year, and he felt deep in his bones that he was approaching the end of his time in this land. Not just the mountain pastures but perhaps his life itself. Tonight, they would finish their camp preparations, and tomorrow, after breaking everything down, they would begin driving their flocks down the mountain.

That fateful day, forty years ago, he had emerged from the desert wastelands to the northwest, seeking water at a well near the foot of this very mountain. Jethro had dug that well, and it was one of several water sources located near the trade routes from Egypt that passed through this part of Midian. It was apparent to everyone that the hand of God was upon him. The Almighty had given him all the strength he needed to rescue his future wife and her sisters from the bandits and slavers who attacked them. They sought not only to steal the sheep but, if possible, to seize the young women and sell them into slavery.

During those early years, his wife and father-in-law gently questioned him about his past, but they did not press the issue when he avoided answering. Everyone in Jethro's family could see that Moses was a good man. He was hard-working and, over the years, had lived a respectable and honest life. Besides, when you begin as a hero, people are willing to let pass matters that, if too closely examined, might diminish you as their champion.

In the early years, that silence had been a necessity, a wall built for survival. What could he have said? That he was a fugitive prince with a price on his head? That assassins from the priesthood of Amun-Ra might still be hunting him? That everyone he had ever loved in Egypt was either dead or lost to him forever? No. The silence had been his only shield, and he had worn it like armor.

But as the years accumulated, one upon another, like sand piling in drifts, the silence had changed. It became less about protection and more about distance, a way to keep the past sealed away where it could not reach him, could not drag him back into the grief he had barely escaped with his life. If he did not speak of Egypt, perhaps Egypt would cease to haunt him. If he did not name his losses, perhaps they would not find him in dreams.

It had not worked. The past was always there, pressing against the walls of his silence, looking for cracks. And Zipporah, his faithful wife, had known. She was too wise, too observant, not to see the shadows that crossed his face when certain words were spoken, the way he would sometimes stop mid-sentence and stare at nothing, lost in some memory he would not share. She had asked, in those first years. Gently, never pushing, but the questions had been there. "Who taught you to fight like that, Moses? Where did you learn to read and write? What drove you into the wilderness alone?"

He had turned aside every question with silence or half-truths, and eventually she had stopped asking. But he knew it hurt her, that wall between them. There were parts of himself he had never given her, rooms in his heart she was never permitted to enter. She had accepted it with grace, but acceptance was not the same as understanding.

The thought brought a familiar ache. So many things left unsaid. So many burdens carried alone when they might have been shared. But what he had denied Zipporah, he could no longer deny his sons.

Sipping from the waterskin, he looked up into the clear blue sky. Only a few clouds billowed in the distance, so nothing obscured the bright blue heavens spread out above him.

But the sky held no answers, only endless expanse, the same sky that arched over Egypt, over the Nile, over the palace where he had once walked as a prince. He wondered, not for the first time, if anyone there remembered him. Ramses would be an old man now if he still lived. Would he sometimes think of Moses, his brother in all but blood, the general who had saved his life at Kadesh? Or had Moses become just another name lost to time, a prince who had vanished into exile to die and was spoken of no more?

Perhaps that was fitting. He had saved his people from the edict, given them a chance at life when death had been decreed. But he had not delivered them from bondage. He had not fulfilled the prophecy his father claimed to have seen, the promise that Moses would be their deliverer. Instead, he was here, eighty years old, sitting in the shade of a tent on a mountain far from the Nile, his people still enslaved, their cries still unanswered.

He had done what he could. Surely that counted for something. He had tried to serve the Most High, had listened when he could hear the Voice, and had acted as he believed he was called to act. But the great work his father had foreseen never came to pass. The failure sat heavily in his chest, an old weight he had carried so long it had become part of him.

"Is it finished?" he asked, the words carrying more resignation than an actual question to the God of His Fathers. His voice was low, almost lost in the stillness, as if he feared the silence that would follow, something he already knew too well. He waited, but the vast stillness remained as mute as it had been for the last forty years. The great invisible Creator, whom his people had worshipped since the days when his ancestor Abraham had left Ur of the Chaldeans, no longer answered him. Moses had heard His counsel many times over the early years, such as when his real mother, the Hebrew who had borne him and nursed him in secret, left this life; Nari lay dying from the cart accident in Perunifer; during the anguish when his Egyptian wife and daughters died; and when his anger mastered him and he accidentally killed the Egyptian overseer.

He had felt the assurances and rebukes of the divine presence that once guided his steps and corrected his path. But the Most High had gone silent. He heard nothing when he wandered through the wilderness after surviving the final effort of the priesthood of Amun-Ra to kill him, when he was out of water and looking into the face of death. Moses had not given up seeking His counsel. During his early years in Midian, he continued to pray earnestly, asking the Creator of All Things what he was supposed to do. He wondered whether there was still some purpose to the life he had salvaged from the ruins of his time in Egypt. Even though he never stopped praying, the Nameless One remained silent. Despite that, each day he hoped to hear something and that the silence would end.

Moses looked at his hands, rough and calloused from the years of hard labor, the hands that had both taken life and held it when new, fresh from the womb of his wife, Zipporah. Was their work finished? Could he accept that his end had finally come? His heart waited, but quiet was his only answer. His question hung in the stillness, alone as it had all the times before.

As he sat there, something within him shifted. The shift felt as if he crossed a great chasm. Spreading out his hands to the emptiness above him, he said in resignation, "It is enough."

A sudden sense of peace filled him. It was not the peace of resignation but something else, something alive. Cool and certain, like water poured over parched earth. It ran down his arms, settled like a mantle across his shoulders, and flowed through his chest into his legs, loosening a tension he had not realized he carried until that moment. His heart gave a sudden, uneven beat, and he drew in a slow breath, tasting God's presence in the dry air as though for the first time in years. Somewhere in the distance, a sheep bleated, the sound thin against the vast quiet.

Forty years of silence and now, finally, he felt that God had answered his petition by acknowledging this final offering of himself.

His hands began to shake. Moses stared at them as they trembled against the worn wood of his staff, and something caught in his throat, not quite a sob, but close. Forty years. Forty years of prayers that fell into silence like stones down a well, never striking bottom, never echoing back. He had prayed in the wilderness when he was dying of thirst, his lips dry and cracked. He had prayed when Zipporah labored with their first son, terrified he would lose her as he had lost his first wife, but no, he would not think of that now. He had prayed at dawn and at dusk, in joy and in desperation, and the heavens had remained as unmoved as the mountain's stone beneath him.

Until now.

That acceptance manifested as a chill that ran down his back and spine, causing an involuntary shiver despite the heat of the day. He tried to speak, but he could not. His breath came shallow and quick. When was the last time he had felt this? The night before his exile, when Miriam and Nazim had come to tell him of the cache in the desert. It was his only hope of survival. No, he could not remember the last time. The Most High's last presence was still clouded in his mind. It was so many years ago. One thing he was sure of: for the last forty years in Midian, heaven had been silent. Though he never gave up, though he still called on the Most High, only silence had answered him.

But this, this was different. This was not rebuke or silence or the weight of divine sorrow. This was acknowledgment. This was the touch of the One who had pulled him from the Nile, who had turned aside the vipers, who had saved him from the Hittite ambush, and Ramses through his hand at Kadesh. The God who had not spoken to him for the last forty years but who had, in this moment, chosen to break that silence.

As the sensation overwhelmed him, Moses let out a low groan and thanked the Nameless One, his voice cracking on the words. His eyes burned, but he did not weep. He had learned long ago that

7

some things went too deep for tears. Instead, he sat there with his shaking hands, his breath uneven and halting, feeling for the first time in all his years in Midian that he was not alone on this mountain. That perhaps he had never been alone, even when the silence was so vast it seemed to have no end.

It was the first time since fleeing Egypt that he had felt anything from the One who had guided so many of his earlier years. And in that moment, Moses understood with absolute clarity what he must do. The silence within himself, the silence he had kept about his past, could no longer hold. If God had broken His silence, then Moses must break his own.

Gershom and Eliezer

"Eliezer, I think we've found them all. Even that old ram that always wanders toward the eastern ravine."

"Good. For once, we won't be scouring the rocks and scrub bushes for strays late into the evening. It's still early. Let's get back to camp and Father."

"He's looking older this year," Gershom said, eyes lingering on the distant ridge where their tent stood in a patch of shade beneath the hot sun. "His shoulders have begun to curve forward, as if carrying invisible burdens. This may be his last summer on the mountain. The way he leans on his staff now, even when the path lies level beneath his feet..."

"I think you're right," Eliezer replied. "Maybe we can get him to talk with us tonight, tell us more about himself. Mother has tried for years, but even she couldn't breach that wall. Even Grandfather Jethro gave up asking years ago. Father says nothing about before he came to Midian. He always turns aside when those days are mentioned, as if remembering costs him something. He remains private about everything before he met our mother."

"I agree. That has always been one of the most frustrating things about him. We know the man but not his making. He's been here forty years, yet remains silent about the time before. All these years in Midian, and still he keeps his past locked away. What do you think he was?" Gershom asked, his voice dropping lower, though no one else was near to hear. "Before he came here, I mean. A soldier? He moves like one sometimes, even now."

Eliezer considered this as they walked. "More than a soldier. Soldiers don't read and write the way he does. I've seen the marks he makes when he tallies the flocks; they're like nothing anyone else in Midian writes. And the way he speaks sometimes, choosing his words like a scribe…"

"A scribe who fights like a warrior," Gershom mused. "Mother said he fought off seven men the day they met. Seven. He didn't just drive them off. He broke a wrist and an arm and knocked two unconscious. He was alone, on foot, and probably half-dead from the desert. What kind of man does that?"

"The kind who's well-trained but running from something," Eliezer said quietly. "Or someone."

They urged the last of the wayward sheep toward the main herd, the animals' hooves kicking up light dust that clung in delicate layers to their sandals and robes, dulling the colors of the cloth. The heat shimmered above the pale stones, and each step seemed to draw more sweat from their brows. The faint clink of bells around a few ewes' necks kept time with their slow progress toward camp, a sound as familiar as their own breathing after all these years. Ahead lay the promise of shade, where the air would be cooler, like a blessing calling to them, promising relief. A long drink from the hanging water bag, kept cool in the shade of the trees around the tent, would be another welcome boon. Their water pouches had run out hours earlier, leaving only the memory of moisture on dry lips. The thought of that first mouthful and a splash on the neck made the last stretch seem shorter.

Preparing To Leave

Moses heard the bells of the approaching strays before he saw Gershom and Eliezer, sweat darkening their headcloths, driving the last of the stragglers toward the main herd.

"Good," he murmured to himself—a habit formed from forty years of solitary shepherding. "They won't be out late into the evening searching for any laggards."

The fading notes of the bells lingered in his ears as he thought about the afternoon's divine touch, that chill that had broken God's long silence, carrying with it both relief and a shadow of what the telling might awaken. That sense of the Most High's return stirred the knowledge of a deeper silence, the one he had kept with his sons, and with all of Midian, about his life before that day at Jethro's well, the day that changed everything.

"It is time," he said, the words settling on the air like something long overdue. His sons needed to know who their father truly was. The thought settled in him with the same certainty as the sun's slow descent behind the ridges, an ending that carried within it the seeds of a new beginning. He drew a long breath, tasting the dry, sunbaked air, and felt the decision take root like something planted deep within him. He would not let the last season pass without his story being told. He would take them on a journey into the forty years he had lived in Egypt, years he had buried so deep that even speaking of them felt like exhuming the dead. He was drawing them into his remembrance of the years that had shaped him into the man who had rescued their mother and her sisters from near disaster.

Moses looked up as his sons approached the hanging water bag. Parched, they drank deeply of the cool water, then splashed it over their heads and necks, the droplets tracing rivulets through the dust on their skin, cooling the day's heat just as truth would cool the long parching of his silence.

Still dripping from the cool water, the two brothers crossed to their father, each taking a camp stool and seating himself on either side of him.

"So, you have finished finding the strays?" Moses asked.

"Yes," Gershom answered. "For once, we will have a quiet evening before our departure."

"That will help," Moses said, his eyes resting on each of his sons in turn, as if weighing their possible responses. "There are things I want to speak with you about."

Both of his sons felt their hearts skip a beat; Gershom shifted slightly on his stool, the wood creaking in the sudden stillness, while Eliezer quietly kept his hands clasped, each giving their father the space to move at his own pace.

"This is my last summer on the mountain." He let the words settle before adding, "My body can no longer support the demands of coming to the high pastures."

"Are you sure?" Eliezer asked, concern showing in his voice.

"I am," Moses said firmly. "We all knew this day would come, and my body tells me it has arrived." He held up his hand before they could respond. "Besides, there is something more important I must do."

Both sons looked at him, questions obvious on their faces, but underneath, a quiet hope began to rise.

"I have been your father for a long time, and you are grown men with your own families. But you know little about me beyond how I rescued your mother and her sisters that day long ago. You also know that I have been a shepherd for your grandfather's and our flocks ever since. The man I was before that moment at the well remains hidden from you."

Gershom and Eliezer felt the fragile hope that had stirred within them grow into excited anticipation, tempered by the fear that their father might yet turn aside from this revelation, as he had so many times before.

"I have decided to break the silence about my earlier life, to bring you into the remembrance of the things that shaped me into the man you have known all your life. You deserve to know who your father was before I came to Midian."

For a long moment, neither son could speak. Gershom and Eliezer looked at each other, then back at their father, as if needing confirmation that they had heard correctly. Their whole life, they had waited. All those years of hints and silences and carefully avoided questions. And now, simply, he was offering what they had long since stopped hoping to receive.

Gershom raised his hand and, with thankfulness in his voice, said, "This has been our hope for some time."

Eliezer nodded his agreement and added, "We thank the God of Our Fathers for this gift; it has long been the desire of our hearts."

"Then let us eat," Moses said. "We have a long night before us."

The two sons rose at once, moving to their packs with the practiced efficiency of men who had made meals in this camp a hundred times before. Gershom gathered dates and dried meat while Eliezer prepared rounds of fried flatbread. They worked in silence, glancing occasionally at their father, who sat watching them with an expression they couldn't quite read—something between resolve and sorrow.

Neither wanted to break the spell with unnecessary words. Whatever was coming, whatever their father was about to reveal, it had waited forty years. It could wait a few minutes more.

Moses Begins Remembering His Past

The meal was finished. After filling their waterskins, they settled into their seats, the afternoon air slowly cooling in the shade. Though anticipation burned within them, his sons remained silent, understanding that forty years of silence could not be rushed in its breaking. They exchanged glances, each waiting for the other to speak, but both held back, realizing their father's silence had to break on its own.

"This will not be easy for me," Moses began. "I have kept these memories locked away for forty years. Much of what I will tell you is hard to remember, and harder still to speak aloud, for it touches wounds long buried. So, you must be patient as I take you on this journey."

Eliezer held up his hand, and his father nodded in response. "May we ask questions to help us understand the whole of it?" he asked carefully.

"Of course. I want you to know who I was, because that will help explain some of what you already know about me. I will try my best to bring you fully into my life in Egypt. Yes, I spent the first forty years of my life along the Nile, as a Prince of the Two Lands, adopted into the household of Pharaoh."

Gershom drew in a sharp breath, his eyes widening. "A Prince of Egypt!" he blurted out, half in disbelief, half in wonder. His words tumbled out before he could master them, and the impossibility of it left both brothers stunned, staring at their father as if seeing him for the first time.

"Yes. It is true. I was a Prince of Egypt." He let their surprise settle, finally becoming a quiet awe between them. "It is a remembrance that I will not easily share. It is filled with many painful memories. To begin, you should know that my life in Egypt, at least at the beginning, was ordered by a special person in the household of my adopted mother, Asati, a royal princess and the sister of Pharaoh Seti, the father of Ramses II. Her name was Nari. She was Asati's chief maidservant, and to her I owe the understanding of my Hebrew beginnings and that of the God of Our Fathers.

"In my early years, I drew close to the Most High, both guided and empowered by His hand. But in the middle years of my life in the Two Lands, I drifted from that closeness. The concerns of daily life, my family, and my place in Pharaoh's court, overshadowed His presence. Pride in my abilities and accomplishments began to govern my choices, blinding me to the warnings that now seem so clear. In God's own time, my arrogance was shattered by tragedy, and at the end of my time in Egypt, when I had just begun to rekindle my dependence on the Most High, I was exiled from the land of my birth. I was forced to make a perilous journey to Midian, where I became the man you have known all of your life."

"Father, this is beyond anything we ever imagined about you," Eliezer said. "So many questions fill my mind. It is difficult to make sense of what you are saying."

14

"I understand," Moses replied, his weathered hands gripping his staff as if drawing strength from its familiar wood. "It is no less difficult for me to make sense of it all. But I felt the touch of our God for the first time in almost forty years this morning, and I know it is His will that this remembrance be shared with you both. Memories are flooding back to me, some triumphant and others carrying unbearable pain. Each had its part in making me who I am. We do not need to rush. The night is long, and we have all of it to share what God deems important for you to know. Of this, at least, I am certain, and in that certainty lies the courage to begin."

He had their full attention as he began bringing them into the story of his life in Egypt.

"My Hebrew parents lived across the river on the eastern outskirts of Memphis. Our family was from the tribe of Levi, which was considered the least of the Hebrew tribes by their brethren.

"The priests of Amun-Ra blamed the descendants of Joseph for the religious turmoil the Two Lands had endured since an earlier pharaoh, the Pharaoh Who is Not Named, had overthrown the traditional gods of Egypt. He had elevated a new singular deity, whom he called Aten, to the status of the supreme god of the land. The priests of Amun-Ra said that these foreign usurpers, we Hebrews, had poisoned their land with the heresy of a single all-powerful god, seeing in our faith an echo of the chaos that had nearly destroyed Egypt. To curry their favor for his ascension to Pharaoh, Ramses I reissued an earlier ineffective edict against the newborn Hebrew sons. As the first pharaoh of a new dynasty, he needed to gain the support of the powerful priesthoods of Egypt, especially that of Amun-Ra, who continued to blame the children of Abraham for their religious turmoil.

"At my father's insistence, because he had prophetic dreams

15

foretelling that I would deliver the sons of Abraham from the edict and from bondage, my parents hid my birth. For three months, they succeeded without any difficulty. But as I grew over the next three months, keeping the secret became impossible. Discovery meant death, being thrown to the crocodiles at the temple of Sobek, to continue the systematic purge of our presence from the land. Egypt, however, depended on our labor, and by killing all newborn males, they would ensure we slowly vanished as a people, giving the Two Lands time to adjust as we diminished. It was a calculated destruction of a people that prevented them from losing their workforce all at once, which could devastate their economy."

Moses paused to let the seriousness of the situation sink in.

"Yet my mother had one hope for me. She learned that Egyptian parents often put unwanted children adrift in small boats on the Nile, while childless mothers would search the river, hoping to find a gift from their gods. This had become common practice in Egypt, as there were severe penalties for killing unwanted children. Instead, it placed the child's fate in the hands of the gods of Egypt, something no one could argue with.

"My mother eventually convinced my father that it was my only hope. She wove a beautiful lidded basket from river rushes, which my father, a carpenter at Pharaoh's shipyard, waterproofed with pitch so it would not sink."

Moses, his eyes distant, as if seeing through the years, continued, "My mother, whose name was Jochebed, told me, years later, about that morning.

"She and Miriam left in darkness, my sister carrying me, and my mother carrying the basket and following behind. The sky was just beginning to lighten in the east when they reached the river's edge at the southern boundary of Asati's estate. They had changed their original path to the river because of a falling star that had struck the west bank of the river near the great lock controlling the water that flowed through the Memphis canals.

"As they stepped into the river to release me, the Nile's flow was gentle, and the water was dark as bronze in the pre-dawn light.

"My mother held me one last time. She kissed my forehead and whispered a prayer over me, commending me to the God of Abraham, Isaac, and Jacob. Then she placed me in the basket and closed the lid. Miriam later told me that her hands were shaking so badly she could barely secure the cover.

"They waded into the shallows. The water was cold. My mother set the basket gently on the current, but it immediately caught in the reeds hugging the bank a short distance downstream. Her heart was torn. She had to hurry back before anyone from the village noticed her absence, but my basket was stuck in the rushes. So, she did the only thing she could. She gathered an armload of reeds for weaving—her excuse if questioned—and left my sister, Miriam, hiding along the embankment to watch over me.

"My mother walked away without looking back. Miriam said she could hear her weeping as she left."

Moses' voice had grown quiet. Neither of his sons moved.

"That morning, three significant events occurred that set the stage for my deliverance. Without all of them, my survival would have been unlikely. The first was personal. Princess Asati, the sister of the Pharaoh, whose estate stood on the east bank of the Nile, opposite Memphis to the west, had a prophetic dream that drove her to the river early that morning. She went to the Nile just north of where my mother had released my basket. Named for Satis, the goddess of the First Cataract, sender of the yearly inundation and

17

the giver of fertility, she believed she had become a stain upon the goddess's name. After five years of marriage, she remained barren—a cruel irony that continually haunted her. Her husband was high-born and, under the Pharaoh, currently served as a chariot commander at the fortress of Buhan, far to the south, near the Second Cataract of the Nile. Because of his wife's barrenness, he had no heir.

"During that night, the princess had a strange vision in which she saw a Hebrew baby boy being given to her from the sacred waters. Unable to free herself from the implications of the vision, she called her chief maidservant, Nari, to rouse the servants for a pre-dawn journey to the Nile. She wanted to take a sacred bath in the Nile and make offerings to the gods to inquire about the meaning of her upsetting vision.

"The second and greatest event shook all of Memphis and eventually the whole of Egypt. A falling star struck the river in the predawn hours against the western bank of the Nile, close to the great locks that controlled the flow of water through the city. Those who saw it said the sky split open with light brighter than day, and the sound when it struck the water shook the very stones of the city. The locks sustained minor damage but remained intact. Water cast up by the strike surged through Memphis's canals, flooding some of the temples close to the city walls. All soon hailed it as a messenger of the gods. For me, its timing was too precise to be a coincidence. It would prove to be the key to unlock the events of the day.

"The third event had far-reaching consequences, extending far beyond that day and shaping not just that morning but also the course of Egypt's future. During the night, both Pharaoh Seti and his wife, Queen Tuya, dreamed of a young Hebrew saving their only remaining son, Ramses, from an unexpected attack and possible death. As the events of the day unfolded, these dreams proved pivotal in shaping Seti's decisions."

Moses paused and asked, "Are you following everything so far?"

Both sons agreed, the intensity in their eyes revealing their struggle to grasp the weight of the revelation. This was only the beginning of the remembrance, and it already went way beyond anything they had expected.

They both took a deep breath, and Eliezer said, "This is almost unbelievable, and if we heard this from anyone else, we would have dismissed it as the ravings of someone gone mad. But you, father, are an honorable man whose word has always been his bond. We must accept this remembrance and all you have yet to tell us as the truth of your life."

Moses looked squarely at both his sons, "Everything you experience with me tonight will be as true as I remember it. I want you to know who I was and not just who I am. You will understand why I am the man you have known when you walk with me through those forty years."

"Thank you, father," Gershom said. "Please don't stop."

Moses took a moment to gather his thoughts before continuing. "As I have looked back on these events over the years, I have seen the hand of the Most High in countless ways in the details of my life: guiding, directing, and bringing about His will.

"A short time after my mother had left, as the sun began to breach the horizon, Princess Asati's group arrived at the water's edge. They quickly prepared for her sacred bath and her petition to the gods for the meaning of her dream. Miriam saw them coming—the servants moving ahead to clear the bank, the princess and her maidservant following, their linen robes catching the first light. She recognized the quality of the fabric, the bearing of the women. This was royalty.

"Miriam tried to reach my basket, but there were too many of them and they arrived too quickly. She could only sink deeper into her hiding place in the rushes and pray. She told me later that her heart was pounding so hard she was certain they would hear it.

"The princess entered the water for her ritual bath while Nari stood watch on the bank. After Asati's purification, she waded upstream and cast specially crafted idols into the current, her petitions to the gods. The golden figures disappeared beneath the surface of the river.

"Then one of the servants noticed my basket wedged in the reeds. 'My lady,' she called. 'There is something in the water.'

"Asati turned. For a moment, she simply stared at the basket, this woven thing caught in the rushes. The rising sun was behind her, light spilling across the water. She looked at Nari, then back at the basket.

"Intrigued, the princess sent one of her servants and two guards to fetch it. When they lifted the basket from the reeds, water streamed from its woven sides. They brought it back and placed it at Asati's feet. The princess tried to open the lid, but it resisted her efforts. Frustrated, she called for Nari's help. Nari produced a heavy comb and worked to loosen the lid. When it began to give, Asati stopped her. She wanted to remove it herself. As she grabbed the lid and pulled, it came off suddenly, and she fell backward, the lid in her hands.

"At that moment, I let out a sharp cry. Nari said later that the princess's breath had caught in her throat. She looked in the basket, and there I was, my hands reaching up toward her. Her dream. The sacred waters. Was this the gift from the gods, appearing at dawn exactly as she had seen it in her vision?

"Every servant froze.

"Nari moved closer, peering into the basket. 'A child,' Nari said quietly.

"Another of the servants who looked inside added, 'A Hebrew child,' and there was fear in her voice. The edict. A Hebrew boy meant death, and even being Pharaoh's sister could not save him.

"Nari told me years later that as Asati looked down at me, her face transformed the moment she met my eyes, and she saw my outstretched hands. All the grief of five barren years, all the shame before her husband's family, all the prayers at a hundred temple altars; everything broke open as she looked at the infant reaching toward her. An infant who had appeared in the sacred waters exactly as her dream had promised.

"Asati whispered just loud enough for Nari to hear, 'The gods have answered.' She reached down and lifted me from the basket, holding me against her wet linen. My crying stopped. She looked at Nari, then at the servants. 'This child was given to me by a prophetic vision from the gods. I will keep him.'

"After a brief, intense conversation with Nari about the implications and the edict, Asati, as she often did, dug in her heels. I was a gift from the gods, and she would keep me, Hebrew or not. The gods had given me to her. The gods would make it work. She named me Moses, which means 'Son of the River,' because the gods had delivered me to her from the Nile itself.

"Then she spotted my sister, who rushed forward and fell at her feet. She explained that the falling star and the chance to see a princess were the reasons she came forward. Both Nari and I later believed that it was the will of the Most High that her story was accepted. When I began crying, that prevented any questions for the time being, and Nari noted that I probably needed to be fed. Miriam suggested a Hebrew nursemaid, as many Hebrew women had milk but no children, thanks to the edict.

"Asati saw that as an answer to prayer and sent my sister, Nari, and me, along with two guards, to find a nursemaid. As we left, she returned home to prepare for the Temple of Satis, where she would inquire of the priests about her vision and my appearance. She believed both were answers to prayer and wanted their confirmation.

"My sister seized the opportunity to enlist our mother as my nursemaid, and from that day forward, for the next two years, Jochebed, my real mother, was with me in the household of the princess. This was just the beginning of the converging events that would drive the day to its climax: the rescinding of the edict.

"At this point, numerous events were unfolding simultaneously throughout the entire city of Memphis. Like the movement of pieces on a hounds and jackals board by a gifted player, each seemed random yet all converged toward a single divine purpose. Seti and his son inspected the great lock where the star had struck. They returned and called for all of the priesthoods in Memphis to send their chief priests and seer priests to a special meeting at the court of Pharaoh to ascertain its meaning.

"Asati sent servants to gather the necessities for a nursery that had, until then, remained unused. The princess, meanwhile, went to the Temple of Satis and told the Chief Priest Sostris…"

Moses paused and said, "There will be many names you may not remember, but focus on what they do, and it will help you keep things straight."

Both his sons nodded.

"She told Sostris about her vision and finding me after her sacred bath and offerings. In addition, two hawks, said to be representatives of Amun-Ra, had circled her bath and were now perched atop the temple gates. Then, while participating in a special ritual set up for her, Princess Asati had another vision and collapsed during the ceremony. This convinced the priests of Satis that the gods were intimately involved in what was happening around her.

"At the Temple of Amun-Ra in Memphis, Nephura, the Chief Priest who would become my most fearsome enemy, dispatched spies throughout the city to gather information on what was happening. Within his temple that morning, an omen both divine and terrible shook the foundations of his authority. When the priests opened the Naos, the god's innermost sanctuary, to perform the dawn purification, a vulture—the sacred symbol of Satis—burst from the shrine and defiled everything in sight, including Nephura himself, spattering his white robes with excrement before the assembled priests. At Nephura's demand, they attempted to conceal the incident, but news of it spread throughout the city.

"An official summons was dispatched to all the temples in the city, and soon all the priesthoods were gathering at the palace to help Pharaoh interpret the morning's cascade of divine signs, including Asati's discovery of me during her trip to the Nile. Word of that had spread everywhere, like fire through dry grass.

"Nephura, whose heart held only darkness, had a plan. He sent assassins, posing as deliverymen, to deliver and assemble a cradle for the nursery being prepared for my arrival. They concealed vipers in the mattress, hoping to eliminate what he saw as the

Hebrew threat before it could complicate matters. Nephura was cunning, and he could see the converging events: the princess finding me, the falling star, the temple defilement, and the royal dreams, all pointing toward a possible rescinding of the edict if left unchecked. That was something he could never allow to happen, and my removal would be the easiest solution.

"I was saved from assassination by divine intervention. My mother, Jochebed, was carrying me into the new nursery, humming one of the Hebrew songs she used to soothe me. The cradle had been delivered and set up early that afternoon. It was beautiful work. A unique design, carved of Syrian oak, which swung from a top bar on two sets of legs that allowed the cradle to swing under it. Jochebed put me on the changing table and told Nari she needed to get something to eat. Nursing demands had to be met. Nari agreed.

"As she turned to go to the kitchen, Jochebed suddenly felt faint, and her balance slipped away. She reached out for anything to catch herself. Her hand found the side rail of the hanging cradle. It immediately spun away from her hand and turned upside down, sending the covers and mattress tumbling out and sliding across the floor toward the bed. With her support gone, Jochebed fell to the floor, striking first her forearm and then her forehead on the tile. Two vipers spilled onto the floor.

"The ear-splitting shriek was out of Nari's lips before she realized it. Clutching Moses in her left arm, she used her right hand to grab the jars of oil and perfume from the shelves and began hurling them at the approaching snakes, the scream echoing through the house and out the high windows.

"Semri, the estate's chief guard, burst through the doorway, his khopesh already drawn. He didn't hesitate, didn't ask questions. The blade flashed once, twice—clean strikes that severed each serpent. Then he was past their still twitching bodies and through the door, shouting for the guards.

"The assassins who had delivered the cradle were fleeing toward the river. Semri and his close friend Nazim caught the first one on the road along the riverbank. The man turned to fight, but Semri took a spear from Nazim and struck him in the shoulder. The assassin fell off the path and down the river embankment. The second assassin was well ahead and fled across the river. Semri left Nazim behind to deal with the first man and pursued the second assassin. He took control of a small riverboat and had them row him across the river. He caught up to the second man on the far embankment, where the assassin tried to fight. The man drew a blade, but Semri was too well-trained. His khopesh took the assassin's hand in one strike. With his blood dripping in the water, the man was suddenly taken under by a crocodile before Semri could do anything.

"After losing the assassin who crossed the river, Semri returned to Nazim and the wounded assassin he was guarding. However, before they could question him, the man took poison and died laughing at them. While Semri had averted Nephura's plot, he had nothing to tie the attempt directly to Amun-Ra's High Priest in Memphis.

"Back at court, as the royal council's debate progressed, the arguments eventually turned to Ma'at, the goddess whose deep requirements for justice undergird all of Egypt. Her demands cut across the actions of Pharaoh and the Egyptian gods. The assembled priests began questioning whether the edict violated the goddess's dictates. When Nephura learned that his plan had failed and then witnessed how the signs from the various gods appeared to align against his position, he was forced to accept the inevitable.

He could not save the edict. Despite this shift, one final thing prevented an easy resolution to the quandary: an earlier prophecy given at the time of Ramses I's ascension to the throne had persuaded even the reluctant to accept the edict. It prophesied that a newborn Hebrew male would not be an ordinary man but someone who would excel above all others in glory and virtue. His name, which was not part of the prophecy, would be remembered throughout the ages, and he would bring Egypt low while raising up his own people."

"Was that about you, father?" Eliezer asked.

"I don't know. Some thought it might be. But after much debate and a final push by Nephura, the council decided the safest course was to raise me in the household of Pharaoh, as his sister's adopted son and a Prince of Egypt. They believed they could use that to mold me into someone more Egyptian than Hebrew. It worked—for a while. While the Egyptian training took root more deeply than they knew, my Hebrew blood and the designs of the Most High ran even deeper still, currents no human design could redirect. The important thing was that the edict was rescinded, and when I became a Prince of Egypt, it set my path for what lay ahead."

Moses watched as what he had revealed began to take hold in his sons' understanding. "I was a Prince of Egypt..." He had not thought about his initial destiny in a very long time.

"Now listen carefully," he continued. "Three people in my adoptive household shaped both my upbringing and survival in those early years: my adoptive mother, Princess Asati, her chief nursemaid, Nari, and the man who trained me as a warrior and protected me from harm until his death, Semri. He was the head of the guard of her estate, and thankfully, he married my adoptive mother within a

26

year after the death of her first husband. Others, such as my
Hebrew sister, Miriam, would later assist me in important ways,
but in the beginning, those three shaped who I would become."

Moses paused, then asked his sons, "Do you have any questions so
far?"

Eliezer leaned forward and said, "Do you have any memories of
those early years, or is this all from what you were later told?"

"My earliest true memory is of reaching for Nari's face when I was
perhaps three years old. I will always remember seeing the
devotion in her eyes. But most of the first five years comes from
what Nari and my adoptive mother told me. Nari kept a careful
account of those early days, believing even then that they held
significance. She would say, 'Moses, you must know where the river
brought you from, not just where it delivered you to.' Years later,
just before my marriage, which Ramses arranged, my Hebrew
sister, Miriam, came to work as a servant at the great estate. Nari
arranged this to help her and my mother as things grew difficult
for them in the years after my father's death."

Moses hesitated when he mentioned his father, but gathered
himself and continued.

"My sister worked at the estate for over ten inundations. That she
was my sister remained a secret to everyone but Nari and me until
the very end. Her presence is why, years later, I eventually met my
Hebrew mother, Jochebed, before she died. When I finally met her,
at Miriam's insistence, she was in declining health, so I was only
with her for one short afternoon. That visit, done quietly to avoid
questions, gave my mother the opportunity to fill in what
happened before my adoption, share memories of my father, her
remembrances from the two years she served as my nursemaid,
and stories of her many prayerful intercessions for me over the

27

years, especially during the battle at Kadesh. I believe that was Nari's ultimate intent in bringing Miriam to the estate—she believed Miriam would convince me to meet my true mother before it was too late. I will say more about both my father and mother later."

"It sounds like Nari knew all your family secrets," Eliezer noted.

"Yes, she did. Nari was one of the most important people in my early life. She saw things others missed and guided me in my understanding of the Most High, a narrow line she carefully walked with me. It became our secret as she helped me understand the true God of creation.

"She died from a cart accident at the Perunifer marketplace, but that is another part of my story. It is a memory that still evokes my anger against the plots of those priests of Amun-Ra who hounded me my whole life in Egypt."

"Thank the Most High that you lived, saved our mother, and became our father," Eliezer added.

"Yes," Gershom added with a thankful sigh, "or we would not be here."

"The Most High has been merciful," Moses said.

"Where did you live after you grew up?" Gershom asked.

"I always lived on my adopted mother's great estate. Later, with Semri's assistance, we extended the walls of the main compound and built a separate house for my future family and me."

Both sons noticed that whenever he mentioned his family, a shadow crossed his features, a grief that settled in the lines around his eyes. They did not press him on that, knowing they would learn the reason eventually.

"When I was five, two things happened that began to shape who I became. I spent every morning at Temple School, where I began to learn what it meant to be an Egyptian prince. For almost ten years, I studied alongside other sons of Egyptian nobles, learning what every highborn son of the Two Lands was expected to know. These subjects included religion, court expectations, protocol, mathematics, and several languages. I already knew both Egyptian and Hebrew, but I also learned Hittite and, most importantly, Akkadian, the language of diplomacy and commerce. Now I speak the language of Midian, which is close to Hebrew in many ways.

"This is also the time that Semri began my training as a warrior. It helped that I was always taller and stronger than the other boys my age. Every afternoon for at least four hours, physical demands replaced the morning's learning. This included combat techniques, weapons mastery, and the endurance a warrior would need to survive whatever he faced. I was taught not just by my stepfather but also by select men-at-arms who had come with him to serve the great estate, each among the best at their specific skills."

Moses sat quietly for several minutes, letting everything he had said work its way through his sons' understanding and the burden it brought to them. It was going to be a long night, and he needed to give his sons time for their hearts to respond to what he was showing them.

Temple School

"Tell us about Temple School. What was that like?" Eliezer asked.

"It started when I was five. School began around eight every morning and went for four hours."

Moses saw the question forming and answered before Eliezer could ask. "Time was important throughout Egypt, and water clocks marked the hours in every temple, palace, and many homes. The priests had mapped the changing times of sunrise and sunset over many years and had worked out the adjustments for each day of the year, noting when the sun first touched and then left the horizon. That meant the priests kept time across all of the temples of the Two Lands within a few minutes of each other. They wanted their priestly activities, including morning offerings, noon purifications, and evening incantations, to be performed at the same time in all their temples. They believed it increased the power of their ceremonies.

"The timing was remarkable," Moses continued, settling back as memories continued to surface. "Each morning, we would hear the bronze gong sound three times from the Temple School's highest tower. That was our call to class."

Eliezer leaned forward. "How many students were there?"

"Perhaps thirty in my group, though the Temple School had several levels. We were sons of nobility, high priests, and military commanders. A few were foreign princes, Nubians, Libyans, even a Syrian or two, sent to learn Egyptian ways." Moses paused, remembering faces he hadn't thought of in many decades. "The priests divided us by ability rather than age. A brilliant student of ten years might study alongside someone less accomplished of fifteen."

"What did you learn first?" Eliezer continued.

"Writing." Moses traced invisible hieroglyphs in the air. "The priests said that without writing, we were no better than beasts. We spent months just learning to hold the reed properly, to mix ink from soot and gum, to prepare papyrus. Our fingers would cramp and ache. One old priest, I don't remember his name, would strike our knuckles with a switch if our characters weren't perfectly formed."

Moses paused, rubbing his knuckles as if they still remembered the sting. "I was seven when I first earned the old priest's approval. He had ordered us to copy a hymn to Thoth, with forty-two lines; each character had to be precisely formed. I worked for three hours straight, barely breathing, terrified of a mistake that would mean starting over. When I finally set down my reed, my hand began shaking so badly I couldn't form another character.

"The old priest took it, held it to the light, and examined every line. The other boys had stopped working to watch. Finally, he nodded once. Just once. 'Acceptable,' he said. That single word felt like victory."

"Harsh teachers," Gershom observed.

"They believed that discipline shaped the mind as a potter shapes his clay. 'The ear of a boy is on his back,' they would say. 'He listens better when he is beaten.'" Moses shook his head. "Though I noticed they were gentler with those of us from the palace. Royal preference, perhaps."

"But surely there was more than just writing?" Eliezer asked.

"Oh yes. Mathematics came next. We studied geometry for building, arithmetic for trade, and taxation. We memorized the flooding patterns of the Nile over the past hundred years. Geography was important, both of the Two Lands and the nations beyond. We learned to track the movements of stars and studied the properties of stones and metals. We knew which could bear weight, which could hold an edge, which turned what color in the fire." Moses counted on his fingers. "Also, medicine, law, debating, and poetry. And always...always, the histories and genealogies of their gods."

Gershom frowned. "Did you believe in their gods?"

Moses was quiet for a moment. "I was taught to. We spent hours learning their stories, feast days, and sacred numbers. Which god governed which hour of the day, which demon god might cause which illness. The priests taught that maintaining Ma'at—the demands of the goddess of divine order—required perfect knowledge of these things."

"Yet you left it all behind," Eliezer said.

"Not all of it," Moses admitted. "The discipline of thought, the systematic observation of nature, the importance of written law, these were valuable gifts, even if wrapped in the falsehood of their gods. The Egyptians understood that knowledge was power. They just didn't understand the source of true knowledge."

"What was the most difficult part?" Gershom asked.

"The examinations." Moses' voice grew quieter. "Every lunar month, we faced the council of teaching priests. They would question us on everything we had studied. For example, we had to recite the founding of Memphis, calculate the volume of a pyramid, name the tributaries of the Nile in order, and demonstrate the seventeen ways to write 'water.'

"I failed my first examination." Moses' voice dropped. "Remember, I was only six. The head priest asked me to recite the genealogy of the gods from Nun to Osiris. I had memorized it perfectly the night before, but when I stood before the council, with five priests in white linen, their faces like stone, my mind went blank.

"I stammered through half of it, mixing up Shu and Geb, forgetting entire generations. The head priest stopped me. 'Unacceptable,' he said. That was all. Just 'unacceptable.'

"I walked back to my seat feeling like I had betrayed Asati, betrayed Semri, betrayed everyone who had fought to keep me alive. That night, Nari found me in the garden, staring at nothing. She didn't say anything at first. She just sat beside me. Then she said, 'Moses, you are not defined by what the priests think of you. Your God has a purpose for you that goes beyond their approval.'

"I didn't understand what she meant at the time. I just knew I would never fail again. And I didn't."

Moses rubbed his temples as if the memory still pained him. "Failure meant disgrace. Some boys were sent home in shame, their families' ambitions crushed. Others were relegated to lesser scribal schools, destined for provincial posts instead of palace or priestly positions."

"And you, father?" Eliezer asked, leaning forward with excitement evident on his face.

"I was Princess Asati's son. Failure would have embarrassed the royal household that had sacrificed so much for my life. So, I studied by oil lamp long after the others slept. I practiced hieratic script until my fingers cramped. I memorized until the words danced before my eyes, even in dreams."

"When did you know you were different? That you weren't truly Egyptian?" Gershom challenged.

Moses' expression darkened. "That's a different story, for later. But I will say this—all that Egyptian learning, all those years in the Temple School, prepared me in ways I couldn't have imagined. When the God of our Fathers would call me, I could speak to Pharaoh in his own tongue, with his own learning. I understood his court, his advisors, his strengths, and his fears."

He looked at his sons, sadness evident on his weathered face. "That call never came. Sometimes the journey seems to lead us far from our destination, only to reveal it was the necessary path all along. You will learn of my failures and my arrogance later, and what it cost me and those I loved."

The Need For Rest

"I need to stop for a while. My bones grow stiff, and my mind needs a rest," Moses said, as he got up and began to stretch his back.

"We will check the sheep," Eliezer said as he and Gershom got up and went to make sure no sheep were wandering off. They walked around the flock, checking for any drifters. Most had bedded down for the night, though some were still grazing. The obvious stragglers were still with the flock.

"What do you think of all this?" Gershom asked. "I never imagined our father had such a past, had been so important. Why do you think he left Egypt when he had such a high position?"

Eliezer considered before answering. "I think he will tell us that remembrance when the time comes. As for the rest, it explains a lot. I always sensed he knew more than anyone here. So often, he just knew what to do, how to respond. Even when he built our first house, he demonstrated knowledge of stone and mortar that surpassed anyone in Midian. The angles, the way he set the foundation, it was all so precise."

"That and so many other things showed his deeper knowledge," Gershom added. "He could calculate so many things. Remember how he figured out exactly how much water Grandfather's new cistern would hold before it was even finished? Ten years at Temple School explains so much of what we've seen. While he didn't train us for war, he did make sure we knew how to defend the flock from predators, and ourselves if needed." His hand went to the large knife they both carried. "Remember the hours he had us work on our staff and sling skills? He wanted us to hit targets most shepherds wouldn't even attempt."

"I do," Eliezer replied. "We should get back before he wonders if we've gotten lost in the dark."

As they walked back toward the firelight where their father sat, Gershom said quietly, "He was a prince, Eliezer. A Prince of Egypt. And now he's here, an old shepherd on a mountain in Midian. What happened to bring him so low?"

"Or," Eliezer replied, "what happened that made him come here to a life so far from what he had known? There is more to this story than we now know."

Questioning the Egyptian Gods

Their father was sitting where they had left him, his staff across his knees, staring into the darkness beyond the firelight.

"Is the flock all right?" he asked as they approached.

"Yes, they have quieted down for the night," Gershom answered, as they sat down on either side of him.

For a moment, no one spoke. Then Eliezer leaned forward. "Father, I have a question. Did you ever argue with the Egyptian priests about their gods?"

Moses thought for a moment before replying. "I learned very quickly not to do that at Temple School. No one enjoys a beating, especially with the switches they used. Instead, I often discussed and debated with Nari. We argued over the differences between the gods of Egypt and the God of Our Fathers. The only priest with whom I ever got into any discussions that mattered was Sostris, the Chief Priest of Satis and my mother's…I mean my adopted mother's patron. He was the only Egyptian besides Nari I ever felt safe discussing these things with, but sometimes the discussions got very intense."

"Very intense? What do you mean?" Eliezer asked.

Moses smiled at the memory. "Sostris often said, 'You don't have to approach everything like a battle, Moses. Discussions don't always have to have victors and vanquished. We can learn from everything.'

"I remember one argument we had the year before Kadesh. I was seeking his counsel on a matter, but I grew frustrated with his answers. I said, 'Why do you speak like this when I ask you for help? You appear to live in a world full of shadows. There seems to be no truth, no resolution, only vague answers lost in a fog of uncertainty. No wonder Ramses doesn't trust the answers he gets from the priests. Talking with one of you is like fighting with mists and vapors.' This was what always frustrated me.

"Sostris replied, 'There you go again, treating this as if it were combat. You may remember that the Pharaoh Seti trusted me, and it was partly my counsel that spared your life and rescinded the edict. Just because you have trouble clearly seeing the arguments doesn't mean they don't have substance, Moses.'

"I argued with him, 'I see them clearly enough. While you aren't as vague as some of the other priests I have to deal with, everything you say is constructed to avoid what, to me, is the obvious meaning. Your words are like soft clay, ready to be molded to the current need. I seek to find solid rock in this marshland. Is all of your religion hidden in this fog?'

"'Sit down,' Sostris said. 'Relaxing a bit will calm down this discussion.'

"I reluctantly agreed and took a seat in front of him.

"Once I had settled, Sostris continued, 'Some things are direct. The incantations we use when passing a soul beyond the judgments of death are very precise. Each one must be accomplished in the prescribed manner. But the gods keep their own counsel on many things. Divination and augury seldom see more than vague shapes in a murky future. Many of us believe that the gods themselves do not know the future, that it remains veiled even to them.'

"'What about the Hebrew God? Do you believe He is so limited?' I asked.

"'I do not know much about him, Moses, but if he knew the future better than the gods of Egypt, why did he allow his people to come into Egypt only to become slaves and suffer so? I think he foresees no better than any Egyptian god.'

"I had no answer for him at that time. I wanted to defend the God of my Fathers, but I had no wisdom to explain His purposes."

Moses paused, then continued. "We reached a standoff that day. Sostris explained that most, but not all, aspects of the Egyptian gods were flexible to the needs of the moment. I had to remember that fate and the actions of the gods were not rigid and unyielding."

"So, he won the argument?" Gershom asked.

"In a way. While I could argue against the fog of his answers, I couldn't grasp how to call it to task. He remained certain in his uncertainty, if that makes sense."

"Was there anything that wasn't flexible?" Eliezer asked.

"One thing for sure. Ma'at. She was both an Egyptian goddess and the principle of truth that held everything together. She stood for justice to which everyone, even Pharaoh and the gods, was subject. While the interpretation of that justice could sometimes be twisted, its demand was absolute. It was the turning point on that fateful day that the edict against every male Hebrew birth was rescinded. Her principles and their demands on everything Egyptian are why I am alive today. We will talk more about her later in this remembrance."

Warrior Training

"I want to hear about your warrior training," Gershom said.

"That was harder than my schooling or the debates with Nari and Sostris, but in a completely different way."

"What do you mean?" Gershom said, expectant.

"Pain. Deep, bone-deep physical pain. Warrior training hurt more than I had imagined possible. Some mornings, it made getting up for Temple School difficult. But Semri, my stepfather, protector, and eventually main male confidant, never allowed me to give in or let up. From the very first day, when I could barely lift a practice sword, he expected me to fight through any physical limitation. He and my adopted mother would often argue about that. Asati wanted to give me time to recover, but Semri refused. On this, he never budged, saying it would forge me into the warrior I needed to be if I were to survive what was coming."

"What was coming?" Eliezer asked.

"We will talk about that later. Do you remember when I mentioned Nephura, the Chief Priest of Amun-Ra, who would become my most fearsome enemy? The threat from him and the rest of Amun-Ra's priesthood, who followed him, shaped much of my life in

Egypt."

"How?" they both asked.

"The whole time I was in Egypt, they tried to kill me. Not openly, but always trying to make it appear as if it were the judgment of their gods. Poison was a favorite of theirs. But mostly they tried to arrange for me to have a convenient 'accident'. Semri's training was important, but it was the Most High, who, in the end, protected me, though sometimes there was a terrible cost to those close to me. But I won't discuss that now.

"Semri wanted me to be physically prepared to meet any challenge. He worked relentlessly to sharpen my reflexes, to make my reactions faster than thought itself. If I had to think about my response, it might already be too late."

"So, you did this every day for ten years?" Gershom asked incredulously.

"We did take a few days off when Semri had to go on a mission for Pharaoh, but most of those times, one of the other warriors in our household guard would take over. In those ten years, I had perhaps twenty days without training. Even on feast days when the temple schools closed, Semri would be waiting at dawn. 'The gods of Egypt take holidays,' he would say. 'Your enemies do not.'

"It was the most demanding thing I have ever faced, even to this day. Nothing else came close. Semri would tell me that I would recover and be stronger for it, and if I didn't, that would teach me my limitations, and we would deal with that if it happened.

"I remember one morning when I was perhaps eleven. I had trained especially hard the day before, and when I woke, I couldn't straighten my arms. The muscles had locked overnight. I tried to hide it at temple school, but by that afternoon, when Semri called me to the training ground, I could barely grip the practice sword.

"He watched me struggle for a bit, and then he said, 'Drop the sword.' I did. He tossed me a spear instead. 'If your arms won't work, you still hold this. We will train your legs today. Sprint to the far wall and back. Twenty times. Begin.'

"I thought he was punishing me. But after running, my arms had loosened. The blood was flowing again. He handed me back the sword. 'Your body will betray you in battle,' he said. 'You must learn to fight through it.'"

"Why didn't you train us the way you were trained?" Gershom asked.

"I trained you the way Midian required. You have different needs. I taught you to read the weather, track animals, and find water in the desert. You know the knife, the staff, and the sling. These are the warrior skills you needed in Midian, as a shepherd. In Egypt, enemies came with poison and daggers. Here, the dangers are sandstorms, drought, and starvation, and for the flock, various predators. These kill as surely as any blade."

Who Was Nari?

"I want to know more about Nari," Eliezer said.

Moses thought for a moment. "I am not sure where to start. Her importance began from the very beginning, on that first morning. She guided my Egyptian mother through that day, bringing my real mother and sister into my life.

"I think she knew from the beginning that my sister was at the river to watch what happened to me, but she never betrayed that knowledge. I also believe she suspected the 'nursemaid' she had fetched was my real mother, but she kept that to herself and often deflected any questions that arose about her. It was much later in our relationship that we discussed what she knew."

"She sounds like a special person," Eliezer said.

"She was. I would not be here or be the man you know without her. I learned most of what I knew about the God of Our Fathers from her. She was the reason I came to believe in Him and eventually began to experience His leading in my life. Later, when I finally met my dying mother, she filled in important details about that first day, along with her understanding of the Most High's involvement.

"I never knew my father, and with everything else going on, he never drew my interest until it was too late—something I later deeply regretted. When I was fourteen, he died from an accident at the shipyard where he worked. For several years after, Miriam and my mother struggled to survive. Even after Miriam married, they continued to struggle to keep food on the table. After Kadesh, when I was sixteen, it became especially bleak for them. Nari, in an effort to help my mother and Miriam survive, arranged for my sister to work at the Great Estate. She was an expert weaver of rushes. Her baskets became highly prized by everyone. She was often asked for a special basket to meet a specific need, and she never failed to deliver.

"But you asked about Nari. Throughout my years at Temple School, when we were alone and away from prying ears, we would discuss the Most High versus the Egyptian gods.

"I remember one evening when I was perhaps twelve. I had been studying the Book of the Dead all day at Temple School. We were required to memorize the spells the Egyptians believed would guide a soul through the underworld. I found Nari in the garden and asked her, 'If the Hebrew God is so powerful, why does He have no book of spells? No incantations to protect the dead?'

"She was quiet for a long moment, her hands running over a reed basket she was repairing. Then she said, 'Moses, the gods of Egypt need spells because they are weak. They must be reminded, cajoled, bribed. The Most High needs no such things. When He speaks, it is done. When He remembers, the dead rise. When He forgets, kingdoms fall.'

"'But how do we make sure He remembers us?' I asked.

"She looked at me then, and I will never forget what she said: 'You cannot make the Most High do anything. You can only be faithful when He calls. And He will call you, Moses. That is why you were pulled from the river. Not to be an Egyptian prince, but to be His servant.'

"I didn't understand what she meant by that. Not for many years.

"As we talked, she would continually remind me, 'Those foolish priests follow capricious gods. They think they must constantly grovel and bribe them with spells and offerings, seeking the smallest boon.'

"I asked her, 'That is not the way with the Most High?'

"'Never! You think baubles of stone and metal can buy Him? He stands above all things of earth. No, when He chooses to move and has called your name, you must have the courage to stand in His path and be swept along in His purpose. He looks only at the temper of your heart, Moses, and the trueness of your word. He expects these to be matched with actions. He cannot be bought with silver or gold; only the blood that runs through your veins can touch His purpose.'

"She had become a servant because her family had followed the

Pharaoh Akhenaten. The Egyptians refused to speak his name, instead calling him '*The Pharaoh Who is Not Named.*' He had overthrown the gods of Egypt in favor of one, singular, all-powerful god whom he called Aten, and he was the sole intermediary between Aten and the people of Egypt. Her family had faithfully followed Aten, abandoning Amun and the other gods to serve the new deity under the heretical Pharaoh.

"When Akhenaten died—some say by poison—the former priesthoods of Egypt rebelled, led by the priesthood of Amun-Ra. They forced the ousting of Aten and the return of the historic gods. All those who had followed Aten were persecuted, losing their positions and property. Nari's family was affected, and she was forced into servitude. Fortunately, however, she became Princess Asati's chief maidservant.

"Some of the priests, especially the priesthood of Amun-Ra, blamed the Hebrews for corrupting Akhenaten and sought their destruction."

"Is that where the edict that condemned all newborn males came from?" Eliezer asked, his voice dropping.

"Yes, but at first it was left to the midwives, who, in fear of the Most High, refused to kill the newborn males, claiming the Hebrew women delivered before they arrived. I remember a story about one of the early midwives who had tried to take the life of the baby boy at whose birth she was assisting. She suddenly fell to the floor and vomited up a stomach full of worms and died. After that, it was said, no midwife dared touch a Hebrew boy being born.

"However, that deliverance was short-lived, though it is why my brother, Aaron, survived.

"A short time later, when a new dynasty came to power, starting with Ramses I, the new Pharaoh, in order to gain the support of the priests of Amun-Ra, posted an edict condemning all newborn males to be offered to the crocodile god, Sobek. Instead of the midwives, they used soldiers to forcefully take the babies. There were informers everywhere, so it was a miracle that my parents were able to hide me as long as they did. The edict that should have meant my death, in a strange twist orchestrated by the Most High, became the means of my salvation. Nari was at the center of it all—recognizing Miriam at the river, supporting my mother as nursemaid, protecting our secret for years."

Moses paused, his voice softening. "I will have more to say about Nari when the time comes. Her wisdom shaped me in ways I didn't recognize. I did not realize how important she was until it was too late. She gave so much of her life for mine, and I will carry that debt until I die.

"When I think, even today, about the events of that first fateful day, I find it remarkable the way the Most High wove all the events together to get the edict rescinded and me into the household of Pharaoh. It was nothing short of a miracle. It showed to anyone willing to look, the Most High's control over even the smallest things."

The Most High Invades Egypt

"Tell us about that, Father," Gershom asked. "Growing up in Midian, these are things about the Most High we have never heard."

Moses shifted in his seat. "Both Nari and I came to believe that the Most High was the guiding force behind the events of that day, pulling together what appeared to be chaos into divine purpose.

What the Egyptians saw as their gods acting to rescind the edict, we saw as the Most High moving His pieces on the great board of Hounds and Jackals to bring about His will.

"My understanding of that day came from many sources over the years. My dying mother told me of my father's dreams and their decision to put me in the river. Nari described Asati's transformation when she first held me. Ramses shared what his parents had dreamed that night before it all started. This was all capped by the star and the signs given to the various priesthoods in Memphis. All of these interventions fit into the will of the Most High. Asati's dream, which drove her to the river, was perfectly timed. Since she had been barren for five years, her heart had been prepared for me to fill the void. She believed her gods, especially Satis, had finally answered her prayers through the sacred river itself. In our discussions, Nari and I came to believe the Most High had prepared every part of the ground, weaving together everything that happened."

"Tell us more about how the Most High worked on that day," Eliezer said.

Moses was silent for a few moments as he thought about what he knew of those events. Everyone in Egypt had an opinion about how and why the events had taken their specific course.

He looked at his sons and began, "Over the years, Ramses told me different things about what the Royal Family believed about that fateful day. His father, Pharaoh Seti, had also shared his own understanding during my early years, especially about the dreams he and Queen Tuya had the night before, concerning my role in thwarting treachery against their son. Those dreams brought Ramses and me together in ways nothing else could.

"Others also shaped my understanding, such as Asati, Nari, Semri, my mother and sister, and, of course, Sostris and a few of his priests, who all shared their beliefs with me. In the end, they either credited the gods of Egypt, especially Ma'at, or recognized the Most High working through their beliefs to bring about His will."

"Our God is so wise," Eliezer said. "He used their beliefs in the gods of Egypt to accomplish His plan."

"But how did He do it?" Gershom asked. "So many things had to happen at exactly the right moment. The falling star, the dreams, finding you in the rushes at the precise time Asati arrived. It seems impossible."

"Not impossible," Moses said quietly. "Inevitable. That is what I came to understand. The Most High doesn't force events. He carefully arranges them. He places the right people in the right places, plants dreams in sleeping minds, and sends signs in the sky that the Egyptians interpret through their own beliefs. And then..." Moses paused, his gaze distant. "He waits to see if we will be faithful when He calls."

"Nari and I would debate this for years," Moses continued. "She believed every detail was ordained: the exact moment the basket caught in the reeds, the timing of Asati's arrival, even my stumbling mother's hand hitting the cradle that spilled the vipers. Nothing was by chance. Everything was the Most High's design. I wasn't always so sure. Sometimes I wondered if He simply set events in motion and watched to see what would happen."

"And now?" Eliezer asked. "What do you believe now, Father?"

Moses was quiet for a long moment. "Now, after forty years of silence from Him, I wonder if Nari was right all along. Perhaps every moment was ordained. That includes the ones I thought were my own choices." His voice grew heavy. "Including the events beyond my control, or even the control of Pharaoh himself. I think this is where faith and trust in the LORD come in. It is not something to be figured out. The complexity is beyond understanding, but instead is something to trust."

The Day That Changed Everything

"Tell us more about what happened that day, Father," Gershom almost pleaded.

"What you must understand is how perfectly everything converged. I will say again, consider the falling star that changed my mother's path to the river. Asati's dream driving her there at that exact moment. My stumbling mother's hand spilling the vipers before I was placed in the cradle. Sostris interpreting prophecy to Pharaoh to support me. Even Nephura—my greatest enemy—suggested I be raised in Pharaoh's household, thereby ensuring I would receive the education and training to fulfill the very prophecy he feared. Nothing happened by chance."

Moses shook his head slowly. "Looking back, I can see that the Most High's purposes are often very different from the ways we would expect. He saves, He adds, and He removes. He builds, sometimes in ways not seen for many years, and He tears down what we might hold on to. I know now that everything that happens, even my speaking to you right now, is part of His will.

"Sometimes, it takes time to understand the Most High's actions," Moses said, almost as a challenge to them. "Can you accept that?"

"I can," Eliezer said.

"But father, what a day that was!" Gershom added, his excitement bursting through his words.

"Yes, it was," Moses answered quietly, looking directly at them, "but there were many more such days about which I still have to tell you."

Moses' Father on his Deathbed

His sons looked at him expectantly.

"It is time to tell you about one of my greatest failures," Moses continued, his head hanging low, his voice faltering.

"When I was fourteen," he began. "My sister came to me and said, 'You must come to the village, Moses,' her hands gripping the side of my chariot as if she could compel me to come by the force of her will. 'This may be the only chance for you to meet your father. He was injured in an accident at the shipyards and could die at any time.'

"I didn't know what to say to her. I made excuses. I could skip school for one morning. I was so far ahead of everyone else that it would not matter. Instead, I told her my tongue gets easily knotted. I added that it would be dangerous for me to be seen in the Hebrew village. What if I were recognized?

"She pulled back from the chariot and looked at me with such fire in her eyes. 'He doesn't care about the danger, Moses. He doesn't care that you're a Prince of Egypt. You are the son of his body, and he is dying. All he wants is to see you before it's too late. To touch your hand. To know you don't hate him for putting you in that basket. He has so much he wants to tell you. He wants to share the secrets of his heart with you. But all you think about is yourself!'

"Embarrassed, I left her and argued with myself for two days. Finally, just after daybreak, I took my chariot and set out for the Hebrew village using Miriam's directions."

Gershom could not help himself and interrupted his father, "But he was your father, and he was dying!"

Moses sighed at his sons as the deep abiding failure he had allowed to happen that day so long ago returned in a rush. He and his sons stared at each other for a long moment, then he continued, "I finally changed my mind and tried to do the right thing. You have to understand the war that was being waged within me. I was genuinely concerned that my presence would put them in danger.

"Anticipation and a strange fear, one whose source I could not place, fought for dominance. Had this been a battlefield, I would have fought without hesitation. A sword against sword, strength against strength, that came easily to me. Heart against heart was another matter. There, my prowess held no sway. My warrior's pride could not serve me in this. Laying aside my sword in the face of an enemy would be easier than this. But Miriam was right; there was no time. It was now or never to know him—and possibly not to know my true self either.

"Because of my hesitation, I arrived at the village too late. He had died several hours before. I will never forget the look Miriam gave me as she met me outside the village, the cold fury that burned in her eyes. I had failed him, and it was something I could never fix, I could never make up for."

Moses stopped, his voice breaking. He looked away from his sons, unable to meet their eyes. When he spoke again, his words came rough and broken. "I failed him. And I can never make it right."

Both his sons moved closer; Gershom placed a hand on his shoulder, and Eliezer on his knee. They said nothing. What words could answer such a wound?

After a time, Moses drew a long breath. "This is why I am telling you all of this," he said, his voice still rough. "I failed my father. I will not fail you." He stood slowly, leaning on his staff. "I need some time alone."

In the firelight, they could see the tears welling up in his eyes.

Failure and Redemption

As their father took his staff and went off into the darkness, Gershom and Eliezer decided to check on the sheep again.

"That was overwhelming," Eliezer noted.

"Yes, it was," Gershom replied. "And this is just the beginning. We need to help him by not overreacting to anything he says. Who knows what sadder revelations await us, and if we are not careful, he may not be able to finish."

"You are right," Eliezer said. "He has been a good father to us all of our lives. His past failures don't change that. It is something we need to remember and not fail him, no matter what he tells us."

"Agreed," Gershom responded.

Moses found relief in the darkness outside the camp, as he carefully climbed a shallow ridge up the mountain. He needed to be alone for a while, to let this emotional storm pass. This was harder than he had expected. He wiped the tears from his eyes. In the telling, memories long buried and some forgotten were surfacing with a force that left him shaken.

He sat down and leaned back against a tree that had grown near a ledge that gave him a place to sit. He let the failure wash over him again. Fresh sobs rose in his throat, and tears he had tried to wipe away began to flow again. This was hard. But he could not stop now. Not after coming this far. His sons deserved the truth—all of it, no matter how difficult the remembering might be. He could not fail them as he had failed his father. Not now. Not tonight.

He recalled the moment earlier this afternoon when he had felt the presence of the Most High for the first time in forty years and prayed aloud a simple prayer.

"Oh God Most High," he whispered into the darkness, "forgive me for failing my father. Give me the strength to finish this. Don't let me fail my sons as I failed him. May your will be done."

The Night Continues

Moses took some time to recover, and as he returned, he stopped to get water. His throat was parched. When he returned to the campfire, his sons were waiting for him. No one said anything as he sat down between them.

After a few moments of silence, Moses said, his voice still raw. "This is harder than I thought, so have patience with me."

Both sons put a hand on his shoulders again. They said nothing, but looked at him with a compassion he could feel.

Moses took a deep breath and began again, "Surprisingly, nothing came of my attempted visit to my parents' household. The fact that my mother had been my nursemaid was enough to excuse my presence as consolation for her husband's death. As I told you, Miriam met me outside the village, and when I learned he had already died, I turned around and left, unable to face their recrimination. As I said before, my distress over my failure haunted me for days. It still haunts me. My training with Semri saved me. What else could I do? I could not change the past. Asati, Nari, and Semri wondered at my obvious upset, but I dismissed it as a private matter. As long as I continued my schooling and training, they let it go.

"My daily pattern held for another inundation. I had finished my schooling and focused solely on my training. Then, at the beginning of my sixteenth year, Ramses called me to court. My warrior training now took up a full day rather than just the afternoon. It was a demanding grind.

"Ramses' call was the beginning of the next phase of my life. Seti had died almost four years earlier, and my cousin Ramses was now Pharaoh. The King of the Hittites, Muwatalli, had sent a challenge to Egypt and Ramses, inviting us to meet him in battle over the shifting allegiance of the fortress of Kadesh in southern Syria.

"When he called me to court, Ramses was beginning to assemble his army to meet Muwatalli's provocation, but he had a problem. He was putting together the largest force Egypt had ever assembled. It included four Egyptian corps named after four gods: Amun, P'Re, Ptah, and Sutekh. Additionally, there was a Semitic contingent drawn from nations surrounding Egypt, some of whom had been conquered in the past. While it included Egyptians and Nubians as charioteers and bowmen, no Egyptian general was willing to take command. They all saw it as a mongrel group destined to fail and refused the assignment. Ramses offered me the command, with Semri as my second.

"If I took the challenge, I would have just over five months to mold this motley group of malcontents and rejects from the other corps into an effective fighting force. Everyone expected me to fail except Ramses and Semri. Ramses believed this command would establish his parents' dreams as a true prophecy, while Semri thought his ten years of hard work would bear the fruit he believed had grown within me.

"I accepted the command. What choice did I have? Ramses was Pharaoh, and more than that, he was my brother in all but blood. If he believed I could do this, I would find a way. My future depended on my success."

Preparation for Kadesh and the Ne'arin

"So, you are now going to be an Egyptian general?" Gershom asked.

"Yes. A sixteen-year-old general destined for failure. Once, with Semri's help, I took command of the Ne'arin, the name given to this Semite corps, two events helped initiate the transformation of this disorganized group into a real army. The first occurred when an Egyptian charioteer killed a young Hebrew over a perceived slight. He acted without thinking, and then his commander supported him, saying he was just a Hebrew.

"Semri and I had envisioned transforming the Ne'arin into a unique force where all our soldiers were treated as equal warriors, each giving their unique skills to the fight we would face. Yes, most Egyptians looked at the Hebrews as no more than slaves, but those who had joined my army, around two hundred, could not be treated that way.

"I did two things: I executed the one who had murdered the Hebrew, giving all his possessions to the family the young Hebrew had left behind, and demoted the Egyptian commander to a common charioteer, giving him twenty lashes as punishment. I expected him to quit, but to my surprise, he accepted the punishment and remained.

"Was that the first man you had ever killed?" Gershom asked.

"Yes, and his execution was one of the hardest things I've ever done. It was necessary and proved to be the foundation for transforming the Ne'arin." Moses paused, seeing it again. "His name was Khenti. He knelt before me in front of the assembled corps. There were nearly 5,000 men watching. Most didn't believe I would go through with it. He knew what was coming. I could see it in his eyes. He didn't beg or protest. He just looked at me with this expression I couldn't read. Contempt? Acceptance? I still don't know.

"I raised my khopesh. My hand was steady. Semri had trained me well for that. But inside..." Moses shook his head. "Inside, everything in me wanted to lower the blade, to find another way. He was Egyptian, like over a thousand of my warriors.

"But the young Hebrew he'd killed had a name too. Yosha ben David. He'd joined the Ne'arin to feed his family. And Khenti had struck him down over an accident. Over nothing.

"The blade came down. It was clean. He didn't suffer. But I did. For days afterward, I could feel the impact in my hands and hear the sound. Semri said it would pass. It didn't. Not really. Even now, remembering this moment, after all these years, I can still feel the strike in my hands."

Moses looked at his sons. "It was necessary. It proved to be the foundation for transforming the Ne'arin. But necessary doesn't mean easy or even right. I still carry his death with me.

"The second event was also significant. The leader of our Sherden, Derden, renowned warriors who even composed part of Ramses' private guard, came to me and offered his warriors as my personal guard. This was noteworthy. Once the Sherden swore allegiance to you, it was a blood oath that they adhered to till death. Derden saw how I responded to the Hebrew's death and agreed with what I was trying to do. This did several things. It gave me immediate status, since a Sherden commitment was rare and valuable. It also gave me protection within the Ne'arin. Semri and I both wondered if Nephura might use a spy or malcontent within the corps to try to kill me. The Sherden made that possibility a lot harder. Fortunately, no attempt on my life was ever made.

"After that, we mixed everyone in the camp. Egyptians shared tents next to Hebrews. Sherden trained alongside Nubians. It took several weeks to settle the resulting conflicts, which included fights, bloody noses, and a few more severe incidents. Gradually, it forced everyone to see each other not by their nationality but as Ne'arin first. Without that change, we had no hope of forging the corps into an effective fighting force.

"It took about a month, but our training began to show real results as the men started helping each other, sharing their skills with those beside them, regardless of nationality. This was hardest for the Egyptian charioteers, who were accustomed to dominating the rest of the corps, treating them as second-class at best. Slowly, but inexorably, the corps became Ne'arin first.

"We even developed a watchword that became our battle cry: *One army, one warrior!* It declared us as united with a single purpose. By the time we arrived at Kadesh, about six months later, every man in the corps shouted it from his heart, because he believed it."

Learning the Art of War

Moses looked at his sons and asked, "Do you have any questions?"

Gershom spoke first. "Isn't there a difference between becoming an effective warrior, which Semri accomplished with those ten years of difficult training, and leading an army?"

"Yes. Absolutely. While Semri had trained me to become an effective warrior, commanding the Ne'arin taught me the art of war. I had excellent teachers in Semri and the three Egyptians he recruited to command the charioteers, the bowmen, and the shieldmen.

"I believe one reason Ramses gave me this command was to help me become something he needed, a commander he could trust who knew how to conduct real warfare, not just fight effectively.

"Kadesh taught me some difficult lessons. There is a difference between planning to fight the greater war and effectively winning an immediate battle. It is like comparing the forest to the process of removing specific trees.

"For example, at Kadesh, we devised a strategy to win the battle, but our primary objective of maintaining Kadesh within Egyptian sovereignty ultimately proved unsuccessful. But, as I will explain later, winning that battle proved decisive to our larger objective. It took just fifteen years to achieve the desired outcome: a peace treaty with the Hittites that lasted over forty years.

"Every war has both a larger objective and the necessity to win battles. I found dealing with battles much easier."

"How so?" Eliezer asked.

"I have a gift for seeing how a battle should unfold. I can see the movements, the weaknesses, and where to strike, as well as when. For me, it was much like any fight, though the stakes were larger and slightly more complicated. I could see the parts of the encounter unfolding in my mind, the give and take, what would work and what wouldn't. That enabled us to decisively win the battle at Kadesh.

"However, the greater war is far more complex and involves extensive planning, as well as the needs of the army throughout the course of the campaign. It involves logistics, supply lines, which battles to fight and which to avoid, and what to do when plans fail. It involves managing not just warriors but grain stores, water sources, and the mood of the troops after a loss. Thinking on that level exhausts me. It's not how my mind works.

"I had to learn some of those skills to prepare the Ne'arin and organize their training most efficiently, but my true ability lay in planning out a specific battle as Semri, and I proved at Kadesh. I was very good at identifying an enemy's weaknesses and planning how to use our strengths against them.

"After Kadesh, the problems shifted to larger war planning, both against the Hittites and, even more importantly, how to deal with the treachery of Nephura and the priesthood of Amun-Ra. Ramses excelled at that type of thinking. He eventually only sought my counsel for specific tactics for individual encounters. I was seldom included in the larger planning. His vizier, Paser, did most of his advising at that level, and he was very good at it."

"I believe it is time to tell us about Kadesh," Eliezer said.

"I agree," Gershom added.

To Kadesh and the Hittite Ambush

"First, I must tell you about our march to Kadesh and the Hittite ambush. Those two things shaped how we prepared for the battle."

Both his sons leaned forward in anticipation.

"Marching with such a large army created numerous problems both for Ramses and for the areas we passed through. We were almost thirty thousand men who stripped the territory along our march of most of the available food. About ten days in, Ramses decided to have the Ne'arin break off and take the coastal route north, reducing the demand on the surrounding countryside. After seeing the growth of our corps over the previous months and our disciplined march, he trusted us to reach Kadesh in time to support him in the battle.

"This actually worked to our advantage. Apart from the main army, we could continue our training because we did not have to conform to the expectations of the rest of the army or Ramses.

"At any time during the day's march, Semri would suddenly shout out attack formation orders. The chariots would fan out on either flank, while the shieldmen would form a wall one hundred wide and thirty-five rows deep. Behind them, the bowmen would form five rows one hundred wide. Meanwhile, the Medjay, specialized soldiers who carried heavy eight-cubit spears tipped with a smooth, rounded bronze point—designed to pierce horseflesh and withdraw cleanly—would split apart and form up on either side, protecting our flanks. No correction was needed from Semri or me as the men took to correcting each other. It soon became a game to see how quickly and efficiently they could complete the formation. This disciplined practice kept the Ne'arin sharp, and the break in the monotony of the march helped us make better time when we resumed.

"As we approached Kadesh, I made a serious mistake. Against Semri's advice, I acted on a premonition that the Hittites had already arrived. I soon found that they were already at Kadesh. I took two friends, creating a three-chariot scout force, and left before first light to explore the outskirts of Kadesh, searching for any sign of the Hittites. Three chariots would not raise enough dust to give away our position, and if discovered, we expected to be able to outrun any pursuers, since Hittite chariots were much heavier and slower than ours.

"Something unexpected turned everything around. Unknown to us at the time, an Amun-Ra spy in our corps overheard my plan and took a horse well before dawn. He rode to find the Hittites and arrange an ambush, hoping to kill me and fulfill Amun-Ra's mission. He found a Hittite patrol and convinced them to ambush us.

"The enemy chariots were waiting in a dry riverbed south of Kadesh. We saw nothing until we were almost on top of them.

"Abasi was driving my chariot. Korum and Horan rode ahead of us. We were moving at a trot, scanning the terrain ahead, when I heard something—a faint jingle of harness, the creak of wood. I raised my hand to signal a halt.

"Too late. They rose from both sides of the riverbed. There were ten Hittite chariots. Six attacked Korum and Horan, while four concentrated on me. I was able to loose one arrow that wounded a Hittite driver, but my friends went down quickly.

"'Go!' I shouted to Abasi. He cracked the whip, but we were being surrounded.

"We began moving up the ridge to our west. It was our only possible escape. It was a slow, difficult climb. We lurched left then right, trying to keep our team moving up the sharp slope. The four chariots that had been trying to surround me could not pursue us in their heavy three-man chariots, so they dismounted and began firing arrows at us. I was able to deflect the worst of their arrows until one struck Abasi in the calf, and he tumbled back out of the chariot before I could grab him. It broke my heart to see the pleading look in his eyes as their arrows struck him down. I had no time to grieve."

Moses ignored Gershom's gasp and went on. "The lighter chariot lurched forward, and I was able to escape over the ridge. When I was clear of the immediate danger, I saw that my right stallion was wounded. Two arrows, one high in the mane and one in his outside ribs, had found their mark. The Hittite commander sent six of his chariots, three around each side of the ridge I had scaled, in pursuit. He expected them to catch up to me and easily finish me off.

"My only hope was to outrun them, even with a wounded horse. I had enough of a lead that at the start, I was out of the range of their bows, but as my wounded horse began faltering, the Hittites were slowly gaining ground. I was sure they would catch me when I saw dust ahead. It turned out to be Egyptian dust. Semri had sent Baktari, the commander of his private chariot guard, to shadow me with ten swift, well-equipped chariots. We signaled each other, and they swept past me and engaged the Hittites head-on.

"They succeeded in destroying the six Hittite pursuers with only one wounded driver, thanks to the advantage of our swifter, more nimble chariots and composite bows. We learned a great deal about the Hittites in the encounter, which provided us with tactics that ultimately turned the tide in the battle of Kadesh the next day.

"While that victory was important, what has stayed with me is that I had lost five good men that morning because I didn't take time to consider Semri's warning. Their deaths joined Khenti's execution as weights I still carry."

Eliezer couldn't contain himself. "I understand the pain of that loss is difficult, but tell us what you learned that was so important? What turned the tide at Kadesh the next day?"

Moses gathered himself past the resurgent grief. "We knew that the Hittite chariot charges we expected to face only carried spearmen. The pursuing chariots had two bowmen each, and they were very poor archers in moving chariots, especially at a distance. Additionally, we found that our composite bows, made of wood and bone, outshot their counterparts by well over fifty to seventy-five cubits. So, even with bowmen in their chariots, we could strike them long before they could strike us. Additionally, we practiced our chariot archery constantly, whereas the Hittites seemed unprepared as they tried to shoot from their moving chariots.

"That night, following the ambush, Semri and I did two things. First, we examined all our assets and devised a plan to counter the vaunted Hittite chariot charge. We also sent out a scouting party to find Ramses and explain what we had learned about the Hittite weakness and our plan to counter their charge.

"We did not expect them to have bows in their chariots as they charged our lines. The ambush group must have been advance scouts. In the past, their charges always included spearmen and relied on devastating assaults to crush ground troops, which had always shattered every shield wall they encountered.

"Our secret weapons would be our bows and our Medjay. Our bows could strike their advancing charge beginning at almost four hundred and fifty cubits from our lines, and our Medjay's spears could devastate any chariots that made it to our shield wall. We put together a trap, getting our seventy-five Medjay, one hundred and fifty of our spearmen, and one hundred and fifty bowmen to a battlefield formation, transported on three hundred and seventy-five chariots for the final three thousand cubits, saving well over half an hour of marching.

"I will try to explain our tactics, since they succeeded in destroying the Hittite northern chariot charge that was supposed to hit Ramses in his unprotected rear. Once we arrived at the chosen trap place, the chariots would unload the spearmen first, then the Medjay. Seventy-six spearmen would create the front shield wall, interspaced with the seventy-five Medjay between them. The remaining seventy-four spearmen supported the backs of their front-line shield brothers. This created a wall of Medjay spears facing the vaunted Hittite chariot charge. Then the bowmen would disembark and form two rows of seventy-five of our best Nubians behind the shield wall. Once they had unloaded their extra passengers, one hundred and fifty chariots would form up on each of our flanks, with the remaining fifty spread out behind the bowmen. We had over five hundred arrows to throw at their advancing charge with each volley we released.

62

"The night of my ambush, we had sent our scouts to find Ramses' camp. Instead, they found Ramses' scout searching for us. After a short exchange of information, Pharaoh's scout returned to Ramses, along with two of our scouts, to pass on our plan and our knowledge of the Hittite weaknesses. We learned that Ramses was camped below Kadesh with only his Vanguard and one corps. The other three armies were at least three hours away and would not arrive until later that morning. Pharaoh was in a perilous position, and we needed to reach Kadesh as soon as possible.

"We didn't wait. The next morning, before first light, we broke camp and, as soon as the light allowed, practiced deploying the Medjay formation three times. That was all the Ne'arin needed to successfully prepare to deploy our trap. All their previous training showed their mettle that morning. The group designated for the trap formed up in front of the corps, and we began a forced march to Kadesh."

The Battle is Joined

"I can see what you mean about how you prefer preparing for the battle. Please tell us what happened, Father," Gershom asked, the excitement evident in his voice.

Moses took a moment to get everything straight in his mind. "Remember, we arose before dawn, packed our camp, and practiced the trap routine three times. The men caught on quickly, so we were able to leave right after first light. We were about three hours' march from Kadesh, and we pushed hard. As we neared the loading point for our trap group to advance, several scout chariots arrived, revealing that Ramses had left his northern flank undefended, expecting us to arrive and close that gap. We couldn't wait any longer and began loading and sending out the chariots, each carrying warriors for the trap formation. It added a few hundred cubits to their travel, but by the grace of the Most High, only a few of the chariots broke down. The planned reserves quickly took over and completed the journey. We arrived just in time. Twelve hundred Hittite chariots were beginning to cross the Orontes River north of the fortress to attack Ramses from the rear.

"Our forces quickly deployed in the plain north of Pharaoh's camp, forcing the Hittites to attack us before trying to move on Ramses. The enemy took a while to cross the river and form up their charge, which allowed us to prepare our defense and begin sending arrow volleys into them at our bows' maximum distance.

"We had pulled every arrow we had from storage. Each bowman and charioteer carried nearly one hundred arrows. They shot volley after volley as fast as they could nock and release. The sight was like a continuous deadly rain, hundreds of arrows darkening the sky above the advancing Hittites. When their chariots got closer, the spearmen and Medjay crouched down so the bowmen could shoot directly at the oncoming chariots.

"That must have been a sight to see," Gershom said.

"Indeed, it was. Semri and I later believed that with enough bows, we could have completely devastated their charge before they reached us. However, while we may have reduced their number by half, our Medjay and spearmen performed beautifully. At the last minute, the Medjay planted their spears, held fast by the feet of our spearmen as their points glistened in the morning sun. Many of the Hittite horses tried to stop or turn to the right or left to avoid our wall of spears, sending the front ranks into chaos and disrupting their charge. Many still ended up on Medjay spears as the chariots behind them began to pile up. About twenty chariots broke through our front lines, only to meet our bowmen and charioteers, who quickly dispatched most of them.

"I ordered our archers to stop, so we could take captives, while many of our chariots picked up a bowman and pursued the retreating Hittites, who had turned around and tried to flee back across the river. In the end, only a handful made their escape. However, we had effectively destroyed their northern chariot force. Almost twelve hundred of their vaunted wheels of death were destroyed.

"While the battle was decided, the fight was not over. One of those who had breached our wall and survived was the Hittite Prince, Hamatarma, brother of their King. He was unwilling to surrender. He challenged me to personal combat, calling me 'boy' and showing me extreme disrespect."

Both his sons leaned forward, anticipating what would come next.

"His remaining charioteers tried to dissuade him, but he would not listen. Derden, the head of my Sherden guard, argued the fight was too dangerous. Only Nazim, my new driver and one of my former trainers, seemed unworried. He actually smiled.

"I had prayed to the Most High, and a strange calm descended over me as I prepared to meet the Hittite. There was no choice but to accept his challenge, or, despite our victory, I would be considered a coward in the eyes of the rest of Pharaoh's army. Besides, I had trained for over ten years to meet this very moment. Hamatarma did not know who he had challenged."

Eliezer could not contain himself. "What happened?"

"It was a short fight, but I remember every moment of it.

"I told my men that no one was to interfere, though Derden still protested. My forces spread out, creating an open space for the confrontation. The Hittite prince came at me first with his sword, a descending thrust at my shoulder. I had practiced this defense a thousand times with Semri. Step back, pivot left, deflect his thrust with my shield, sending his sword harmlessly into the dirt. My khopesh swung up, knocking off his helmet and leaving his head bleeding.

"He pulled back and circled, claiming I was lucky. His second attack was even more vicious, as he charged at me with his shield, attempting to crush me with sheer force, like a Hittite chariot charge. Semri and I had practiced against this maneuver for many years. Using my shield, I pretended to give way, rolling onto my back. As Hamatarma began to fall forward, I planted both my feet in his groin and used his momentum to flip him over me backward. As he flew over me, I hooked his shield with my khopesh, wrenching it away. He hit hard, flat on his back, the wind knocked out of him. My years of training had done their work.

"I was on my feet immediately, saying, 'Do you yield? This doesn't have to end in death.'

"His men shouted at him to surrender. Even in Hittite, I could hear the desperation in their voices. But Hamatarma was a prince, and pride is a cruel master. He looked me in the eye and yelled, 'Never!' He then spat at my feet, cursed my God, and called on his deity as he prepared his final assault.

"That's when I felt it. The Most High overshadowed me. A strange calm settled over me. My breathing steadied. Time seemed to slow. I could see his final charge before he made it. He came at me with everything he had and made a wild, direct thrust, his sword striking forward with all of his strength.

"I sidestepped. His blade cut empty air. As he passed, off-balance from the force of his swing, I hooked his sword hand with my khopesh and twisted. The blade flew from his grip. He turned, reaching for a dagger at his belt.

"I gave him no time. My khopesh came around in a single fluid arc, Semri's training moving through my body without thought, and struck him across his neck. He dropped face-first into the dust.

"The silence that followed was absolute. No one made a sound."

Moses looked at his sons. "He had left me no choice. I took no pleasure in his death. Others considered this a pivotal moment. They believed that this was when I came to terms with my destiny. For me, it was a difficult moment. I responded by ordering the prince's body to be respectfully prepared and placed in his chariot, to be honorably returned to his brother, the King."

"What about the rest of the battle at Kadesh?" Gershom asked.

"Understand that what I know about that comes from what others told me. As intense as our fight in the north was, the Egyptians to the south faced darker moments. What we had learned about enemy weaknesses and our tactics with bows and Medjay had been passed to Pharaoh, and he sent the report to his three corps arriving from the south that morning.

"All three corps left at first light and began their march north. The rest of the Hittite chariots, twenty-five hundred of them, assembled out of sight across from the southern ford of the Orontes. Their plan was to strike the first Egyptian corps, P'Re, broadside as they marched toward Kadesh. From past experience, they expected their charge to destroy the center of the Egyptian line and throw the remaining troops into such disarray that they would break and run, leaving the corps useless in further conflict. It didn't unfold the way they expected.

"Two things worked against the charge. First, the ford would only allow a hundred chariots at a time to cross, so their attack was twenty-five rows deep, which slowed the charge considerably, limiting its initial effectiveness. Secondly, P'Re was at least partially prepared for the attack. They had placed their Medjay into the second column of their eighteen-column march. If, as they expected, an attack came from the river, their shieldmen could turn and form a wall while their Medjay would intersperse their spears through the defensive wall. It almost worked, but without practicing the maneuver, they were slow to respond and only partially formed their defense. It did slow the front ranks of the charge, creating momentary confusion, but the Hittites eventually broke through and plowed through the remaining columns, many of whom turned and ran, with some even throwing down their weapons.

"But P'Re didn't collapse as expected. The corps split. Paser, Ramses' vizier, commanded the front section in an organized retreat north toward Pharaoh's camp. He sent two hundred chariots out into the plain to the west to harass the Hittites with speed and bows.

"General Piankh commanded the rear half, rallying behind the remaining shieldmen and Medjay. He had five hundred bowmen and two hundred fifty chariots. He sent two hundred more chariots to harass the Hittite flank. That meant four hundred Egyptian chariots now attacked the Hittite charge from all along their western flank as they turned toward Pharaoh's camp.

"Piankh's bowmen and the remaining fifty charioteers began hitting the Hittites crossing in front of them with devastating volleys of arrows. While too many were crossing the river to stop the charge, they did considerable damage to their ranks, as did the four hundred Egyptian chariots harassing their flanks as they surged north.

"Meanwhile, the Ptah corps, following behind P'Re, saw the attack, and their general, Hasani, sent his five hundred chariots to join the harassment of the chariots heading north. The Egyptians now had nine hundred chariots attacking the flanks of what remained of the original twenty-five hundred Hittite chariots that had begun the charge.

"The Hittites had never seen such resistance. Their force was actually two units. The first thirteen hundred were commanded by Spetrin, the King's middle brother, who led the surge north. The rear twelve hundred was commanded by the King's youngest brother, Hattusili. He bore the brunt of the P'Re bowmen as they finished fording the Orontes and turned north.

"As they approached Ramses' camp, Amun's shield wall and Medjay were prepared, having practiced the defensive maneuver that morning. But it was his one thousand bows that did the most damage, as they unleashed volley after volley of arrows into the approaching chariots, adding their toll to that of the nine hundred Egyptian chariots harassing the enemy flank.

"That did not stop Spetrin, who still expected to break through the Egyptian shield wall, while his brother and twelve hundred northern chariots would attack Pharaoh's rear. Our defeat of the northern force, unbeknownst to him, made that impossible. They had no hope. While several hundred initially succeeded in breaking through the defenses, the Amun bowmen made quick work of most of them, including the King's brother, as they got tangled in the closely packed camp tents. Some managed to flee north through the chariot lane established by Ramses, attempting to join the retreat led by Hattusili, who was also trying to flee back across the Orontes.

"Ramses and his personal guard took their chariots and left the camp. They began engaging the stalled enemy below the camp. The Hittites, with only spears, had no way to counter the Egyptian bows. It was a slaughter, with Ramses taking many kills himself, proving to his army that he had a true warrior's heart.

"The Hittite retreat was disastrous as they passed back across where the prepared P'Re bowmen waited, revealing the true ability of the Nubian archers for all to see. These bowmen, called by many 'Archers of the Eye' for their exceptional skill, gave the retreating Hittites no chance. Fewer than two hundred actually made it back across the ford, but all were missing drivers or spearmen. Hattusili lost his driver and fellow spearman. He only survived because he had newly forged iron armor that deflected the arrows shot at him, except for the one that struck his right arm. Sadly, for him, both his brothers perished."

"So, the Hittites lost almost thirty-five hundred chariots?" Gershom asked.

"Yes, almost three thousand five hundred chariots were destroyed. We gathered between all our forces about five hundred captives, most of whom were the only survivor from their chariot. But the worst was yet to come. We had to deal with almost ten thousand Hittite dead, as well as thousands of horses. "We spent the rest of the morning and most of the afternoon stripping all the enemy dead and piling them into mounds throughout the plain to be burned. Only the King's two brothers were honorably returned. The rest met their end in funeral pyres that burned well into the evening. The cooks and many warriors assigned to assist them spread out and began butchering the fallen horses, so everyone feasted on horse steaks for several days."

Moses could see that the description of stripping and burning so many dead physically upset his sons. "I know this is upsetting."

Surprisingly, Eliezer responded while making a face, "So many dead horses. Did you eat horse meat?"

"We all did. Horse meat is good eating."

"I could never eat such a beautiful animal," Gershom said.

"What about the ten thousand Hittite dead?" Moses asked.

"They were the enemy, and it was kill or be killed," Eliezer said. "The horses were victims."

Moses studied his sons for a long moment, then softly said, "You see the horses as innocent because they had no choice in the battle. But neither did most of the men. They were commanded by their king, bound by oaths, driven by duty to their families, and fear of being called cowards. Many were fathers like me or sons like you. War makes killers of us all if we want to survive, not by choice but by the demands war brings. The horses at least died quickly. Many of the men did not."

He paused, letting that settle. "I envy that you can still see death so simply—enemy or victim. After Kadesh, I never could. The Hittites I killed had mothers and some wives, sons, and daughters who would weep for them. Every horse that fed us would have pulled a plow or cart if it hadn't pulled a chariot. War teaches you that everything beautiful can be fed into war's grinder, and everyone you kill was once someone's beautiful child."

He hadn't meant to chasten them, only to show them their innocence, but he could see they took it as a rebuke. He stood up and said, "I need to take another break," then took his staff and, after getting some water, went up the rise outside the camp again.

"That was difficult," Eliezer said.

"I know, but we are going to hear many difficult things tonight, and I'm sure there are more to come," Gershom replied.

"You are right. We asked for this, so we need to be careful not to judge what he says too harshly. Compared to Father, we have led a simple life here in Midian, filled with safe routines. Death stalked him his whole life in Egypt, something we cannot begin to understand."

"Let's get some water and go and check the sheep again," Gershom suggested.

They both got up, each getting a water pouch, and went to check on the flock.

The Spy and Amun-Ra

Moses looked at the star-filled night sky. The moon had not yet risen, so he enjoyed the quiet darkness. It soothed his troubled mind. The further he progressed in his time in Egypt, the more difficult this became. Some of the hardest parts were yet to come. He offered a quiet prayer to the Most High, hoping it would be heard.

> *"O Most High, help me to complete this task while being patient with my sons as they react to what I show them. No matter how hard it is for me to remember and share these events in my life, it is also hard for them to learn about their father in this way. Be merciful and remember my sons and me during this difficult night. Amen."*

After praying, he carefully made his way back to the campfire. His sons had not returned from checking the flock, so he sat down, took a long drink of water from the water pouch, and waited for them.

His sons quietly returned and sat down on either side of him. Eliezer asked, "What's next?"

"There is more you need to know about Kadesh. You may remember I told you about the spy who went to the Hittites and set up the ambush that killed my friends and driver."

"We remember," Gershom said.

"After Baktari's men dispatched the six chariots pursuing me, we found their camp and killed those remaining. It was then that we captured Amunen, the spy and traitor who had helped arrange the ambush. We stripped him to look for poison, the preferred way for Amun-Ra's plotters to make their exit, but never found any. We brought him back to our camp and put him under the guard of my Sherden, the only ones we trusted to keep him alive.

"We didn't tell Ramses anything yet. We needed to question him to learn what he knew. I left that to Semri, who found out from his tentmates that he was deathly afraid of ants and the desert had a particularly vicious variety. One of Semri's men dug up a nest and put them in a bag.

"They stripped the spy and strung him between two poles, his hands tied high and his feet low. He was defiant for a while, until Semri produced the bag of ants, taunting him with them. He took a little honey on a spoon, spread it onto the spy's left foot and lower leg. The man immediately began to scream, but Semri did not relent. Dipping the spoon into the bag, he drew out a few of the red ants, worse than demons, I might add, that still clung to the honey. To make his point, he lifted the spoon in front of Amunen's face, letting him see the ants' mandibles working, their bodies already agitated, and then, bending down, wiped them on the honeyed foot. The ants began crawling through the thick syrup and up his ankle, a few biting as they went. The spy's screams were unlike anything I had ever heard. It was something primal, broken. He thrashed so violently that he passed out."

73

Moses paused, seeing the look on his sons' faces. "I know what you're thinking. After everything I said about the weight of killing, how could I allow such cruelty?

"The truth is, we needed to know what he knew. This wasn't an enemy soldier on a battlefield. This was a spy in my own camp who had sent my friends to their deaths. Amun-Ra's agents had tried to poison me, to arrange 'accidents,' for years. I needed names. I needed to know who else in my command might betray us.

"Does that justify it? I don't know. Semri thought it did. The man was never really hurt. A few bites on his ankle were nothing compared to warriors' wounds in battle. We used his own fear against him. Semri reminded me that intelligence saves lives. We had no way of knowing what we would learn, but we needed the truth, and that kind of abject fear provided it. Maybe he was right, or maybe I was wrong to agree." Moses looked away. "But some nights I can still hear that man screaming. Some things you do because you must, not because you should."

Gershom spoke quietly. "Did you have to be there? When Semri...when the ants..."

"No," Moses said. "I could have stayed away. But these were my men who died. This was my command that was compromised. I needed to look Amunen in the eyes and know he understood what his betrayal had cost."

Moses took a breath. "Let me continue."

"Semri's men wiped his leg clean, and then they threw water in his face to revive him. After holding the bag in front of his face again, Amunen begged us to allow him to tell us everything. We had brought a scribe along to record everything, and it took almost five pages of papyrus to document his complete confession, which he and Semri signed and inked with their thumbprints. The scribe made a second copy, which both signed again. I had my leather master make two pouches to hold the confessions, which allowed Semri and me to keep them on our persons until we could give them to Pharaoh."

Truce, Honoring the Dead, Cowards' Justice

Moses waited for most of the shock and reaction to the torture to pass. After his sons had been quiet for a few minutes, he said, "I want to now tell you how we honored our dead and executed justice on the cowards who had fled when the Hittites broke through P'Re. Ramses met with all five of his corps' generals, including me, about how to deal with those who had deserted the battle."

Moses paused. "I know what that may sound like. We had just fought side by side with some of these men, and now we were condemning them to death. Brothers executing brothers.

"But Ramses was right about one thing. Everyone knew that if desertion went unpunished, discipline would collapse. Every soldier needs to know the man beside him will hold the line. At Kadesh, some had broken and run. Their cowardice had nearly cost us everything.

"Still, I found no satisfaction in it. Fortunately for us, we had no cowards to add to their number. Ne'arin's discipline had held. Some of the condemned protested their innocence. Others wept. A few met their end with defiant pride, claiming they had only done what any other man would do.

"Who's to say they were wrong? In their place, would I have held? I'd like to think so. But I had Semri's training, the Sherden guard, the divine presence in battle. They had none of that. Just orders to stand against thousands of Hittite chariots."

"How many were executed?" Eliezer asked quietly.

"Over three hundred," Moses said. "From P'Re alone, two hundred and ninety. There were only a handful from Amun at Pharaoh's camp. P'Re's general, Piankh, personally supervised every execution. He said it was his responsibility. They were almost all his men, his failure.

"Ramses had to do this. He was very concerned about maintaining the integrity of his army while demonstrating to everyone, friend and foe alike, that cowardice would not be tolerated. Since we were meeting with Muwatalli that day at noon to work out a truce, and the ransoming of prisoners still awaited, the execution of deserters risked dividing the army, but not to do so risked more.

"Scribes recorded every accusation, and it was made clear that anyone who falsely accused someone would face execution themselves, in an effort to prevent any attempts at vengeance.

"We separated the honored dead from those killed while fleeing using body position and the location of wounds. A man struck from behind while running away bore different marks than one who died facing the enemy.

"Early that morning, all five armies assembled, and we burned the honorable dead with offered prayers and a strong ritual that Ramses led with dignity and honor. Then came the execution of the condemned and the burning of their bodies with those deemed to have died dishonorably.

"Muwatalli and Muršili, his Chief Scout, watched from a rise beside the fortress. Muršili later told Paser they were impressed by our unity. It was the kind of discipline the Hittite confederation could never achieve with its contending kingdoms.

"Later that day, after some political maneuvering, we agreed upon the truce. The next day, the Hittites brought enough treasure to ransom four hundred and fifty of their prisoners, leaving fifty to return with us to Memphis. Ramses distributed the portion for the troops that afternoon, which caused celebration throughout the camps, as everyone would return home with physical treasure, not just stories of their prowess. The Ne'arin were assigned to transport the remaining fifty prisoners back to Memphis—all of whom, surprisingly, had volunteered. Ramses gave us the responsibility of keeping them safe on the long journey home.

"The terms of the truce left Kadesh under Muwatalli, so while we had become the first army to successfully withstand the Hittite chariot charge, we had failed our primary objective. Keeping Kadesh within Egyptian influence was why we had engaged in this war. That failure, and the problem of Amun-Ra traitors assisting the Hittites, created a difficult situation for Ramses when he returned to Memphis.

"That evening, while the army celebrated the ransom, Paser informed Ramses that Muršili, Muwatalli's Chief Scout, had warned him that Amun-Ra spies were throughout our army and had been sending reports to the Hittites ever since we left Memphis. Paser also instructed Semri and me to bring the spy and his confession to Ramses, which we did. This confirmed what Muršili had revealed. Pharaoh ensured the spy was protected by his own personal guard, while the confessions were entrusted to Pharaoh's Chief Scribe, who was also assigned a guard.

"I remember the night we brought the confession to Ramses. He read it by lamplight in his tent, his face growing darker with each line. When he finished, he looked at Semri and me. 'How many?'

he asked. 'How many priests of Amun-Ra can I trust?'

"Neither of us had an answer. The confession named seventeen conspirators spread throughout the army and a few in Egypt, but there were hundreds of Amun-Ra priests across Egypt. Any of them might be loyal to the Chief Priest rather than to their god or Pharaoh.

"'We're marching home with an army that might tear itself apart,' Ramses said. 'If word of this spreads before we leave Kadesh, we'll have Egyptian fighting Egyptian before the Hittites are out of sight.'

"He was right to be concerned. The spy and his confession needed immediate protection. That was our only direct evidence of the Amun-Ra conspiracy. Those named in the confession needed to be apprehended, though some had already disappeared.

"The question Ramses had asked was more difficult: which priests could he trust? He immediately assigned guards to all Amun-Ra priests in the army until they could demonstrate their loyalty to Pharaoh rather than to Nephura and to protect them from any retribution.

"All of this uncertainty seriously complicated our march home and endangered the hard-won unity Ramses had just accomplished. The possibility of the army dividing along temple lines and erupting into open conflict was very real."

"How did you solve that problem?" Gershom asked.

"Fully addressing the problem had to wait until the army was well south of Kadesh. The army needed to start for home while the truce still held, so Muwatalli wouldn't be tempted to use any outbreak of conflict as an excuse to attack a divided army.

"While Ramses used his most trusted men to search for any traitors who could be identified immediately, scribes recorded the names of anyone from the four corps who disappeared. We were left to handle any Ne'arin issues ourselves."

Leaving Kadesh and Traveling Home

"Our immediate task was to head home as quickly as possible. All five corps spent the next day preparing for the march to Memphis, and the following morning, the entire army departed from Kadesh. The main army followed the same route home, while we took the coastal route south again.

"Semri and I, along with our commanders and my Sherden guard, conducted a thorough review of our troops and support personnel. We noted several disappearances, and we felt reasonably assured that any remaining traitors had fled.

"Four days south of Kadesh, Ramses assembled the whole army and explained the problem. By then, about fifteen people had disappeared, including one of the priests he had been protecting, along with a number of horses and some of the captured Hittite chariots. He ensured that everyone understood it was only the traitors following Nephura, not true followers of Amun-Ra, who were at fault. The remainder of the journey passed without a major incident.

"We later learned that the traitors had sent messenger pigeons to Nephura in Thebes and to his replacement in Memphis, Ameny, warning them that we had caught a spy who had confessed. I had one advantage that only Semri and I knew about. My scribe had secretly made a third copy of the confession. While it lacked Amunen's signature, it contained everything he had revealed. This gave Semri and me the names of all those the spy had exposed, allowing us to verify that no traitors remained in the Ne'arin and to prepare for any lingering danger their families might pose upon our return.

"No Amun-Ra treachery disrupted our journey home. Both the main army and the Ne'arin faced only the usual travel hardships we had encountered on the journey to Kadesh. Yet when we returned to Memphis, a day behind Pharaoh, nothing was the same. But that belongs to the next part of my remembrance."

Moses looked at his two sons and said, "Before we move on to the part of my life after Kadesh, are there any questions you need to ask about what you have learned so far?"

Gershom and Eliezer looked at each other for a moment. Gershom shook his head. Eliezer, however, asked, "How did the rest of the army react to your defeat of the Hittite prince?"

"That was embarrassing. The story of the fight spread quickly throughout Pharaoh's four corps. I became a Kadesh legend, and with each retelling, my prowess grew with every exaggeration added to the tale. By the time we arrived in Memphis, the commanders began trying to downplay the significance of the clash, fearing it would overshadow Ramses. There was nothing I could do. We were on a separate march, and Semri and I were able to keep the response of the Ne'arin from getting out of hand. We argued that I had acted like any other Ne'arin warrior, and that my victory was no different than what we expected from everyone in the corps."

Moses paused and looked at his sons. "Knowing that, I need you to understand that the reality of war is different from the stories of glory. It is like surgery; while sometimes necessary, only a madman or a surgeon enjoys cutting into living flesh or revels in the slaughter that war demands.

"I remember what Ramses once said to me: 'Do not glory in war or battle itself, but take glory in what we defend, in the defeat of the destroyer who would lay waste to that which we protect. No, we glory not in war but in Egypt, and my troops glory in their Pharaoh, who is Egypt before the gods.' Ramses paused and then went on, 'Warriors glory in courage and stout hearts tested by blood and death, and in those who stand with them against fear and evil, but do we glory in war itself? May the gods forbid it.'"

Moses could still hear Ramses' voice as if he were speaking now. "Ramses was realistic about serious conflict. He once told me, 'War is a malevolent master. Though sometimes necessary, it is a disease upon the land. It can devour all that is good and noble, leaving only weeping and destruction in its wake, despite the glory we rightfully take in victory and the courage it takes to achieve it. Yes, even as victors we celebrate, remembering how our hearts rose to meet the challenge, yet we are diminished by the demands that war makes upon us—and that is the truth of it. No, only a fool glories in war for war's sake.'"

Moses paused, then asked, "Is there anything else?"

Gershom spoke up. "Why do you think the fifty Hittites volunteered to come to Memphis and await ransom?"

"I discussed that very question with Nazim, my new driver. He was a regular soldier, so I felt he would have a more grounded insight into their decision. He believed that after such a terrible defeat, it was their only way to restore some measure of honor. I agree. It demonstrated they still possessed courage."

Moses waited, but his sons had no more questions.

"I will now tell you how everything was different after returning to Memphis."

Returning to Memphis After Kadesh

"When we returned to Memphis, not all the Ne'arin had families to return to. We needed to maintain the corps, knowing that Ramses would eventually need to engage the Hittites again. No one could be released until Ramses allowed it, under penalty of desertion. After several days, when the official celebrations had subsided, Pharaoh called his generals together to plan their next steps.

"Fortunately, none of Egypt's nearby vassals had used the opportunity of Ramses' absence to create any problems. The only immediate concern was dealing with the treachery of Nephura and his followers, who were scattered throughout the temples and among Amun-Ra's followers. Any incursion back into Syria could not begin until next spring, if then, and would most likely not involve a massive force like the one that went to Kadesh. Any of these strikes would need to be quick and unpredictable, requiring concerted efforts to prevent the enemy from identifying our targets in advance.

"Pharaoh's vizier, Paser, had left for Memphis with a small chariot force while the army was still ten days' journey from the city. Publicly, he arrived early to prepare for the army's celebration. Privately, he needed to ascertain how far knowledge of Nephura's treasonous actions had spread. He also wanted to activate the embedded agents he and Semri had successfully placed around Nephura in the first few years after the edict was rescinded.

"Paser didn't include me in these plans, but later I learned his strategy. If he moved too quickly to implement Nephura's death with a 'god event', it could drive the rest of the Amun-Ra agents and committed supporters deeper underground, making them harder to root out. He needed to balance mapping out the treasonous network with cutting off the leadership. There was one other hope from my perspective. Maybe the Most High could take out Nephura and Ameny in a sandstorm on their way to their western desert temple complex, where they could best protect themselves from Ramses' retribution. That would be a 'god event' that could not be laid at the feet of Pharaoh. The more I considered this possibility, the more it became my diligent prayer request as we approached Memphis."

Both brothers leaned forward. "What happened?" Gershom asked.

"We were three days from Memphis when a messenger arrived. Nephura and Ameny had left Thebes two days earlier, heading west toward their temple complex in the desert. It was the one place they felt safe from Ramses. They had a caravan of perhaps forty people: priests, guards, servants, supplies for a long stay.

"The messenger said a sandstorm had struck them in the western desert. It was not a normal storm. It came out of nowhere without warning—a wall of crushing sand. It was like the hand of a god striking them down. The caravan had vanished. Search parties found nothing. No bodies, no survivors, no trace. Just...gone.

"When Semri told me, I said nothing. I went up on the rise where I could be alone and knelt in the sand. I felt the presence of the Most High. Not speaking, not commanding, just present. Confirming.

"I had prayed for this. Asked the Most High to strike down my enemy. And He had answered. You would think I'd feel triumph, or relief, or vindication. Instead, I felt...fear. Not of Nephura anymore, but of the God who would reach down from heaven and sweep away forty people because I had asked Him to.

"Semri found me there an hour later. 'You prayed for this,' he said. He knew. He always knew.

"'Yes,' I told him. 'And now I know what it means to be heard by a God who can bring to pass His will. It's terrifying, Semri. More terrifying than any battle.'"

The brothers sat in silence. Finally, Eliezer spoke, his voice quiet. "You prayed for God to kill them. And He did."

"Yes."

"All forty of them? The servants, the guards. They weren't all conspirators, were they?"

"They were," Moses said. "If Nephura took them with him, he trusted them, knew they were loyal to his cause. I prayed for Nephura's death. The Most High answered by taking everyone with him."

He looked at his sons. "When you pray for justice, be very careful. Because sometimes the Most High grants exactly what you ask for, and you discover you weren't prepared for the weight of getting it."

Gershom asked, "Did the Egyptians believe their gods did this as judgment?"

"Yes. That was the common explanation. However, despite solving one problem, it created others. While it would give all the other supporters pause, it would also drive them, as I had surmised earlier, deeper underground. Only the most committed would remain active, and they still pursued my death until they believed I died in the desert, while fleeing to Midian.

"Ramses decided he still needed to exaggerate his warrior actions at Kadesh. He felt that would give him the prominence necessary to counter any lingering support for Nephura's position anywhere in the Two Lands. Since he planned to elevate my position at court, he didn't want any further fallout from holdouts who still adhered to Nephura's opposition to threaten me. He also wanted to use my new legend to his advantage.

"Life went on. Months passed. Ramses consolidated his power, rotated troops, and negotiated the ransoms. Then, about six months after the sandstorm, he summoned me.

"'You need a proper Egyptian wife,' he said. No preamble, no discussion. Just a command dressed as advice. 'I'll arrange it.'"

Both sons noticed the darkened expression on his face as he continued.

"He made a fine choice. Her name was Nashwa, which means happiness."

Moses bowed his head a moment before going on. "She was the daughter of a hereditary prince, Heqan-Akht, who came from a well-placed family. He adored Ramses, which made it easier for her to accept the arrangement.

"Nashwa was tall and beautiful, yes. But it was more than that. She carried herself with elegant grace and spoke with quiet intelligence. She could discuss the trade routes through Punt as easily as the proper offerings to Hathor. When I first met her, she smiled at me. Not the practiced smile you see at court, but something genuine. I was lost. My heart was overwhelmed. I had expected duty. Instead, I found the woman my heart longed for.

"As part of the contract, Ramses agreed to appoint Heqan-Akht to an important role in Pharaoh's court, Viceroy of Kush, ensuring the position was filled with someone he could trust. The negotiations and the need to add my family quarters to the Great Estate's compound meant we didn't complete the contract until after the next inundation. Semri and I had to both oversee the Ne'arin and build my future house. We had plenty of help, but I was very demanding and needed to oversee every aspect, which greatly slowed progress."

"What do you mean by contract?" Eliezer asked. "We have a ceremony invoking God's blessing and much feasting."

"While marriages in Midian and among the Hebrews in Egypt are religious as well as family events, it is not so for Egyptians. Their marriages are legal and social contracts in which the gods take no direct part, except perhaps Ma'at, which undergirds everything, especially the fairness of negotiations. In the case of political unions like mine, the families formally negotiate terms and sign a contract. Ramses, who arranged the marriage, negotiated on behalf of our family."

Moses paused, taking a deep breath before continuing. "It is very difficult to remember my wife, even after all these years. The first woman who takes your heart never leaves you."

Moses paused, looked up at the stars, and clasped his hands together. He sat silently for several minutes.

Eliezer waited for a while, then gently asked, "I know it's hard, but can you tell us what happened to her, Father?"

"I would prefer to wait. That tragedy happened almost nineteen years later. Don't be impatient. Let my remembrance unfold as it occurred. It is obvious that I lost my family, but let that moment come at the proper time."

Both his sons nodded in agreement, despite their urgent desire to know right now.

"There were other significant events occurring during this period. Fifty prisoners remained to be ransomed. Ramses was confident that Muwatalli would not attempt any further incursions until all the prisoners were safely home. This gave the army breathing room and allowed him to send three of the four Egyptian corps home, keeping Sutekh's corps at only half strength, while regularly rotating troops home while keeping them on notice for quick recall. Since Sutekh never fought at Kadesh, it was the best choice for the army's morale. That rotation gave everyone who needed it a chance to return home to their families.

"While almost all of the Hebrews, Nubians, and Egyptians had family to return to, many of the Ne'arin had no one in Egypt, so we did our best to ensure that everyone with a family got time off to go home. We were also concerned that if too many Ne'arin were gone for too long, we might begin to lose the 'one army, one warrior' solidarity we had so painstakingly built. Ramses wanted to keep the Ne'arin as battle-ready as possible. He trusted their ability, proven at Kadesh, to quickly adapt to whatever the situation demanded. The Egyptian corps were more regimented and less flexible, though they had adapted admirably during the Hittite charge.

"It took longer than expected to raise the ransom. The Hittites waited until they had enough to ransom everyone, rather than repeatedly offering partial ransoms. Ramses and I both agreed that this was intentional. Muwatalli needed to maintain internal kingdom unity if he still wanted to launch attacks to the south. We both believed this was true, but it worked to our advantage to extend the period during which we faced little threat of a Hittite incursion.

"I remember the day the prisoners finally left for home. We'd kept them for almost eight months. Some had become friends with their guards. I watched one of the Sherden guards embrace a Hittite he'd been assigned to watch over. They'd been teaching each other their languages. War is strange that way. You can respect the enemy even though you may need to fight him again.

"That gave Ramses the time to consolidate his version of Kadesh and inscribe it on temple walls for all to see. It allowed the questions surrounding Nephura and Ameny's demise to fade, and the narrative of the gods' judgment to take hold."

My Marriage

"The next event in my life that mattered was my marriage to Nashwa. In the months before the contract signing, we spent time together—walks in the estate gardens, quiet conversations about what we hoped our life might be. She asked about Kadesh, about the Ne'arin, about my adoptive mother. I asked about her childhood, her interests, and her fears.

"Our time together was important, and it made the transition to the Great Estate's household an easy one. As for the formal contract, I left everything to Ramses and her father.

"Her name proved to be not just a hope given at birth, but an expression of her attitude toward life and, eventually, toward me. The woman was genuinely happy and seemed to find the best in every situation. I believe the Most High guided Ramses in choosing my wife. She was the woman I needed. She brought joy into the difficult life I had led up to the moment she became part of me.

"Our union and the celebration Ramses set up at the palace took place immediately after the second inundation following our return.

"Asati couldn't help herself and offered a great deal of advice on how to begin my relationship with Nashwa. Primarily, her counsel came down to 'take it slow; be patient and let her guide you.' Semri agreed, drawing on how his own marriage to Asati had begun. 'Patience,' he said with a smile, 'yields lasting fruits.'

"Our marriage festivities made one thing clear to everyone: Ramses knew how to put on a celebration. It was six days, during which Nashwa and I stayed at the palace instead of traveling home each night. "There was excellent wine, and we had so many delicacies from the palace bakery. The chef outdid himself, coming up with something new each day to tantalize the attendees.

"While most celebrations slowly ebb as guests departed, ours sustained its energy throughout the week. Almost everyone stayed to experience each new treat and, of course, to court Ramses' favor.

"I recall a particular moment from the third night. The musicians were playing, guests were dancing, and Nashwa took my hand. 'Come with me,' she said. She led me out to the palace gardens, where it was quieter. The music drifted faintly behind us.

"'Are you happy?' she asked.

"I looked at her. Though I had only known this woman for six months, she had completely overwhelmed me and would now share my life. 'More than you can ever know,' I said. And I meant it. For the first time in years, despite everything that had gone before, I felt real peace.

"She smiled that genuine smile of hers. 'Good. Because I am too.' She leaned against me, and we stood there in the garden, listening to distant music and feeling the cool night air. It was a perfect moment, and despite the later tragedy, I now realize that I still cherish it. This was a gift from the Most High.

"Ramses' excellent planning also helped focus attention on Heqan-Akht's future ascension as Viceroy of Kush, which would take almost two years to finalize. His appointment also elevated the status of my new family.

"Fortunately for our marriage, we had well over a year and a half before Ramses initiated new attacks on Hittite holdings in Syria, giving us time to learn about each other and grow together as husband and wife."

Moses stopped, looked at the ground, and allowed his head to sink even further down.

The brothers sat in silence, watching their father. It was obvious to both his sons how much their father had loved his first wife. His earlier comment about the depth of one's first love played out in front of them. He sat with his shoulders bowed, unable to lift his head, lost in a memory both sweet and unbearably painful. Gershom reached out, placing a hand on Moses' shoulder. Eliezer did the same from the other side. They said nothing. What words could answer such grief?

The New Syrian Campaign

They sat together in silence for several minutes. Finally, Moses lifted his head. "I'm sorry. Some memories are...harder than others."

"We understand," Gershom said quietly.

Moses took a long breath. "Where was I? Oh yes, the campaigns. After Nashwa and I married, there was little time for peace. Within months, Ramses was planning new strikes into Syria. Because the initial campaigns following Kadesh lasted two full seasons, once they began, there was little time for family. Those first campaigns were wildly successful, and after two spring campaigns, we took almost a year off from further Syrian operations. It was not until we were forced to march north and retake Dapur, which had reverted to Hittite control, that we set out again. This time, Ramses took six of his young sons with him to introduce them to the art of war as he successfully retook the city."

"How were you involved in these battles?" Gershom asked.

"Most of the time Ramses would take one or two Egyptian corps on the campaign, depending on the target, sometimes feinting with one corps as a decoy to hide his real intentions. He always took the Ne'arin. He trusted us to guard his flanks and rear. This proved crucial at Dapur, when a hastily assembled Hittite relief force tried to attack us from the rear.

"I remember it vividly. We were holding Ramses' rear when the Hittite relief force appeared, perhaps five hundred chariots. Semri looked at me and said, 'Like old times.'

"But it wasn't. At Kadesh, I had nothing to lose except my life. Now I had Nashwa waiting at home. For the first time, I understood what soldiers with families felt before battle. I now knew the gnawing fear that you might not return.

"The battle itself was quick. Our new iron arrows and improved tactics made the difference. But experiencing that fear was new. After that, I carried it in every confrontation.

"The Hittite chariots now included both a bowman and a spearman, but they still had significant disadvantages in both tactics and equipment. Their chariots did not change their heavy construction, as they were designed to carry three people. That made them harder to maneuver in the open field than our faster, more nimble platforms. Most importantly, they had not yet perfected the composite bow, which meant they lacked the extra distance and force of our arrows. They also were not very good at shooting on the run, something we had long ago perfected. This gave us a decisive advantage in all engagements.

"We made improvements as well. The Ne'arin adjusted their shield construction and tactics to counter Hittite arrows more effectively, thereby protecting our archers and chariots, which proved crucial in holding our defensive positions.

"Egyptian metal smiths began working with the captured iron. The amount surprised everyone. They were able to melt it down and recast it for other uses. The metal smiths adapted their furnaces to produce more heat by adding a larger, more efficient bellows, which more than doubled the airflow needed to melt and recast the iron.

"After much consultation, it was decided to use most of the material to make stronger arrow points. That would magnify the advantage of our composite bows. Testing showed that at close range, the new arrows could even pierce the captured Hittite iron armor. They enhanced sections of Ramses' armor with iron, but because he didn't like the growing weight, these were limited to the most critical areas: his heart, neck, and groin.

"These Syrian and Canaanite engagements were different from Kadesh, where we had defended against an attack from a massive Hittite chariot force. Now we were on the offensive, launching quick, precise strikes before opposing forces could fully prepare or seek reinforcements.

"After securing our Syrian objectives of Dapur and Tunip, we marched south through Canaan to deal with Egyptian vassals who had wavered after hearing distorted reports claiming we had lost the battle of Kadesh, while conveniently leaving out the fact that this was the first time anyone had ever defeated their vaunted chariot charge and forced Muwatalli into a truce.

"These were rapid strikes against smaller forces. Within weeks, Ramses struck up and down the coast—Merom, Salem, Acre, Ashkelon.

"Some cities surrendered before we even engaged them. Our reputation, established at Kadesh and reinforced by these subsequent victories, had spread. We were swift and decisive. We exacted their punishment, applied mercy where appropriate, and secured willing submission to Pharaoh. We were gone before any effective opposition could organize. By the time the year's inundation had passed, we were finally able to return to Memphis.

"The Ne'arin performed admirably throughout. Our new iron arrowheads proved devastatingly effective, and our improved shield tactics, which we continually refined, held against Hittite arrows. Slowly, Ramses' Egyptian corps began incorporating the best of what the Ne'arin had to offer. The Egyptian army was becoming an even more formidable force than the one Muwatalli had encountered at Kadesh.

"When we returned from these early campaigns, something interesting began to happen. Rather than being resupplied with castoffs from the other corps, Egyptians and Nubians began volunteering to join us. Eventually, we had to turn men away. Semri and I did not want to establish a second corps, and there were historical and practical limitations on the size of corps in Egyptian armies."

Moses looked at his sons and asked, "Do you want to take another break?"

"No!" they both said in unison. "How much longer did you fight these campaigns?"

"Other than some minor skirmishes, this was the end of major battles. We maintained the army's full strength for several years longer through extensive training and regular competitions between the various corps.

"During those years, Pharaoh's Vizier, Paser, worked diligently to reshape Egypt's image of me. But just as important, with the leadership of Amun-Ra gone and the activities of those who might still be seeking my demise driven deep underground, the constant threat was reduced from a continuous shout to a rare whisper.

"Now that the serious campaigns were over, it was time for me to step back from commanding the Ne'arin. They needed someone to lead them into the future, and I needed to spend time with my family."

"How long did that take?" Gershom asked.

"That took nearly two years. We needed someone the men would follow—someone with tactical skills and the temperament to lead. Ramses suggested Khamwaset, a young commander who had distinguished himself in the Syrian campaigns. He was ambitious but sometimes reckless. I convinced Ramses that Khafre was the best choice, and with the respect of the charioteers, he was best suited to maintain the 'one army, one warrior' core of the Ne'arin."

"Did you train him yourself?" Gershom asked.

"Semri and I both worked with him. We took him through exercises, let him lead the corps practice, and gradually gave him more responsibility. By the third year, Khafre was leading most operations, and I was only there on rare occasions in an advisory role. It was the right time for the transition. The Ne'arin needed a general they could trust and who believed in their uniqueness.

"I released Derden and the Sherden from their oath to me. He objected and wanted to move to the estate with a protective detail, but I told him no. He needed to look to his new general, not me. Semri continued to work with them. He had a hard time letting go of his attachment to the corps.

"Eventually, the event that sealed Ramses' reign happened. He signed the treaty with the new Hittite king, Hattusili. It was a peace that held the entire time I remained in Egypt."

Moses paused. "That treaty, after fifteen long years following Kadesh, gave me the time with Nashwa I wouldn't have had otherwise. Years I'm grateful for, even though..." He stopped, quashing the anguish before it could rise again.

Early Married Life

Moses sat quietly, letting his sons take their time in making sense of everything he had shared.

Then Eliezer asked, "We know discussing your marriage is difficult, but can you tell us what that time was like for you?"

Moses looked at them directly. "It's alright. It's something you should be aware of.

"After the campaigns ended, life settled into something I'd never known before—peace. Real peace, not just the absence of war. Life at the Great Estate had continued in Semri's absence and mine. Nashwa became a favorite of Asati and Nari, as she lived up to her name. She brought light and lifted the mood wherever she went. She and Asati spent many evenings laughing, talking, and playing board games.

"One thing did cast a small pall over Asati's and Nashwa's time together. She had not yet conceived before I left for Syria, and Asati feared that barrenness might plague my new wife as well. Nashwa would have none of it. She explained that the women in her family had always been slow to have children. She assured Asati there was nothing to fear. Her cheerfulness soon overcame Asati's concerns.

"Each time I returned home during those first campaigns, I found a household that had been further transformed by her presence. There was a lightness that permeated the Great Estate, a warmth it had previously lacked. I could see it in the servants' ready smiles, and I was not alone in noticing.

"The success of those Syrian and Canaanite campaigns helped wash away the memory of our failure to retake the fortress of Kadesh. The battles themselves had become almost routine, if war can ever be thought of as such. We struck quickly, secured Egyptian interests, and returned before our enemies could mount effective resistance. Ramses relied on the Ne'arin to guard his flanks and rear while the main corps engaged frontally. The tactics we had proven at Kadesh became an important part of Egypt's standard approach in warfare.

"Between campaigns, Ramses kept me at court, not my favorite place. Necessary work, but my heart was always at the estate. Ramses assigned me duties to keep me visible. I advised him on military preparations, reviewed reports from frontier garrisons, and attended ceremonies where my presence reminded nobles and foreign dignitaries of Egypt's strength to wage war.

"During the fourth year of our marriage, Nashwa finally conceived. I clearly remember the evening she shared this with me. We were seated in the estate's garden. She took my hand and placed it on her belly, though there was nothing yet to feel. Her eyes held such joyous certainty that my heart leaped, and I believed her before any physical signs appeared. Asati wept with joy when we shared the news with her. Even Nari, usually so reserved, embraced Nashwa with uncommon warmth.

"Those months progressed with surprising ease for my wife. I found myself more anxious than I had ever been before any battle. I could face Hittite chariots and Syrian defenders without hesitation, but the thought of my wife in childbirth terrified me in ways I could not put into words. Semri noticed my unease and kept reminding me that for women, childbearing was a natural part of life. He constantly told me, 'She will be fine.'"

Moses leaned back as he recalled this happy time, and a sad exuberance softened his face.

"When her labor began," he continued, "Asati sent Semri and me away. She argued that we would only be in the way, and from the look on Semri's face, he agreed. We spent the time in intense training, working off the anxiety, neither of us speaking except out of necessity. With every cry that reached us from the house, we fought harder. Semri would attack, I would defend, then we'd switch. Neither of us wanted to think about what those cries might mean. The sun moved across the sky. Still, we fought. My arms ached. I didn't care. As long as I kept moving, I didn't have to imagine what was happening inside.

"The birth took most of the day. When Nari finally found us and told me I had a daughter, I felt something I had not expected. Yes, there was relief, but a fierce protectiveness rose from deep within me, surprising me. I commanded the Ne'arin, fought intense battles, but this little child had conquered me before I even saw her face.

"I hurried to our bedroom, flushed with expectation. Nashwa lay exhausted but triumphant. She held our daughter wrapped in fine linen, and when she looked up at me, I saw in her eyes something I recognized from the battlefield. She had the look of someone who had faced ultimate choices and prevailed."

"What did you name her?" Eliezer asked quietly.

Moses paused, and for the first time since recounting his wife's story, he smiled. The memory was still tender despite all these years. "Merti. It means 'beloved.' Nashwa chose it. She said our daughter was beloved before she ever drew breath."

The smile faded as quickly as it had come. "None of my Hebrew family knew my daughters. Even Miriam, who worked at the estate for years, kept her distance, fearing she would expose our relationship if she showed them too much attention. That is one of my great regrets." Moses shifted his weight. "Their memory now lives only with me. Merti was careful and thoughtful, even as a small child. She would watch everything before deciding how to act. In that way, she reminded me more of Nari than of Nashwa or me.

"The first weeks after her birth, I didn't know what to do. I could command men in battle, but I had no idea how to act around something so small and fragile. Nashwa would laugh gently at my awkwardness. She was patient and taught me how to hold Merti properly and how to interpret her different cries. It was another language, one that I slowly learned to speak.

"Two years later, we had a second daughter. This time, I chose the name: Sitra, which means 'protection.' By then, I was learning to be a father, though Nashwa still had to correct my missteps. Sitra was the opposite of her sister. Where Merti watched and waited, Sitra acted first and thought afterwards. She kept Nashwa busy from the moment she learned to crawl.

"Those were good years. I attended court when required, continuing to advise Ramses on military matters. But my heart was always at home. I would return from court to find Merti carefully arranging her toys while Sitra scattered them everywhere. Nashwa would look at me with amusement, as if to say, 'They are like night and day, like you and Semri.'

"This was clearly shown by one evening when Merti was perhaps four. She had arranged all her dolls in careful rows, each one positioned just so. Sitra, barely two, toddled over and scattered them with one sweep of her arm. Merti didn't cry or yell. She just looked at her sister, then at me, with this expression of weary patience. She seemed to say, 'You see what I deal with?' Then she calmly began arranging them again.

"Sitra, meanwhile, had already moved on to climbing onto a table she had no business being on. I caught her before she fell. She laughed. The girl was fearless, always fearless.

"Those early years passed quietly. Merti grew into a girl who loved stories, especially the ones Nari told about the old ways of Egypt. Sitra preferred to follow Semri around, watching him work with the guards. She declared she would be a warrior like her father.

99

Nashwa and I would exchange glances, knowing that would never happen, but we were careful not to discourage her spirit.

"I grew comfortable after years without incident. The underground followers of Nephura had been silent for so long. No attacks, no poisoning attempts, no suspicious deaths among those close to me. I believed they had given up or died off. I eventually learned I was wrong. We will talk about that later.

"You should know that these years of comfort affected me in other ways, striking at the heart of my relationship with the Most High. I tell you this now with shame. The Most High had pulled me from the Nile for a purpose. Nari had told me that years before.

"But I was comfortable. I had Nashwa, my daughters, and my position at court. I saw the suffering of the Hebrews at work sites, but I turned away. I told myself there was nothing I could do. That Pharaoh would never listen. That my position was too precarious.

"The truth? I didn't want to risk what I had. I chose comfort over calling. And the Most High let me make that choice, for a time.

"Then Miriam came to me one morning at the estate. I saw her approaching and knew immediately something was wrong. She didn't wait for pleasantries.

"'Your mother is dying,' she said. 'You need to come.'

"I felt something twist in my chest. My real mother. The one I'd failed to see when my father died. 'I can't,' I said. 'It's too dangerous. If anyone sees me in the village…'

"'She's dying, Moses.' Miriam's voice was flat. 'Do you want to fail her a second time?' Her words bit deep.

"When Nashwa learned my former nursemaid was dying, she encouraged me to go and see her. She gave me the cover I needed and destroyed my only real excuse."

Meeting My Real Mother Before She Died

"So, you did go?" Eliezer said.

"Yes. Miriam's message had been clear: I could delay no longer. Early that morning, after explaining to Asati, Nari, Nashwa, and Semri that I was going to pay respects to my dying nursemaid, I took my chariot and set out alone for the Hebrew village. While it was not a lie, it was far from the whole truth.

"The journey did not take long, but with each turn of the wheels, the weight of what I was doing pressed down on me. Not just this visit, but all the years I had avoided it. I had not been to Jochebed's village since the day I arrived too late to meet my father. After that failure, my focus shifted to my duty to Ramses, the events at court, the ongoing campaigns, my marriage to Nashwa, and finally, my children.

"I had gone early, and as I approached the village, I saw groups of Hebrew workers leaving for their day's labor. Some glanced at my chariot with the wariness all Hebrews showed toward Egyptians of rank. None recognized me. Why would they? They may have heard about me and my Hebrew heritage, but this was only the second time I had come to the village. I was alone, without retinue or announcement. They had no way to know who I was.

"Miriam was waiting at the edge of the settlement. She offered no greeting. I hobbled my horses, and she simply turned and led me through the narrow paths between the humble homes. I was reminded how different this world was from the estate and my life as a Prince of Egypt. Everything here was sparse and worn. There were no gardens, no decorative pools, no courtyards at all. The homes were functional shelters, nothing more.

"'We asked the others to leave,' Miriam said as we reached a small dwelling of mud brick. 'She has been asking for you since yesterday. I told her you would come.' There was reproach in her voice, though she kept it carefully measured.

"I stepped to the doorway. There I hesitated. My hand rested on the doorframe, but I could not make myself step forward. Miriam waited, but finally said, 'She is your mother, Moses. Whatever you have become, she is still your mother.'

"Miriam reached for the door, opened it, and gestured for me to enter. Jochebed sat at a simple wooden table in the small room, an empty chair waiting opposite her. Her eyes lit up when she saw me. She gestured toward the open seat, and I saw relief wash over her face as I sat down. She was drinking something from a cup, and as I sat, a hacking cough wracked her, which she tried to stifle.

"My sister asked, 'Are you alright, Mother?'

"'I'm fine. You can leave.'

"Miriam shrugged, stepped back outside, and closed the door, leaving us alone.

"For a long moment, neither of us spoke. I studied the grain of the wooden table, its roughness. Jochebed took another sip from her cup, her hands trembling slightly as her cough tried several times to assert itself. I did not know where to begin or what to say. So many years had passed, and this was our first contact beyond her work as a nursemaid, when I was too young to remember. The silence held until she set down her cup and looked directly at me.

"'You have grown into a strong man,' she said. Her voice was rough and worn by illness, but there was warmth in it. 'When I put you in that basket, I prayed that God would protect you. I did not know if I would ever see you again, or what you would become.'

"'You did what you had to do,' I said. The words felt inadequate even as I spoke them.

"'I did what I hoped would save your life,' she corrected gently. 'Whether it was right or wrong, I cannot say. But you are here. You are alive, and for that I thank the Most High.' Another cough shook her, and she reached for the cup again.

"I waited until the cough subsided. 'I should have come earlier, but I was unsure of the consequences, and to be honest, I was afraid of what it might do to me. However, Miriam said you were sick and wanted to see me.'

"'I am dying, Moses.' She said it matter-of-factly, without a hint of self-pity. 'I wanted to see my son before I died. Not the Egyptian prince. Not Pharaoh's commander. Just the son I birthed.' She paused. 'Is that too much to ask?'

"'No,' I said quietly. 'It is not.'

"She studied my face for a moment, then smiled slightly, though it seemed to cost her effort. 'You look like your father. Amram would have been proud, though I think he would have been confused by the path you have chosen.' She gestured around the small room. 'This, and his work at the shipyard, was his world. He never knew the palaces you live in.'

"'Tell me about him,' I said. 'I know nothing about him. The chance I had to meet him before he died, to my shame, I squandered.'

"She held up her hand. 'That is not important now. You are here. You are forgiven.' Her words struck deep, touching a heart still broken over that failure. As her absolution eased some of the awkwardness between us, it did not completely disappear. But her eyes were filled with love, not reproach.

"She told me about Amram's strength, his quiet faith, his devotion

103

to his family and to his people. She spoke of their life together, of Aaron and Miriam as children, and of the hard years of labor our people endured under Egyptian taskmasters. She smiled when she said, 'His carpentry skills and valued work at the shipyard freed us from the worst oppression.' She ended by telling me about his dreams, his belief that I would save our people, and that it was not just about the edict. It was a short mention, but it stuck with me ever since.

"Then she shifted and asked me about my life. I told her what I could: my training, my interaction with Ramses and the Ne'arin, and learning the art of war. I spoke warmly of my wife and daughters, the joy evident in my words. What I did not speak of was my growing distance from my heritage or the questions that had begun to trouble me.

"'There is something you should know,' she said. 'When you were at Kadesh, the Most High woke me with a dream about you being surrounded by bearded attackers, and for several hours I interceded on your behalf.'

"I drew in a sharp breath, startling her. 'I knew the Most High had saved me from that ambush, but Miriam never told me about this.'

"'That was not all. For several days, He guided my continued intercession for you and those with you. You have been very blessed, Moses. My prayers were just a small part of that blessing.'

"'But an important part. Thank you for telling me this.'

"'When I look at you, I can see you have accomplished so much,' she said. 'The Most High has blessed your whole life, not just helping you in times of danger.'

"'That is true,' I replied, not willing to tell her about the growing distance I now felt.

"We continued to talk until two hours had passed. Jochebed grew tired. She rested her head on her arms at the table, her breathing labored. I suggested she lie down, but she waved me off. 'I can rest when you are gone,' she said. 'I want to look at you while I can.'

"Eventually, a quiet knock came at the door. Miriam opened it partway. 'Moses, if you stay much longer, people will begin to wonder.'

"I looked at Jochebed, torn. She reached across the table and placed her hand on mine. Her skin was thin as paper and cool to the touch. 'You should go,' she said. 'I do not want to cause trouble for you, your family, or Miriam.'

"'I will try to come back,' I said.

"'I would like that.' Her eyes were bright, emotion shining through despite the pain evident in her body. 'But if you cannot, I understand. You must protect your own life, your own family. You have done me a great kindness in coming today. If that is all, it is enough.'

"I stood, reluctant to leave, though I knew I should. Miriam stepped fully into the room. 'Moses, there is something you should know,' she said. 'Nari knows the truth. She has always known. I thought it might ease your mind to know that someone in your household understands.'

"I stared at her. 'Nari knows?'

"'She guessed it from the beginning,' Miriam said. 'She has kept your secret faithfully. You are not as alone in this as you might think.'

"I looked back at Jochebed. She was watching me with a mother's tenderness. For a moment, I felt like a child again, though I had no memory of being her child. 'Goodbye, Mother,' I said quietly.

"'Goodbye, my son,' she whispered. 'Go with the Most High.'

"I followed Miriam outside and closed the door behind me. My sister stood a few paces away, her arms crossed, her look filled with questions. The morning sun was higher now, and the village had grown quieter with most of the workers gone to their labor.

"'Thank you,' I said. 'For convincing me to come. Her concerns were all answered, but most importantly, she forgave me for my earlier failure.'

"She nodded but said nothing for a moment. Then, Miriam simply asked, 'Will you come back?'

"'I don't know if I can. You said yourself that people will wonder.'

"'They will wonder regardless, but it is good for her that you had these two hours,' Miriam said. 'But I understand. You have your life, and we have ours.' There was no bitterness in her voice, only a statement of fact and a sad resignation.

"'How long does she have?'

"'Days. Perhaps a week.' Miriam looked toward the door. 'She has held on to see you. That was what mattered to her. To know her grown son.'

"I looked down at my hands, then back at my sister. 'I wish things could be different.'

"'So do I.' She met my eyes. 'But they are not. Go, Moses, before you raise too many questions.'

"I nodded and walked to where my horses waited. As I removed their hobbles and climbed into the chariot, Miriam quietly said to me, 'She has always loved you, prayed for you. Remember that.'

"I did not trust myself to respond. I simply raised my hand in acknowledgment and turned the horses toward home.

"The estate was quiet when I returned. I unhitched the horses, put away the chariot, and led the stallions to the stable myself. I avoided the groom. I needed a few moments alone before facing anyone.

"As I walked toward the main house, I saw Nari in the garden near the kitchen. She was alone, gathering herbs. She looked up as I approached, and I saw the question in her eyes. She said nothing, but she set down her basket and waited.

"I stopped a few paces from her, glancing around to ensure no one could hear us. 'As I told you this morning, she is dying,' I said quietly. 'It was more than paying respects. She needed to see me.'

"Nari's expression softened. 'I thought that might be why you went.'

"'Miriam told me you've known. That you've always known.'

"'Yes.' She stepped closer, her voice low. 'From the beginning at the river, I suspected. I was able, with the help of your God, to divert any suspicion away from Miriam and your mother.'

"'You never said anything.'

"'It was not my place to speak of it. It was yours to carry or to share.' She paused. 'How was she?'

"'Weak. Tired. Dying. Only a short time left,' I said, my voice rougher than I intended. 'But she forgave me for not coming sooner. For missing my father.'

"Nari reached out and briefly touched my arm, a gesture of comfort. 'Then you have been given a gift.'

"I nodded, unable to speak. For a moment, we stood together in silence. Then she picked up her basket. 'The others will want to know how your visit went. You should think of what you will tell them.'

"'I will say she was grateful for my visit, for remembering her, and that she is at peace.'

"'That is true enough,' Nari said. She gave me a small, knowing look. 'Go rest, Moses. You look weary.'

"I watched her walk back toward the kitchen, carrying her basket of herbs, and felt a measure of gratitude. I was not as alone as I had previously believed."

The Treaty with the Hittites

Moses looked at his sons and said, "As I alluded to earlier, something very important happened about fifteen years after Kadesh. It was the treaty between Egypt and the Hittite Empire. It created peace between the two empires that lasted for almost forty years, well into my time here."

"Why was that important?" Eliezer asked.

"Peace with the Hittites changed everything. In the years after Kadesh, the Hittite King Muwatalli refused to heed the counsel of his surviving brother, Hattusili, and continued to harass the borders of our kingdom. He could not forget the death of his two brothers during Kadesh, especially when he learned I had defeated Hamatarma in single combat. It was an affront he never got over.

"Hattusili, however, had experienced our strength and tactical advantages and believed it would benefit both of us to pursue peace and learn from each other. When his brother, the King, died, Muwatalli's son Urhi-Tesub became king, but he proved ineffective. Hattusili eventually seized power from his nephew, and one of his first acts as the new Hittite King was to pursue peace with Egypt, partly to secure Egyptian recognition of his legitimacy, but Hattusili was, above all, a practical man.

"Interestingly, Ramses and Hattusili never met. The treaty was negotiated through intermediaries and by the exchange of letters. Ramses sent Paser and me as heads of our delegation. Before any negotiations began, Ramses received a letter from Hattusili, who argued there were several advantages to guaranteeing peace. The Hittite King had been wanting this treaty ever since Kadesh, biding his time until he took power.

"First, he said it would free our armies to deal with internal issues such as bandits and malcontents. No longer having to look over our shoulders at each other, we could focus on making our kingdoms safer for everyone. That would facilitate trade and travel in general."

"Our grandfather and the other Midianite shepherds saw the benefit from that," Gershom said.

"So true," Moses said. "Second, he argued we should consider sharing our special skills with each other. That meant the Hittites could help with all things iron, while we could help them build better bows and stronger, faster chariots. Ramses understood that their knowledge of iron, from finding the ore to producing finished goods, including not just weapons but also plows and many other useful items, would save years of learning it on our own. Egyptian lightweight chariot frames were remarkably strong, and their wheels were unmatched. Using Hittite iron at stress points on chariots and carts would make them even stronger, improving their performance and enabling them to haul larger loads. Both countries benefited."

"Is that knowledge why our carts are so strong?" Gershom asked.

"It is. Much of what you see around our camp, as well as the way we build, the tools we use, and, as you noted, even the wheels on our carts, comes from what I learned in Egypt. The peace treaty made it possible for that knowledge to spread even further," Moses replied.

"Lastly, Hattusili made a combined financial and personnel argument. Wars and campaigns were costly and drained treasuries. Peace would mean those resources could be used elsewhere—places that would yield valuable returns, not be lost in blood and sand. But there was an even bigger return. No war meant no men dying in large numbers. Their countries would not lose the best of their fathers to death on the battlefield. Instead, they would be at home, raising strong families and enriching every aspect of life in their realms."

"Hattusili was very thoughtful, though he had fifteen years to craft his arguments," Eliezer said. "So, you were part of the negotiations?"

"Yes, I was. By then, I had become one of Ramses' chief advisors, especially with the aging of Paser. It took Ramses a long time to trust anyone new, and there were few people he trusted with matters of such importance. It significantly raised my stature at court. It was an honor I couldn't refuse, though it took me away from my family.

"Those trips to Kadesh were hard on Nashwa. Merti was eleven, Sitra nine. Every time I left, Sitra would ask when I was coming back, and Merti would just watch me with those careful eyes of hers, saying nothing.

"Nashwa never complained. She'd kiss me goodbye and say, 'Come home safe.' But I could see the worry. A year of negotiations meant being away from home for months, and every time I returned, my daughters had grown a little more, changed in ways I'd missed.

"That was the cost of peace, for me, at least. Hattusili spoke of fathers coming home to raise their families instead of dying on battlefields. He was right. But even in peace, duty takes its toll.

"Ramses had chosen his next vizier. His name was Khay, and he was from a distinguished military family. He had recently been elevated to First Royal Herald. But Ramses hadn't yet tested him with matters this important. His inclusion as an observer in the treaty mission would be that test."

"How long did the negotiations take?" Gershom asked.

"It took almost a year. The meetings were held in Kadesh, and the round-trip travel consumed most of our time.

"I recall a particular moment from the third meeting. Paser and I sat across from Hattusili's representatives. These were hard men, warriors like me. We'd been debating terms for hours. The Hittite general, Sapalulme, kept insisting they needed military access through our northern territories. Paser refused.

"The talks stalled. We sat in silence, neither side willing to move. Finally, Sapalulme looked directly at me. 'You fought at Kadesh,' he said. 'You know what we're capable of.'

"'I do,' I replied. 'And you know our capabilities. That's why I'm here negotiating peace instead of preparing for war.'

"He studied me for a long moment. Then, to my surprise, he smiled slightly. 'My brother died there. In the retreat across the ford. Your Nubian archers.' He paused. 'I would have killed you for that, once. Now I'm sitting here trying to make sure no more of our brothers die. Strange, isn't it?'

"'Not strange,' I said. 'Overdue. I lost my closest friends and my beloved driver.'

"He nodded his head, understanding my loss.

"That broke something loose. Within the hour, we'd found a compromise on the territorial question. Sometimes war makes enemies. But shared loss—that can make peace.

"Eventually, a silver tablet was created, which Hattusili sent to Ramses for his approval; he received it from my own hand. After Ramses approved the treaty, a counterpart in Ramses' own name was drawn up, engraved on another silver tablet, stamped with Ramses' seal, and forwarded to Hattusili. Ramses chose Khay to deliver it—the young herald's first mission of true consequence. It was Ramses' way of raising the stakes in testing the man he intended to make his next vizier.

"That treaty changed everything. Its benefits were everything Hattusili had argued for. It ushered in real peace, and for the first time in my years there, Egypt felt truly safe. Trade caravans, sometimes under military escort, moved safely between our kingdoms, and the army, especially our chariots, now campaigned against bandits and brigands, instead of Hittites.

"There was peace for the rest of my time in Egypt. They were the best years of my life with Nashwa and my daughters. Years I didn't know that I should have treasured more carefully."

Moses paused, his expression darkening. "But peace doesn't last forever. And sometimes the greatest threats don't come from foreign kingdoms. They come from closer to home."

Time to Rest

Moses looked at his two sons. "I am tired and need to rest for a while. Sharing this with you is more exhausting than I thought it would be."

Gershom and Eliezer exchanged a nod. "We understand," Eliezer said. "We can check on the flock again and begin packing for leaving tomorrow. Take all the time you need."

"Thank you for your patience," Moses said. He slowly stood and stretched his back and joints, pushing past their stiffness and complaints. There was enough moonlight to climb carefully up the same shallow ridge he had used before. He found the same tree, sat down, and leaned back against the trunk, placing his staff across his lap. The moon was high overhead, its cool light bathing the area in a quiet peace. The weariness of the day and his sharing with his sons had finally caught up with him, and before he realized it, he was asleep.

Gershom and Eliezer made their way quietly to the pasture and found the flock had bedded down for the night.

"No need to stay here," Gershom said, turning back toward camp. Eliezer silently followed. Neither knew what to say. The weight of what they were learning sat heavy between them. The deeper they went into the story, the more they understood why their father had kept quiet all these years. With that understanding, they also realized some of the more difficult parts of his story were still to come.

When they returned to camp, their father was not there. They lit two lamps and began collecting their gear for the return home. They spent about an hour gathering everything they would not need in the morning. They decided to take down their tents and pack them away. They doubted they would get any sleep tonight, but if exhaustion overtook them, they could rest under the open sky.

After packing the cart with the things they would not use before leaving, they sat down and waited for their father to return. An hour passed, and still no sign of him. Gershom took a lamp and started toward the ridge their father had climbed. "I bet he has fallen asleep. We should wake him if we want to hear the rest before the night is over. Once we start home, I doubt he will be willing to make the effort again."

"Wait for me," Eliezer said, as he grabbed a lamp.

Lamps in hand, they climbed the ridge. Off in the distance, they saw their father asleep, leaning against a tree. As they drew closer, the lamplight reached him, and he stirred.

Gershom stopped, letting him wake up on his own.

Moses lifted his arms and stretched. "Sorry," he said. "I must have been more tired than I thought."

"It's alright," Eliezer said. "You needed the rest. Are you ready to return to camp?"

"Yes, I am ready. Go on back. I will follow shortly."

Gershom and Eliezer turned around, and the brothers carefully made their way back down the ridge.

Moses sat against the tree a moment longer and offered a prayer to the Most High.

> *"Tonight, O Lord, you have been gracious to me, helping me pour out my heart to my sons. You know how difficult the remainder of this remembrance will be. Thank you for bringing to mind so much of what I had forgotten. Grant me the strength to continue opening my Egyptian past to my sons. Forgive my failures and have compassion on my pain. I surrender this effort and my remaining days to you, entrusting myself to your mercy."*

Fighting through his body's rebellion, Moses stood up and, using his staff for support and the moon to light the path, slowly followed the ridge down to their camp.

His sons were waiting for him around the campfire. They were silent as he sat down between them.

Jochebed Dies and Nari's Importance Increases

Moses took a breath and looked at his sons. "Four days after my visit, Miriam came to the estate for her regular duties and told me my mother had died peacefully two days after I saw her. Nari gave her permission to miss her next few days of work and take time to grieve."

He paused, remembering. "Part of me wanted to go to the burial, to pay my respects, to be there. But I knew that wasn't possible. Miriam's message to me was clear: Stay away. Too many questions would be asked. Too much attention would be drawn to our family. She assured me Mother would have understood and that she had already said her goodbyes to me.

"I sent a small amount of silver and gold hidden in a sealed message to Miriam through a trusted servant to assist with the burial and support her household during this difficult time.

"I stayed away. It was the right decision, but it felt like another failure. First, my father; now, my mother. Both were buried without me present."

Moses fell silent for a moment. When he continued, his voice was quieter. "The grief was harder than I expected. Not because I had known her well—we had only those two hours together. But because of what might have been. Because now that she was gone, I would never have another chance."

"Did you talk with Nari about this?" Eliezer asked. "What about the rest of your family?"

"I had already told them my nursemaid was dying, so when Nari told them she had died, they offered their condolences, but nothing more. They had no reason to suspect anything deeper. There was no reason. The only person who truly understood was Nari."

Moses looked at his sons. "From that point forward, she became more important to me than I can properly express. She was the only one in my household who knew the truth, who understood the weight I carried."

"What did she do?" Eliezer asked.

"She listened. She gave me space when I needed it and companionship when I could not bear to be alone. She never asked intrusive questions, but when I needed to talk, she was there. She understood loss. She had lost her own family when she was young, caught up in the backlash against Akhenaten. And she understood what it meant to live between two worlds."

Moses shifted his position, his joints protesting. "In the weeks after my mother's death, Nari and I would sometimes talk in the garden when no one else was near. Small conversations, but they mattered.

"I remember one evening in particular. I had just come from court, where I'd witnessed Hebrew laborers marching past the first southern gate to the port. They were exhausted, barely able to walk. One tripped and fell. The overseer kept kicking him until he got up.

"I found Nari in the garden. She took one look at my face and said, 'What happened?'

"'I saw my people being mistreated,' I said quietly. 'And I did nothing.'

116

"She was silent for a moment. Then she asked, 'What could you have done?'

"'I don't know. Something. Anything.' I looked at her. 'When does wisdom become cowardice? When does protecting my family become abandoning my people?'

"'I don't have an answer for that,' Nari said. 'But I know this: you cannot save everyone. And sometimes the price of trying will cost you everything you have.'

"She was right, of course. But it didn't make the guilt any easier to carry.

"As the days passed, she would ask how I was managing, and I would tell her the truth. It was a relief to have someone with whom I didn't need to pretend."

"Did the others in your family notice?" Eliezer asked.

"If they did, they said nothing. Most of our daily life continued as usual. Nari was careful. She never drew attention to our conversations or made them seem unusual. To everyone else, she was simply the household manager going about her duties. But to me, she became a close friend and confidant, perhaps, besides Semri, the only true friend I had ever had."

He paused again, then added, "It was during this time that I made a hard choice. I chose not to examine the problems that oppressed my people too deeply. I told myself it was a distraction I couldn't afford.

"That conversation stayed with me. But so did my choice. Day after day, I chose my family over my people. I chose comfort over calling. I chose Egyptian Moses over Hebrew Moshe.

"I tell you this with shame. The Most High had saved me from the Nile, protected me at Kadesh through my mother's prayers, and

117

given me years of peace. I repaid Him by turning my back on the very people my father claimed God had called me to save. I told myself I was being wise, protecting what mattered. However, wisdom and cowardice can appear very similar when you're desperate to justify your own excuses.

"In Egypt, and for me, it was a time of transition. My life moved on. With peace established, Semri and I shifted focus from preparing campaigns to assisting Khafre in maintaining the Ne'arin's readiness. Ramses told me it was time to let go. He was thinking long-term and wanted me to move away from anything Ne'arin, to become a trusted counselor at court. Paser was now old enough that he would soon have to relinquish his position, and Khay was just beginning to be ready to take over. Ramses still wanted me around to protect his back."

My Family and Court Life in Egypt

Moses looked at his sons. "That said, the next few years were the happiest time of my life in Egypt. I had position, respect, family, and purpose. Looking back, I can see I was trying to build a life I thought would last the remainder of my years."

He shifted on his seat. "My role at court changed gradually. I still attended military councils, and though no longer needed by the Ne'arin, I continued to advise Ramses on Ne'arin matters. However, as time passed, Ramses began meeting with me to discuss other issues—trade negotiations, building projects, disputes between Nome governors. He wanted a second opinion from someone who wasn't afraid to disagree with him but whom he trusted to be completely honest. Paser was barely vizier, and he finally slowed down, so Ramses was positioning me to fill some of the gaps until he felt Khay was finally ready to fully assume his duties."

"Did you still train with Semri? What were your days like now?" Gershom asked.

"Semri and I would train just enough to keep my skills from eroding. Most days, I would rise early and spend time with my daughters. They were still young enough to want my attention, and I relished every moment.

"There was one morning when Merti was about thirteen. I found her in the garden at dawn, sitting with a scroll she'd borrowed from the palace library. She was reading about the old kingdom's architectural techniques.

"'You're up early,' I said, sitting beside her.

"She looked up, excited. 'Father, did you know they moved stones weighing hundreds of talents to build the pyramids? How did they do it without breaking them?'

"I smiled. 'Clever engineering. Ramps, rollers, leverage. And many, many workers.'

"'I want to understand it,' she said. 'Not just know what they did, but understand how they did it.' She looked at me seriously. 'Is that strange? For a girl to care about such things?'

"'No,' I said. 'It's wonderful. Never apologize for wanting to understand how the world works.'"

Moses paused, a faint smile crossing his face. "Sitra was different. One afternoon, I found her in the training yard with Semri, attempting to lift one of the practice swords. It was far too heavy for an eleven-year-old girl.

"'Teaching my daughter bad habits?' I asked Semri with a smile.

"'She asked,' he said with a shrug. 'I told her she's too young. She

119

disagreed.'

"Sitra looked at me defiantly. 'Why can't I learn? You trained soldiers younger than me.'

"'Boys,' I said. 'Soon to be warriors, with real muscles.'

"'That's not fair,' she shot back.

"She was right, of course. It wasn't fair. But it was the world we lived in. 'I will get you a lighter sword,' I said gently. 'When we've found one you can wield, I'll teach you what I can.' It was at least partially an empty promise. I knew she'd never wield a sword in anger. But seeing her fierce little face, I didn't have the heart to tell her that.

"I wish I'd taught her right then. She had the spirit for it.

"Those memories have stayed with me. My thoughtful daughter, hungry to understand everything. My fierce, spirited daughter, a natural warrior though born a girl. I didn't know then how little time we had left.

"Asati had gradually stepped back from managing the estate as Nashwa took over. With Semri often away helping the Ne'arin's new commander and me, married with children who demanded my time, Asati found companionship among the wives of other court officials. She was often at court with her new friends. I began to rely on her observations from the palace councils. She saw subtle maneuverings I would miss. She also heard things from the wives that I had no way of knowing.

"I did my best, whenever possible, to stay at home. After the morning meal, I would go to court if summoned, but mostly I would do a short stint with Semri to maintain my fighting skills and then spend time with my wife and daughters."

Moses paused. "I had good reasons to avoid Court. The sessions

120

were mostly tedious, filled with disputes over irrigation rights, complaints about tax collectors, and endless presentations from officials seeking favor. Fortunately, I seldom had to speak in front of a large group. Except for soldiers, regardless of their number, or discussing battle plans with the corps, I had a hard time speaking to more than a handful of people, especially at court. I would get nervous, and if it got too bad, I might even begin to stutter. The hero of Kadesh was afraid to speak in front of a crowd of councilors.

"However, my time there was not entirely wasted. I learned to watch faces: who looked nervous when Ramses frowned, who schemed for advantage, who genuinely served Egypt, versus who served themselves. I began to know when to speak and when to stay silent. Ramses valued my input, but he didn't always take my advice. At first, that was hard, but I soon learned to accept whatever happened. My role was to give him options, not to make decisions for him."

Moses fell silent for a moment, then continued in a quieter voice. "As I said, my family life during those years was all I could hope for. My daughters asked endless questions. I would tell them tales, some from our campaigns for Sitra, and some from my time in Temple School for Merti. Nashwa would smile when she joined us. My doting on my daughters made her happy."

"Were you happy?" Eliezer asked.

Moses considered the question. "I thought I was. I had built a life that worked. But I had divided everything: my Hebrew heritage in one place, pushed deep, nearly to the point of denial. My Egyptian life filled everything else, and I kept them both separate. It seemed sustainable." He paused. "But there was always an undercurrent of tension. Deep in my soul, I knew I was abandoning my calling from the Most High."

"What about the people who wanted you dead?" Gershom asked.

"While nothing obvious occurred, I eventually learned that Nephura's supporters never forgot. They were patient, quietly waiting for an opportunity. Occasionally, I would hear rumors of someone asking questions about me and, in later years, making veiled threats. Semri still had his sources and kept me informed, and I stayed alert. We continued our daily training, but years passed without incident. I began to think perhaps they had given up, or that Ramses' protection was too strong to challenge."

Moses paused and looked at his sons. "I was wrong about that. They were simply waiting for the right moment, for something they could exploit. And eventually, they got exactly what they needed."

The firelight flickered across his weathered face as their father fell quiet, a sudden sadness becoming obvious. Both sons sat motionless, dreading what was coming next.

Nari Dies

Moses' silence continued for a long moment. When he spoke again, his voice was heavier, and sorrow was evident in every word. "About five years after stepping back from commanding the Ne'arin and spending more time at the estate, everything changed. Nari died."

He looked down at his hands. "It happened in the market at Perunifer. Sephra, one of our servants, regularly went there for household supplies. This time, Nari went with her. She needed specific herbs for medicines. Some were for Nashwa, who had been unwell, and others for the household stores. Nari didn't trust that

Sephra would be careful enough to get the right ones, so she decided to go with her on this trip to the port markets."

Gershom and Eliezer said nothing, waiting.

"They were in the market square when a cart came through at too high a speed. Too fast for that crowded space. Witnesses said the driver seemed to lose control, that the horse bolted. The cart barreled straight toward where Nari and Sephra stood examining herbs at a merchant's stall."

Moses paused, his jaw tightening. "Sephra saw it coming first. She shoved Nari aside, taking the full impact herself. She was killed instantly. Nari was thrown clear but struck her head on the stone edge of a fountain. She had other injuries as well—her ribs, her arm."

"Did they bring her back to the estate?" Eliezer asked quietly.

"Yes. Sephra was well known at the market, having been there weekly for over twenty years, and was immediately recognized. The herbalist, at whose stall they were struck, immediately closed his shop. Along with several others, using makeshift stretchers, they carried both women back to the estate—Sephra's body, and Nari, still alive but unconscious. The guard on duty saw them approaching and sent out a cart to speed their return. We summoned the best physicians. They set her broken bones, treated her other wounds, but the head injury..." He shook his head. "She woke briefly that first night. Recognized me. She tried to speak but couldn't form the words properly. She soon slipped away again, only regaining consciousness one more time."

Moses' voice grew quieter. "For three days, I rarely left her side. Nashwa and the household staff took turns caring for her, but I was there through most of it. At night, when no one else was in the room, I prayed. I begged the Most High to spare her. I promised anything—anything if He would let her live.

"My daughters were devastated. Merti sat by Nari's bedside for hours, holding her hand, talking to her even though Nari couldn't respond. Sitra couldn't bear to enter the room. She'd pace outside the door, then disappear to the training yard to work off her grief with a practice sword. They'd known Nari their entire lives. For them, losing her was like losing a beloved grandmother."

He fell silent for a moment. "On the third night, I was with her alone, and she woke again. For a few moments, she was almost clear-headed. She looked at me, her voice hoarse and weak, and said, 'Moses, you must be careful. I don't believe this was an accident.' Before I could ask her, she convulsed and went unconscious again. Within the hour, she was gone. I sat with her body until dawn, unable to move, unable to pray, unable to do anything but stare at her still face and realize how alone I now was."

Gershom leaned forward. "She thought it wasn't an accident?"

"Those were her last words to me." Moses looked at his sons, the memory almost too painful to bear. "Semri investigated immediately. The cart driver had fled the scene. No one could find him. He was well known in the marketplace. The horse that supposedly bolted was known to be docile and well-trained. The merchant whose stall they had been at remembered seeing a man watching Nari and Sephra, who disappeared before the cart came through. The merchant was certain the man was watching them, not shopping. When Semri tried to find this man, no one knew who he was. The most suspicious thing was that the driver, his cart, and his horse were never found. They had disappeared."

"I'd wager that Nephura's supporters arranged it all," Eliezer said.

"Almost certainly. But we had no proof. The driver was gone, the witnesses vague, and officially, it was simply a tragic accident in a crowded market." Moses' hands clenched. "Sephra gave her life trying to save Nari. If she hadn't pushed her aside, Nari would have been killed instantly instead of lingering for three days. I don't know if that was a mercy or a curse."

"How did you..." Gershom started, then stopped, unsure how to ask.

"How did I manage after she died?" Moses finished for him. "I didn't, not well. Nari was the only person at the estate who knew my secrets, the only person with whom I could speak honestly. Semri may have guessed some of it, but I couldn't discuss these kinds of things with him. With Nari gone, I was completely alone, even in my own home, with my family around me."

Moses paused. "Nashwa knew something was wrong. She saw my grief and assumed I was mourning a faithful and trusted servant, which was true, but she couldn't know the real meaning of my anguish. Eventually, I had to hide the depth of my mourning, because showing too much would raise questions I couldn't answer."

"The household must have been in chaos," Eliezer said.

"For a time, yes. Nari had managed everything so efficiently that we hadn't realized how much we depended on her. Nashwa took on the additional duties, but it was a struggle at first. And Sephra's death devastated the rest of the servants. We tried to console them, but it took some time to overcome her loss."

Moses looked at his sons. "After Nari died, I changed. I withdrew even more from my Hebrew background. I focused entirely on my immediate family. I was all the more isolated. I stopped even the

125

minimal contact I'd had with Miriam. It was too dangerous. If they could reach Nari, they could reach anyone. I convinced myself I was protecting my sister and her family by pulling away from everything Hebrew, by becoming as Egyptian as possible."

He fell silent again. "Semri and I concluded that her death was meant to be a warning. They wanted me to know they could reach me, that I was never safe. And it worked. I became more careful, more controlled, more closed off. But that control came at a cost. When it finally broke..." He shook his head. "You'll understand soon enough."

The fire crackled between them, and neither son knew what to say.

Moving Forward Without Nari

As the three of them sat quietly, staring into the fire, Moses broke the silence with an admission. "Pockets of Amun-Ra resistance had never stopped. For forty years, I had lived under constant threat, sustained by the Most High's, Semri's, and Ramses' protection. I believe there were times I was protected and never knew it. Nari and Sephra's deaths were a more public attack. Semri and I kept what we discovered to ourselves. Their deaths showed that Nephura's supporters could reach us if they were willing to sacrifice their own people in the process. Alerting my family would only introduce fear into our lives and most likely not protect anyone from a determined attack. It was a burden only Semri and I bore, though Semri did alert his sources to be more vigilant."

Moses shifted his weight; his joints still protested, but after sitting for a while, he needed to relieve his stiffness. He stood up, stretched his back, then sat back down.

"Are you alright, Father?" Eliezer asked.

"Just the stiffness you get in old age from sitting too long in one position. I will be fine. Let me continue. "Following their deaths, Semri and I made changes. Nothing obvious that would alarm the household, but additional precautions were necessary. We varied my routes to court, never following the same pattern twice in a row. When we ate outside of the estate, Semri would often taste my food, claiming he was checking the seasonings for me. His willingness to put his life in danger deepened our relationship. I tried to get him to stop, but he would have none of it, saying he was getting old and if saving my life was his last act, it was a worthy way to leave this life. We limited access to certain areas of the estate. The servants stopped going to markets or public places without taking at least one guard. Semri always had a trusted guard with me, no matter where I went."

"Did anyone notice?" Gershom asked.

"If they did, it wasn't obvious. They likely attributed it to my increasing responsibilities at court. Ramses was relying on me more, and it made sense that I would be more more protected."

Moses paused, taking a deep breath, "The exhausting part wasn't the precautions themselves. It was living with constant vigilance. Always watching. Always wondering. Was today the day they would try again? I could never fully relax, even in my own home."

"What about Semri?" Eliezer asked, "With his willingness to sacrifice himself, he must have been carrying a heavy burden as well."

"He was, and he became more important to me than I can express. With Nari gone, Semri was the only person I could speak honestly with, the only one who understood the threat we faced." Moses looked at his sons. "Our relationship deepened during those years. We still trained together most mornings, but it became more than just maintaining our skills; it was a way to stay connected. It was a time when we could talk freely, when I didn't have to pretend."

"What did you talk about?" Eliezer asked.

"Everything. The threats we were tracking, the political maneuvering at court, my daughters, and his concerns about the Ne'arin under their new leadership were all interconnected. He tried to help me process Nari's death, though that grief never fully left me. He understood I was isolated, even surrounded by my family, and he did what he could to ease that loneliness. But he couldn't replace what I'd lost with Nari. No one could.

"I recall one morning when we were training, and I made a careless mistake. I dropped my guard, left myself open. Semri could have struck me easily. Instead, he stopped.

"'What's wrong?' he asked.

"'Nothing. I'm fine.'

"He planted his practice sword in the ground and looked at me directly. 'You're not fine. You haven't been fine since Nari died. Moses, you're going to break if you don't find some way to release this pressure.'

"I wanted to argue. But standing there in the training yard, with the sun barely up and no one else around, I couldn't maintain the pretense. Not with Semri.

"'I don't know how,' I said quietly. 'If I let go of control for even a moment, everything could fall apart.'

"'It's going to fall apart anyway,' he said. 'The question is whether you choose how, or whether it chooses for you.'

"He was right, of course. But I didn't listen. I couldn't."

Moses sighed, "The next year passed without incident. I

maintained rigid control over everything: my schedule, my emotions, my interactions. At court, I was reliable, measured, and trusted. At home, I was present but often distant. I loved my daughters, watching them grow, but there was a wall between us that I couldn't bring myself to lower."

"How did that change things?" Eliezer asked.

"Merti grew more serious, more interested in learning. She would ask me questions about court, about trade, about how decisions were made. Sometimes I wondered if she sensed something was wrong with me and was trying to understand.

"Sitra remained bold and became even more physical. She still wanted to watch Semri and me train and would ask about campaigns and battles, wanting to hear the same stories repeatedly, as if memorizing every detail. However, she also convinced me to start sword training with her, and after finding a practice sword she could handle, we began some basic exercises together.

"Nashwa devised a system to manage the household, stepping fully into Nari's role, although she never replaced Nari's presence. I am thankful she continued to live up to her name, and her ready smile helped the household to begin to recover. But a wall began to build between us. As intimate as we were as husband and wife, there were things she could never know, a part of me that would remain forever secret to her."

Moses paused. "Asati, by then, was rarely home, leaving everything to Nashwa. Without Nari to anchor her at the estate, she formed her own circle at court. She was creating the life she had never had. I saw her at formal occasions, but we were also drifting apart. I told myself it was natural, but the truth was, I had begun letting go of her, and I let it happen."

"How did your court duties grow?" Gershom asked.

"They continued to expand. Paser was fading fast, and Khay still wasn't fully trusted to replace him, so Ramses increasingly turned to me for counsel. I attended more meetings, mediated more disputes, sat in on decisions about building projects, trade agreements, and military deployments. It was what I had wanted since childhood. I wanted to be trusted, to be valuable, and later, to secure my family's future. But it felt hollow. It felt like I was going through the motions, doing what was expected, but something inside me had died with Nari."

He looked at his sons. "Semri saw it. He would sometimes ask me during our morning sessions whether I was managing. I would tell him I was fine, that I was simply focused on my responsibilities. But we both knew I was hiding the real truth. I had built a life that appeared successful from the outside, with a position, respect, a family, and influence. But inside, I was increasingly empty."

Moses shifted again, wincing slightly. "The rigid control I maintained was becoming unsustainable. I think I knew that even then. Semri certainly knew it. He would tell me I needed to find some way to release the pressure, to stop trying to control everything so tightly. But I didn't know how. The only way I knew to survive was to keep everything locked down, keep moving forward, keep pretending I was fine."

He paused, staring into the fire. "That kind of control can only last so long before something breaks. And when it finally broke..." He shook his head slowly. "My remaining support fell apart in a single morning."

The fire crackled. His sons waited in silence for him to continue.

Semri's Death

Moses drew a slow, deep breath. "Three years after Nari died, I lost Semri. He was getting old, though he refused to acknowledge it. He insisted we continue training together most mornings, though the sessions had grown shorter and less intense. He would joke that he was just pacing himself, but I could see the truth. It was impossible to hide that he was slowing down."

"How did it happen?" Gershom asked quietly.

"We were training one morning, practicing basic forms, nothing too strenuous. Sitra had not joined us that morning. Afterward, we sat under our usual tree to rest. He was in a reflective mood. Later, I thought he may have known what was coming and was offering me his final advice.

"He told me he was proud of what I had become, that he and Asati had made the right choice all those years ago at the river."

Moses' voice grew softer. "Then he looked at me directly and said, 'Moses, you carry too much weight alone. When I'm gone, you need to find someone you can trust. Don't let yourself become completely isolated.' His 'when I'm gone,' when I thought about it later, wasn't a casual remark but a warning."

Moses paused. "I told him he wasn't going anywhere, that we'd be training together for years yet. He smiled at that, but there was sadness in his eyes. He knew better than I did."

"We talked for a few more minutes about small things—the weather, a minor issue with the estate staff. Then he stopped mid-sentence, put his hand to his chest. I asked if he was alright. He said he just needed to catch his breath, that he was fine. He drank some water that I brought him and thanked me. Then he smiled at me once more and said he was glad we'd had these years together. Finally, he closed his eyes."

The silence stretched out before Eliezer asked, "Did you know right away?"

"Not immediately. I thought he was resting. But after a moment, I realized he wasn't breathing. His heart had simply...stopped." Moses paused, the grief rushing back, uninvited. "I sat with him for a long time before I called for help. I didn't want to let him go."

"What did you do as you sat there with him?" Eliezer asked gently.

"I thought about all the years we'd had together. How he had trained me from the time I was a boy, protected me through countless dangers, and become the closest thing to a real father I'd ever known. I thought about his warning—about not letting myself become isolated. And I prayed. I thanked the Most High for giving me Semri, for all those years of friendship and protection. And then I asked Him..." Moses' voice faltered slightly. "I asked Him why He kept taking away everyone I could trust. First, my birth father, then my mother, then Nari, now Semri. I was angry, though I knew I had no right to be."

He fell silent for a moment before continuing. "Eventually, I called for help. The household staff came running. Someone went to fetch Asati. Fortunately, she had not gone to court that morning."

"Asati must have been devastated," Eliezer said.

"Asati was destroyed. I learned at that moment how much she loved him. They had been together my whole life, but Semri and Asati had kept their life together private, so I never understood its depth. She had lost her brother, Pharaoh Seti, years before. Then Nari was killed. Now she had lost her husband. There was no one who could take his place. She went to her room and cried for hours.

"Merti and Sitra were also heartbroken. Semri had been like a grandfather to them. He would tell them stories and show them things he'd learned in his years of service. Sitra especially loved watching us train together. When she learned he was gone, she wept inconsolably. I tried to comfort her, but I had nothing to give. I was empty inside.

"The household mourned for weeks. Everyone on the estate had great respect for Semri. His funeral was large and well-attended. Ramses himself came to the burial to pay respects. He spoke of Semri's years of loyal service to the royal family."

"But for me, Semri's death was more than losing someone I cared about. He was the only person I had left who knew even part of the truth about me, who understood the threats we faced, who had helped me navigate everything. With him gone, I was completely alone. I had no one to honestly talk to, no one whom I could trust with my deepest secrets."

"What about the security measures he'd put in place?" Gershom asked.

"They began to fall apart almost immediately. Semri had maintained the connections, the sources of information, and people who would warn us if they heard anything suspicious. With him gone, those connections dried up."

Moses leaned forward slightly. "About two weeks after Semri died, I tried to meet with one of his key contacts, a merchant who worked in the port district and had access to information from everywhere in the harbor. Semri had met with him regularly for years. When I approached him in the market, he looked at me with barely concealed fear and shook his head. He quickly walked away, not wanting to be seen anywhere near me. I realized then that whatever trust Semri had built with his people wouldn't transfer to me. They would see me as a court official, someone too visible, too dangerous to be associated with."

"I was unsuccessful in finding any others willing to talk. Within a few weeks, I was operating blind. I didn't know who might be watching or planning something. My family and I were vulnerable in a way we had never been before."

"Was there a way to rebuild what he'd created?" Gershom asked.

"I tried. However, I didn't have the necessary contacts or skills. Additionally, increased court duties consumed a greater portion of my days. My daughters still needed their father, even though I was barely present most of the time. And truthfully, I think part of me had given up. I was exhausted from years of vigilance, from the constant fear and isolation. Semri's death broke something in me."

Moses paused, steadying himself. "About a month after Semri died, Asati came to find me. I was in the training yard, going through my basic forms alone. She watched me for a moment, then asked if we could talk. We sat together under the same tree where Semri had died."

Their father fell silent. When he began speaking again, his voice reflected the failure he had felt. "She said she was worried about me. She understood I was grieving, and she was grieving too, but there was something else happening with me, something she couldn't reach. She asked me what was wrong, what she could do to help. She was trying so hard, despite her own grief, to draw me back into our family life."

"What did you tell her?" Eliezer asked.

"I told her what I told everyone. I was fine, I just needed time. The same empty words I always said. She looked at me with such sadness, such helplessness. She knew I was not being truthful with her, but she didn't know why, and I couldn't tell her. There was so much she could never know. The distance between us in that moment felt insurmountable, even though we were sitting side by side."

Moses looked at his sons. "She tried several more times over the following weeks to reach me, but I couldn't respond. I was drowning, and I didn't know what to tell her."

"How long after Semri died..." Eliezer started, then stopped.

Moses understood the question. "Not long. Three months. Semri died, and three months later, everything else fell apart."

He fell silent, staring into the fire, his heart heavy. His sons quietly waited for him to continue.

The Secret War Claims His Family

Moses was silent for a long time. When he finally spoke, his face was strained, and his voice was hollow. "Three months after Semri died," he began, "Nashwa told me she wanted to take the girls to visit her father in Nubia. He was getting old, and she hadn't seen him in over a year. He had last come to court to counsel with Ramses on gold-caravan routes from the south. She asked if I would come with them."

He stared into the fire. "I said no. I told her I couldn't leave, that my duties at court were too pressing. The truth was, I was barely functioning. I was drowning, going through the motions of my responsibilities. The thought of all those days on a boat, nowhere to go, making conversation, pretending to be present when I felt like I was going under—I couldn't do it. Even sharing time with my wife and daughters wouldn't help. I had nothing left to give."

"Did she understand?" Eliezer asked.

"She was disappointed, but she didn't press. She had learned not to press me about anything by then." Moses' jaw tightened. "She made arrangements for passage on a cargo boat heading south. The captain was known to us, having regularly transported goods for the estate. Merti and Sitra were excited about the journey. They would see their grandfather and visit new places. I remember Sitra asking, 'Are you certain you can't come, Father? Won't you change your mind?' I told her I would try to join them later, though we both knew I wouldn't."

"When did they leave?" Gershom asked.

"Three days before the storm. It was early morning. Nashwa organized everything efficiently. She put together their supplies and gifts for her father. I selected two of my most trusted guards and escorted my family to the dock. Nashwa kissed me goodbye. The girls hugged me. Merti said something about bringing me back a story. Sitra made me promise to practice my forms while they were gone." His voice cracked slightly. "Then they boarded. I watched from the dock as the boat pulled away. I waved. Nashwa waved back and stood watching me from the rail until they rounded the bend."

Moses fell silent for a moment. When he continued, he could barely get the words out. "That was the last time I saw them alive."

Neither son spoke. The fire crackled between them. Moses sat silent for a long time. "I need a moment," he finally said.

His sons said nothing, just nodded, giving him the space to grieve all over again. Finally, their father regained control and said, "Five days later, a messenger came to the estate. Their boat had capsized

136

in a storm south of Memphis. There were survivors, but..." He stopped, unable to continue for a moment. "I took the chariot the guards kept by the gate and rode out immediately. I didn't wait for my chariot to be readied, nor did I bring any guards with me. I just took off, driving the team as hard as I dared."

"What did you learn?" Eliezer asked quietly.

"The news had spread throughout the port. Perunifer was abuzz with conflicting reports about what happened. Amid the confusion, one account emerged. The boat had pulled to shore when they saw the storm approaching. The captain was experienced and knew how to seek shelter. But everything went wrong.

"They had successfully anchored and taken down the sails by the time the storm hit with full force. Then, for reasons no one understood, the anchor rope broke. Unable to maintain their mooring, the boat was swept back into the river by the driving wind. The crew tried to control their direction with the rudder. They struggled to turn the boat into the Nile's current, but as they fought against the rising waves and the wind, the rudder snapped, sending them broadside into the flow of the river. The boat capsized in the wind and sent everyone into the churning water."

Moses' hands clenched. "After the storm passed, they pulled four bodies from the river: Nashwa. Merti. Sitra, and one of the guards. Two crew members barely survived by clinging to debris. The captain, three other crew members, and the second guard were never found."

"How did you..." Gershom started, then stopped.

"How did I manage?" Moses finished. "I didn't. Not at first. When I saw their covered bodies lying on the dock, something inside me shattered completely. I lifted the linen cloths, one by one. Merti looked like she was sleeping. Sitra…" His voice broke. "Sitra still had that same fierce expression, even in death. As if she'd fought the water until the end. Nashwa's face was pale, peaceful.

"After I looked at Nashwa, my legs gave out. Someone caught me. I don't remember anything after that."

He paused, steadying himself. "Ramses, with some help from Asati, managed their burials. Four days after the funerals, I was finally able to leave the estate. One of my guards brought me to where the two surviving crew members were being cared for. One was badly injured, incoherent. The other, a young man named Khonsu, did not look well, but he was able to speak. He was shaken, traumatized, yet was able to tell me what happened."

"What did he say?" Gershom asked, trying to be gentle.

"He described the storm, much as I had heard earlier. 'We pulled to shore as a precaution. My Lord, we did everything right. We took down the sails and set the anchor. That should have been enough. It was a violent storm, and as the wind and waves mounted, the anchor held, as expected. Then, without warning, the rope gave way—not gradually frayed but suddenly, as if deliberately weakened. When we tried to steer into the current with the rudder, it barely responded. Then, under the strain of wind and current, the rudder post snapped. We lost all control.'"

Moses looked at his sons. "I asked him directly: could this have been sabotage? He hesitated, then said yes. He said 'I inspected the boat before we left Memphis, and everything was in excellent condition. The anchor rope was less than a month old. The rudder was in good condition and had been properly maintained. I cannot believe that both failed in the same storm, one after another. That should have never happened.'"

"Did he know when sabotage could have been done?" Eliezer asked.

"He told me the boat had docked for the night before at a waystation, the second day south of Memphis. The crew, my family, and their guards had gone ashore for the evening. 'We left one man on watch,' Khonsu said. 'There was no reason to do more. I am sorry, but that man drowned in the capsizing, so there is no way to know if he suspected anything. It is possible someone could have tampered with the boat in the darkness while we were gone. They could have cut the rope to weaken it. But how they could have damaged the tiller without the man on watch knowing—that I cannot explain.'

"What did you do?" Gershom asked.

Moses' voice grew harder. "I tried to investigate further. Even in my grief, even while part of me wanted to die with them, I needed to know. I went to the waystation and questioned everyone. No one had seen anything suspicious. A few boats had been docked there that night, travelers coming and going. Anyone could have approached the boat in the dark."

"I searched for connections to Nephura's supporters. Tried to find any evidence, any witness, anything that would prove this wasn't just a tragic accident. I spent two weeks barely sleeping, barely eating, just pursuing any thread I could find."

He fell silent, then continued more quietly. "I found nothing solid. Suspicions, possibilities, but nothing I could prove. Eventually, I had to give up and return to the estate."

"How did Asati handle it?" Eliezer asked.

"She was destroyed all over again. First Semri, now her grandchildren, and the woman who had become like a daughter to her. The entire estate went into deep mourning. Servants were weeping openly. The household staff had known Merti and Sitra since they were born. Nashwa had been their mistress and treated them kindly. The grief was overwhelming."

Moses' voice grew hollow again. "When Ramses stood with me, he tried to offer comfort. He said he would have the Chief Scribe of Investigations and Secrets investigate personally. He said if this were murder, he would find whoever was responsible. He meant it. I could see that he was genuinely trying to help. But we both knew the truth. Whoever had done this had been careful. They'd made it look like an accident. And without Semri's network, without any way to track them, we had little to go on."

"Ramses tried to help in other ways. He offered me time away from court, offered resources, and offered to station guards at the estate. But none of it mattered. My family was gone. The people I had been trying to protect by distancing myself from my Hebrew heritage were all dead. Only Asati, Miriam, and the brother I had never met, Aaron, remained, and I wasn't close enough to rely on any of them for help."

He looked at his sons, his face haggard even in the firelight. "In the weeks after I returned from my investigation, I started to unravel completely. I couldn't sleep. When I did sleep, I dreamed of them drowning, of reaching for them and not being able to save them. I stopped going to court. Stopped eating properly. Asati tried to care for me, but I was unreachable.

"I would go to the training yard and go through the forms that Semri and I had practiced for hours, trying to exhaust myself into unconsciousness. Sometimes I would just sit in their rooms, holding their things. Sitra's wooden practice sword. Merti's scrolls. The smell of Nashwa lingered in her clothes and on our bed. I couldn't let them go."

Moses was quiet for a long moment. "The guilt was the worst part. I should have been with them. If I had gone on that journey, maybe I would have noticed something wrong with the boat. Maybe I could have saved them. Or maybe I would have died with them, and that seemed preferable to what I was living through.

"Ramses came to the estate several times. He would sit with me, try to talk to me. Sometimes I would respond, sometimes I couldn't. I remember one time he said, 'Moses, you cannot let this destroy you. They would not want that.' And I told him they were gone, so what they wanted didn't matter anymore. He left after that, and I remember the worry in his eyes."

He paused. "That's when I knew I was losing myself. But I didn't care. I had nothing left. My parents gone, Nari gone, Semri gone, and now my wife and daughters were gone. Only Asati was left, and I couldn't speak to her about what I was feeling because she didn't know the secrets I carried."

Moses looked at his sons. "For the next year, I was a ghost. I occasionally attended court when Ramses insisted, but I was going through the motions. Everyone at the estate walked carefully around me, as if I might break at any moment. And I might have. Asati kept trying to reach me. Ramses tried. But I had nothing left to give either of them. I had failed everyone I'd tried to protect, and now they were all gone.

"Then something happened that I didn't expect."

The fire had burned low, and in the darkness, his sons could barely see his face.

Moses Spirals Downward

Gershom got up and added wood to the campfire. They were all silent as he stirred the fire back to life, illuminating their surroundings.

Moses watched the flames grow, and their warmth and glow helped calm him. After a few moments, he was able to continue. "That year after my family died was the darkest time of my life. I was barely present, barely functioning. Asati kept the estate running. Ramses gave me leave from court. I existed, but I wasn't alive. No one who had known me before would have recognized me."

He paused. "But that couldn't continue. About a year after their deaths, Ramses came to the estate. He told me firmly that I needed to return to court. Not for Egypt's sake, he said, but for my own. Staying at the estate, drowning in grief, was killing me. He said I needed purpose again, responsibilities to force me back into the world. He even suggested I go and inspect the Ne'arin."

"Did it help?" Eliezer asked.

"Not really. First, I returned to court and went through the motions. I attended a few council meetings, offered advice, and fulfilled my duties. But I was still hollow inside. The work that had once given me purpose felt meaningless. What was I protecting? What was I building? Everyone I'd been trying to secure a future for was gone.

"As Ramses suggested, I went to inspect the Ne'arin. When I got to their camp, it did help at first. Watching them train, being among warriors again, rekindled some of my old sense of self. But it didn't last. It had been years since I had commanded them, and they had moved on to new leadership. I was now just a memory, a story, or a legend from the past. In some ways, it deepened my sense of loss. What Semri and I had spent so much time and energy producing worked fine without us. It was the last remaining touchstone, and it too was gone.

"I had sunk as low as I could go. However, something unexpected began to happen. Something I hadn't foreseen. The walls I'd built so carefully between my Egyptian life and my Hebrew heritage began to crumble. I had spent years after Kadesh keeping those two aspects of myself separate and suppressing the Hebrew part of me. Now, with everyone I loved gone, with nothing left to protect or hold onto, I couldn't maintain that separation anymore."

"What changed?" Gershom asked.

"I started seeing things I'd trained myself not to see. Hebrew workers in the streets bent under heavy loads. Hebrew families lived in poverty, while even the lowest Egyptian lived in relative luxury and freedom. The casual cruelty with which Egyptians spoke about the Hebrews reminded me of the way they spoke about their cattle. It was as if the children of Abraham were animals, not people. I had witnessed all of this before, of course, but I'd looked past it, blinded myself to it, told myself it wasn't my concern or there was nothing I could do. I argued that I had to focus on my own family, my own position, and its duties."

Moses' voice grew harder. "But now I had no family to protect, no position worth preserving, no one who needed me. And suddenly, everywhere I looked, I saw my mother's people suffering. No, my people suffering. And the rage inside me, the grief that had nowhere to go. It started attaching itself to what I was seeing."

"Did anyone notice the change in you?" Eliezer asked.

"Asati did. She would watch me when I came to the evening meal, which was not often but often enough to notice that I was different, that I'd become harder somehow. I was not just grieving anymore, but she sensed a deep anger. She tried to get to the bottom of what was happening. She asked me what I was thinking about, what was troubling me beyond the obvious loss."

143

"What did you tell her?" Eliezer asked.

"Nothing truthful. I gave her vague answers about struggling with the meaninglessness of court politics, about questioning my purpose. She told me she loved me and tried so hard to reach me, but she couldn't. How could she? There was a wide gulf between us now. She had no idea who I really was. She knew almost nothing about my Hebrew ancestry or its impact on me. I was her adopted Egyptian prince, the valiant warrior who had saved Ramses. She couldn't comprehend how much watching my birth people suffer under Egyptian oppression mattered to me now."

Moses fell silent for a moment. "The internal conflict between my two worlds was becoming unbearable. It was tearing me apart. I would sit in council meetings, listening to officials discuss Hebrew labor quotas, Hebrew building projects, Hebrew problems—always spoken of as if they were managing livestock, not human beings. And I just sat there, silent, nodding, playing my part while my stomach churned and the anger deepened."

"Then I'd go back to the estate and see the respect everyone showed me, the deference, the assumption that I belonged to this world of privilege and power. I felt like a fraud. Worse than a fraud—a traitor. My mother had risked everything to save me, had poured out her heart in prayer for the Most High to protect me. And what had I done with her gift? I'd become one of the oppressors. I'd lived a comfortable life while my people suffered."

He paused. "The rage kept building. I had no outlet for it, no way to release it. I couldn't talk to anyone about it. And I couldn't act on it without destroying what little I had left, and I worried I could bring harm to Asati or even Ramses. So, it just continued to fester inside me, growing stronger every day."

"How long did this go on?" Gershom asked.

"Months. Maybe eight or nine months of this slow spiral. To most people, it seemed I was functioning. I still went to court, at least on the outside, I fulfilled my duties, and maintained appearances. But inside, two things were happening: who I had been most of my life was coming apart, while at the same time, anger was building into unfocused rage at the injustice leveled against the Hebrews. The grief over my family, the rage over Hebrew suffering, the guilt over my own complicity, it was all swirling together into something dark and dangerous."

Moses looked at his sons. "Part of me knew I was heading toward something catastrophic. But I felt helpless to stop it. Or maybe I didn't want to stop it. Maybe I wanted something to happen, anything to break through this endless, hollow grief and emptiness punctuated only by anger and growing rage.

"During those months, I began visiting places I'd never been to before. Construction sites. Brick-making pits. Quarries. The worst were places where Hebrews labored alongside other workers. I told myself I was inspecting royal building projects, fulfilling my duties to the court. But that wasn't the real reason."

"Why did you go there?" Gershom asked.

"I wanted to see it for myself, to understand what my people endured daily. At construction sites, I would stand at the edge and watch. Hebrews weren't the only workers there. Laborers from other conquered peoples also worked under forced servitude. But the Hebrews were treated differently. Always differently."

Moses' voice grew quieter. "The non-Hebrew workers would get rest when they needed it. They had water brought to them regularly. If a tool broke or materials ran short, work would slow down until the issue was fixed. However, when Hebrew workers requested the same consideration, they were denied, told to work

145

faster, work harder, make do with what they had."

"What about the overseers?" Eliezer asked.

"The overseers." Moses' jaw tightened. "I watched them closely. Some were merely harsh. Others seemed to take pleasure in using their authority to lord it over my brothers. They would shout insults, mock them for being slow or weak. I heard one overseer tell a Hebrew worker that his people were born to serve. This was the natural order. He should be grateful Egypt let them live at all."

He fell silent for a moment. "I went to the brick pits several times. Stood there watching Hebrew men and women making bricks in the sun. The work was endless. They mixed mud and straw for bricks, laid a batch out in rows to dry, and then started over. Their hands were raw, their backs bent. Children who should have been at home were hauling water and straw."

"The Egyptian overseers would talk about the Hebrews as if they were barely human. They laughed about how many bricks a Hebrew could make before collapsing, placing wagers on whether an old Hebrew man would survive another day in the heat.

"One afternoon at a brick pit south of Memphis, an old Hebrew man—he must have been sixty or more—stumbled while carrying water to the brick makers. The jar fell and shattered. Water soaked into the dirt.

"The Egyptian overseer strode over. 'You clumsy fool! That water was for the workers. Now they'll slow down because you can't carry a simple jar.'

"The old man went to his knees. 'I'm sorry, master. I'll get more. I'll work faster…'

"The overseer kicked him. Not hard enough to break bones, but hard enough to send him sprawling. 'You'll work twice as long tonight to make up for this. And no food until the quota is met.'

"The old man said nothing. Just picked himself up, bowed, and left to get another jar. No one helped him. No one objected. This was normal. This was how things were.

"I stood there watching, my fists clenched at my sides. I wanted to intervene. I wanted to strike that overseer, to make him feel what that old man felt. But I didn't. I just stood there, another Egyptian observer, complicit in my silence."

Moses' hands clenched into fists. "I tried to stop going to these places, because whenever I did, the rage inside me grew. But I couldn't help it. I would return to the estate, wash off the dust, dress in fine linen, and sit down to an abundant meal. And the contrast would tear at me. Aaron, my brother, made bricks in pits like those. And here I was, living in luxury, doing nothing."

"Did you try to do anything?" Gershom asked carefully.

"What could I do? I was one man. If I spoke out against the overseers or tried to intervene, questions would be asked. My position, my safety, Asati's safety—everything would be at risk. And for what? To help a few workers for a day? The system was too large, too entrenched. So, I did nothing but watch and let the rage build."

He looked at his sons. "But I kept going back. Week after week. I think I was looking for something, though I didn't know what. Perhaps I was looking for an excuse. Maybe I was looking for permission. Or maybe I was just punishing myself, forcing myself to see what I'd been avoiding all these years."

For a moment, Moses stopped speaking, then said, "One morning, it all came crashing down."

The fire crackled, and his sons waited.

Death of the Overseer

Moses stared into the fire, his voice dropping to barely above a whisper. "That fateful morning began with a dream. I was standing at the brick pits, watching Hebrew workers under the sun. But in the dream, I saw faces I knew—my mother, Miriam, all bent over the mud and straw. An overseer was shouting at them, raising his rod. I tried to move, to intervene, but I couldn't. I was frozen. I could only watch them suffer."

He paused. "I woke before dawn, already seething with anger. The rage from the dream hadn't remained with the dream—it had followed me into waking. I lay there in the darkness, feeling it pulse through me. I told myself I wouldn't go out that morning. I would stay at the estate, attend to my duties, avoid the brick pits and construction sites."

"What changed?" Gershom quickly asked.

"I came down for the morning meal. One of the servants brought me water to wash my hands. He bowed so deeply I thought he might fall over. Called me 'my Lord Prince' with such reverence, such deference that something in me snapped. I was being treated like a prince of the court while my people were being treated like animals. The contrast was more than I could take. I recoiled at the servant's deep respect with the dream's memory still vivid in my mind. I couldn't bear it."

Moses' hands clenched. "I left the estate without eating. Took my chariot and rode toward the brick pits outside the city. I told myself I would just observe, as I had been doing. But I think part of me knew something was different that morning. The rage was too close to the surface."

"What happened when you got to the first pit?" Gershom asked.

"I watched for a while and saw the same familiar scene. Hebrew workers were bent to their labor, overseers standing over them with rods. One overseer was particularly harsh, striking a man who wasn't moving fast enough. I stepped forward and spoke. I told him to ease up. If he expected production that day, the workers didn't need beating; they needed reasonable rest breaks and water.

"He recognized me immediately. His whole demeanor changed. He bowed, apologized, and said my advice would indeed boost production. He put away his rod and called for water to be brought. The other overseers suddenly became solicitous, asking if I needed anything, if there was a problem with the work."

"Did it help?" Eliezer asked.

"For those workers, in that moment, yes. But it actually strengthened my upset. They only altered their behavior because it was me, because I was a Prince of Egypt. I knew when I left, it wouldn't take long before they would fall back into their regular pattern, and the abuse would begin again. It might take a few days, but it would return to how it was before I intervened. I was just a temporary interruption that they would soon forget.

"I went to a second pit. The same thing happened. The overseers recognized me, moderated their behavior, and showed me deference. The Hebrew workers looked at me with a mix of hope and confusion. They didn't know who I was or why I was there. To them, I was just another Egyptian who strangely had given them momentary relief."

He became quiet for a long moment before continuing. "Then I went to the third pit. It was farther from the city, more isolated. When I arrived, I stopped below a ridge and hobbled my horses. As I walked over the ridge to the pits, I saw an overseer beating a Hebrew worker with his rod. The man had fallen, couldn't get up, and the overseer just kept hitting him."

"What did you do?" Gershom asked.

"I shouted for him to stop, and started walking toward him. The overseer, surprised by my shouting, turned, saw me, but didn't recognize who I was. He didn't see a prince—he just saw another Egyptian interfering with his work. He left the Hebrew worker and came toward me, his face twisted with anger."

Moses' voice grew harder. "He got right in my face. I could smell beer on his breath. He said, 'Who do you think you are? This is my pit, my workers. What gives you the right to interrupt me?'

"I told him I was Moses, advisor to Pharaoh, and he needed to stop beating that man. But he either didn't believe me or didn't care. I tried to calm down the situation before it escalated. I turned and walked back over the ridge toward my chariot, but he followed me, not letting the situation go. As he caught up to me at my chariot, I turned around. Before I could say anything, he pushed me and told me to get out of the area before he had me removed. All the rage that had been building for months—the grief, the guilt, the helplessness—it all came together in that moment."

Moses stopped, his hands trembling slightly. "I didn't think; I reacted. I pushed him back. I didn't think it was very hard. Just to get him away from me, to make him back down. He stumbled backward and his foot caught on something—loose sand, a rock, I don't know. He fell, and his head struck the wheel of my chariot with a sickening crack. He hit the ground and lay there for a moment. After a moment, he got up. He was groggy, swaying. He said something I couldn't understand, took a step, and then fell again. He hit his head on the chariot wheel a second time."

Moses' voice dropped until it was barely audible. "This time he didn't get up."

Neither son spoke. The fire crackled between them.

"I rushed over. He wasn't moving, and there was blood on the wheel. As I turned him over, there was a deep gash across the back of his head that was bleeding profusely. I panicked, which showed how far I had fallen. My first thought was to bury him in the sand in this low defile, which I actually did. I created a shallow trench, slid him in, and covered the body with sand. I wasn't thinking; I was just reacting. The lack of sleep and all the pressure were catching up with me. I, Moses, hero of Kadesh, had panicked completely.

"Next, I wiped the blood from my chariot wheel with sand. Then I led my horses away from the site, trying to obscure the tracks. I must have walked them a hundred cubits before I finally mounted the chariot and rode back to the estate. Halfway home, my mind still in a fog, I stopped and used water from my bag to scrub the wheel clean, though a dark stain remained.

"When I returned to the Great Estate, I told my servants not to disturb me. I spent the rest of the day alone, replaying what had happened. I kept going over and over what had happened, playing the 'what if' game with myself. That might be useful after a battle with your leadership to adjust your tactics in the future, but personally, it is a downward spiral at that point because you can't change what happened. Following that path was pointless. There is no escape from the decisions you have made.

"I got almost no sleep that night. By dawn, I knew I couldn't leave him buried there. Whatever consequences I faced, I had to deal with them properly. I needed to bring him to Ramses, explain what happened, and face whatever judgment came.

"I left before the household woke. When I arrived at the swale below the ridge leading to the brick pit, work was just beginning. I hobbled my horses a short distance away, then went to where I'd buried the overseer. I started uncovering the body, intending to load him in my chariot. That's when I heard voices on the ridge above.

"I was standing next to the partially uncovered body when two Hebrews appeared on the ridge crest, arguing and exchanging blows. I yelled at them to stop. They stopped and looked at me, and one of them said, 'Who made you judge over us? Do you intend to kill us as you killed that Egyptian?' He pointed at the man half-uncovered at my feet.

"I knew there was no way to control my version of the story now. Just then, an older overseer appeared. He ordered the two Hebrews back to the pits while I stood over the body. He looked down at me, and recognition dawned on his face. 'Lord Moses, what happened here?'

"I stood there, looking down at the dead man, not sure what to say. I had hoped to bring the body in my chariot back to Ramses and have some chance to explain what happened. But suddenly, I wasn't thinking about being discovered or my failed plan. I was overwhelmed with the memory of the charioteer I had executed."

"The charioteer?" Eliezer asked.

"Do you remember how I told you about how years ago, during training for the Kadesh campaign, one of our charioteers killed a Hebrew supply driver over a perceived slight. Just struck him down without thinking, over something trivial. I was the one who judged that case. I was harsh. I took the charioteer's life as punishment because he had killed someone in anger without thinking."

Moses looked at his sons. "And now I had done a similar thing. I had killed a man in anger. Yes, it was an accident. I only meant to shove him back. I hadn't meant for him to die. But the charioteer probably hadn't meant to kill the supply driver either. He'd just struck out without thinking, and the man had died. Just like this.

"The guilt hit me like a physical blow. I tried to explain it was an accident, that I'd only pushed him away, that I didn't mean for him to fall. But even as I said the words, I knew how hollow they sounded. I knew where this was leading."

Moses paused. "The older overseer came down to where I was and tried to assess the situation. I explained what had happened as best I could, admitting I had panicked and thought of hiding the body, but I admitted I could no longer do that. He looked at me with something like pity and said, 'There are no witnesses to what happened, my lord. But from what I have seen, your actions do not suggest an accident.'

"There was noise on the ridge as some of the other overseers came to look down and asked what was going on. The older overseer instructed the others to be silent and then told them to return to their duties. He would explain later.

"He came closer and pulled me aside, away from the body. His face was grave. He said, 'My Lord Moses, this is very serious. We searched for him last night when he did not return. Some of the Hebrews said they saw him following someone over the ridge, but when we searched the area, we found nothing —no tracks, nothing. We were hoping he would turn up this morning, but not like this. You have to understand. This man was the chief overseer here. He has an important family and connections. There will be serious questions and an investigation. His family will demand it. And I must tell the truth about what I saw.'

"I knew what he wasn't saying. It didn't matter that I was a prince or that it was an accident. I had killed an Egyptian chief overseer, tried to hide his body, and there were no witnesses to come to my defense. My enemies at court, Nephura's hidden supporters who had been waiting for years for me to make a mistake, and now I had given them exactly what they needed."

Moses stared into the fire. "Everything I had built, everything I still tried to protect—Asati, Ramses—would now fall apart. And the worst part was, I couldn't even say I regretted it. The overseer was dead, and I felt guilty about that. But standing there near that brick pit, surrounded by the suffering I had ignored for so long, part of me felt something else too."

He looked at his sons. "It felt like I had finally done something. After months of watching, of building rage with nowhere to put it, I had acted. And that terrified me more than anything else."

Gershom started to say something, but stopped. Eliezer leaned forward and asked, "What did you do?" Concern filled his voice.

Return to the Great Estate

Moses looked at both his sons, took a deep breath, and then went on. "As I turned to go, I asked the overseer, 'What will you do with the body?'

"'I'll report that we found him this morning. That's the truth. What I saw when I found him...' He paused. 'I will tell the truth about that, too, my Lord. But you should be gone when I do.'

"I started to protest, saying I should stay and that I needed to explain. But he cut me off. 'Explaining will not help. Not here, not now. Go home, alert your family, and then go to Pharaoh Ramses. Tell him what happened before the reports reach him. That is your only chance. But you must go now.'

"I knew he was right. I climbed back into my chariot. My hands were shaking so badly I could barely hold the reins. The ride back to the estate was a blur. Everything was more intense: the sun beating down, the dust, the chariot's motion. My mind kept replaying what happened—the overseer falling, that crack, his eyes staring at nothing.

"When I arrived at the estate, I must have looked terrible. A servant took the horses, and I walked, almost stumbling, toward the house. Asati saw me from the courtyard. She knew immediately something was seriously wrong. She ran to me. She took my arm and asked what had happened."

"What did you tell her?" Eliezer asked.

"Everything. We went to her sitting room, and I told her everything—the dream, the anger, going to the brick pits, the confrontation, the push, the fall. I explained to her that the man was dead, that it was an accident, but that it didn't matter. I admitted to trying to hide the body and going back this morning to retrieve it. I told her I wanted to take it to Ramses to explain, but I was discovered. Then I told her the worst part: 'Do you remember the charioteer I had executed years ago, the one who had killed a Hebrew driver in anger?'

"She went very still. For a long moment, she said nothing, just looked at me. She knew what I was implying. Then she asked, 'Are there witnesses?'

"I said, 'Yes, there was the older overseer and the two Hebrew workers. Then there was the Hebrew who was beaten the day before. He saw the overseer chase after me.'

"She asked if anyone would testify that it was an accident. I admitted I didn't see how. We were alone when it happened, and no one saw anything until I returned this morning. We sat there for nearly an hour, talking through every detail, every possibility."

"What did she do?" Gershom asked.

"I could see that she was frightened for what might happen, but she was also thinking. This was not the same Asati who had been so dependent on Nari for everything. She had spent years at court, developing a deep understanding of politics and power. She said, 'This is very bad, Moses. Very bad. Your enemies will use this. They have been waiting for a long time for a chance like this.'

"I admitted I knew that. Then she did something I didn't expect, which showed how different she had become.

"She called for Nazim. He had left the Ne'arin two years earlier and had returned to the estate, where he helped manage security and train her guards. He was old by then, but still sharp, still loyal. When he arrived, Asati told him what had happened."

"What was his reaction?" Gershom asked.

"He listened carefully, asked a few questions about the details, such as how many witnesses, what they had seen, and whether anyone had tried to stop the fight. Then he looked at me and said, 'My Lord Moses, what do you need from me? I am at your service. We can gather men, we can secure the estate, we can prepare for whatever comes. Just tell me what you need.'

"I told him I didn't need anything. This wasn't something that could be fixed by gathering men or preparing defenses. I had killed a man. Yes, it was an accident, but I had still taken a life in anger. I deserved whatever punishment was coming. Nazim started to argue, but I cut him off. I said, 'Remember the charioteer I had executed for killing a Hebrew in anger? How can I claim I should be treated differently? I'm guilty of the same crime.'

"Asati had been listening to this exchange, and suddenly she spoke. Her voice was firm, almost sharp. 'Moses, stop! Stop talking about what you deserve. This is not about what you deserve. This is about what happens next, about how we protect you, about how we minimize the damage.'

"She came to me and took my hands. 'You need to go to Ramses. Now! Immediately! Before the official reports reach him, before the council starts meeting, before your enemies can control the narrative. You need to go to him as his trusted ally, tell him exactly what happened, throw yourself on his mercy.'"

Moses looked at his sons. "I told her. 'It won't matter. Even Ramses can't protect me from this. The law is clear. I killed an Egyptian over a Hebrew. It will not matter that it was an accident. I had acted in anger. There will be a trial, a judgment.'

"She said, 'But if you go to him now, if you show remorse, if you explain it was an accident—he might find a way. He owes you his life from Kadesh. That must count for something.'

"I looked at Nazim. He understood and averted his eyes.

"Did you leave immediately?" Eliezer asked.

"No. Part of me wanted to stay at the estate, to wait for whatever was coming, to accept the punishment I deserved. But Asati kept pressing. Then she said the only thing that mattered. 'If not for yourself, do it for me. Do it so I know you tried. Do it so Ramses at least has a chance to try and help you before the council forces his hand.' Nazim added his voice to hers, said she was right, that going to Ramses was the only possible course.

"I bowed my head and relented. I agreed to go. Asati called for my chariot to be readied. She told me to change my clothes, to wash, to make myself presentable for the court. While I was changing, I heard her giving Nazim instructions: 'Station men at the estate gates, be ready for anything and send word if anyone comes looking for Moses.'

"When I came back down, she was waiting. She embraced me, something she rarely did. She looked me in the eyes and said, 'Moses, you are my son. Whatever happens, remember that. You will always be my son.' I could hear the fear in her voice, but also strength and love.

"'I will return as soon as I can. I will tell you what Ramses says.'"

Their father fell silent again as the turmoil rushed back. It took him a few moments, but he continued. "I climbed into the chariot and rode to the first ferry across to Perunifer. The sun was past its peak by then, and the heat of the day was settling over the city. As I waited to cross on the ferry, I worked out what I would say to Ramses and how I would explain what had happened. But my mind kept returning to the overseer's face, to the sound of his head striking the chariot wheel, to the blood on the sand where he fell.

"I knew, even as I rode toward the palace, that nothing would ever be the same. The life I had built, the positions I had held, my relationship with Asati and Ramses, it was all ending. As I made my way through Memphis, I was riding toward that end, not knowing what would come next."

Ramses Pays His Blood Debt From Kadesh

Both Gershom and Eliezer sat silent, not looking at their father, not looking at each other. Finally, Gershom said quietly, "If these things had not happened…"

He didn't finish. He didn't need to.

They knew that without the flight from Egypt, they would not exist. The conflict was obvious in their faces—grief for what their father had endured, guilt for being grateful it had happened.

"The Most High works in ways we cannot see at the time. What you're feeling, there's no shame in it."

Eliezer nodded but said nothing.

After a long moment, Gershom spoke. "What happened when you reached the palace?"

"It was late afternoon when I arrived at the palace. The guards recognized me immediately and let me pass. I went directly to Ramses' private chambers, where he conducted informal business. But as I approached, I heard raised voices. I slowed, uncertain whether to continue.

"A servant saw me in the corridor. His face went pale. He said, 'My Lord Moses, perhaps you should wait. Pharaoh is speaking with a messenger from the brick pits.' My stomach dropped. The report had already arrived. I was too late to control what Ramses heard, too late to explain my side of the tragedy before others shaped the story.

"I told him I would wait. He led me to a small antechamber. It bordered the main hall, and through the walls, I could hear Ramses' voice, angry, demanding details. I couldn't make out all of the words clearly, but the tone was unmistakable. He was furious."

"How long did you wait?" Gershom asked.

"Perhaps half an hour. It felt like days. I sat there, listening to the muffled voices, trying to prepare what I would say. But my mind kept returning to the brick pit, to the overseer's fall, to the blood on the chariot wheel. And underneath that, a deeper realization was growing."

159

Moses looked at his sons. "I had spent months feeling abandoned by the Most High, wondering why He wasn't acting. But sitting in that antechamber, I understood the truth. He had not turned away from me; I had turned away from Him. The distance had grown steadily over the years—after my mother died, after Nari and Semri died, after my wife and daughters died. I had pulled back from the God who had sustained me. And now, in my moment of greatest need, I felt alone because I had made myself alone."

"That must have been difficult to realize," Eliezer said quietly.

"It was devastating. It meant this was my fault—not just the overseer's death, but everything that led to it. I had spent my life trying to live between two worlds, and in the process, I had betrayed both. I wasn't Egyptian enough for the Egyptians who hated me for my Hebrew blood. And I wasn't Hebrew enough for the Hebrews who I had abandoned for comfort and position."

"Finally, the door opened. The servant appeared and said, 'Pharaoh will see you now.' His face was somber. He knew what I was walking into.

"I entered Ramses' chamber. He was standing looking out into his garden, his back to me. The messenger had left. For a long moment, he didn't turn around, didn't acknowledge me. When he finally spoke, his voice was tight with controlled anger. 'Moses. I have just received a disturbing report from the brick pits south of the city. An overseer is dead. And a witness says you killed him.'"

"What did you say?" Gershom asked, unable to wait.

"I told him it was true. I had gone to the brick pits and confronted an overseer who was beating a Hebrew worker. The overseer challenged me, followed me when I tried to leave, and pushed me. I pushed him back. He tripped and fell, striking his head. It was an accident, but he was dead.

"Ramses turned to face me. He had never looked at me that way before. There was anger, yes, but also something else. A deep sadness mixed with disappointment. Even betrayal. For the first time since I had known him, he yelled at me, 'An accident! You pushed an overseer hard enough that he fell and struck his head and died, and you call it an accident?'

"I told him I hadn't meant to kill him, that I had only wanted him to back away, to stop threatening me. Ramses walked toward me slowly. He said, 'And why were you there, Moses? Why were you at the brick pits confronting overseers? What business is it of yours how Hebrews are treated?'"

Moses' voice grew quieter. "That question hung in the air between us. Because we both knew what he was really asking. He was asking about my loyalty, about who I really was, about whether I had become what his enemies had always claimed—a Hebrew pretending to be Egyptian."

"How did you answer?" Eliezer asked.

"I told him the truth. I said I had been visiting construction sites and brick pits for months, observing how Hebrew workers were treated. That I couldn't watch it anymore without doing something. The overseer had been beating a man who had fallen, and I had intervened.

"Ramses stared at me for a long moment. Then he said, 'You fool. You absolute fool. Do you understand what you've done? You've given them exactly what they have always wanted. Nephura's supporters have been waiting for this for over twenty years since their leader disappeared in that sandstorm. And now you've handed them proof that you're not Egyptian, that you're a Hebrew

161

who killed an Egyptian defending your people.'

"He was right, of course. I told him I knew. I understood what this meant. He turned away from me, paced to the window, and back. He said, 'There will be a council hearing. Tomorrow. They're already demanding it. The overseer's family has connections and influence. They want justice, or what they call justice. They want you executed.'

"I said I understood. I reminded him of the charioteer case from my early days training the Ne'arin, emphasizing that this was no different. I knelt and said I would accept whatever judgment came to me. He spun and stared directly at me, 'Accept it? You'll accept being executed? Just like that? After everything we've been through, after everything you've done for Egypt, you'll just let them kill you?'

"I told him I had no choice. The law was clear. I had killed an Egyptian over a Hebrew. Years ago, I had executed a similar judgment, saying that killing someone in anger without just cause could not be forgiven. How could I now claim I deserved different treatment?"

"How did he react to that?" Gershom asked.

"He went very still. Then he said, quietly, 'That's what they'll use against you. The fact that you executed an Egyptian for killing a Hebrew, and now you've killed an Egyptian while defending a Hebrew. They'll say you've always been a Hebrew sympathizer, that you've always been working against Egypt's interests. And I won't be able to defend you against that charge, because apparently, it's true.'

"We talked for another hour. He asked whether there were any other witnesses, what exactly they had seen, and whether anyone could testify that it was an accident.

"I answered as honestly as I could, though we both knew the answers weren't promising. Finally, he told me to go home, to put my affairs in order, to return the next morning for the council hearing."

"As I was leaving, he called me back. His voice was different—not angry anymore, just sad. He said, 'Moses, I have never forgotten Kadesh, how you stopped the attack on my rear. I owe you my life. But I don't know if even that will be enough to save you from this.'

"I told him, 'I don't expect you to save me. I brought this on myself.'

"He looked at me for a long moment, then said, 'Get out. And pray to that God of yours, because you're going to need Him. He is your only hope since no Egyptian god will help you now.'

"I returned to the estate as night was falling. Asati was waiting. I told her about the meeting, about what Ramses had said, about the council hearing the next day. She asked if there was hope. I told her I didn't think so, but that Ramses would do what he could.

"That night was the longest of my life. I couldn't sleep. I paced my rooms, thinking about everything that had happened, everything that had led to this moment. And I prayed. For the first time in months—maybe years—I truly prayed. Not demanding, not angry, just asking. Asking the Most High for wisdom, for strength, for whatever would come next.

"The next morning, I dressed carefully. Asati helped me, her hands shaking as she adjusted my robes. Nazim was waiting with the chariot. He asked if I wanted him to come with me. I told him no, that this was something I had to face alone."

Moses looked at his sons, the sadness in their eyes clear to see. "The council chamber was packed when I arrived. Officials, nobles, and priests had all come to see the judgment of Moses, the Hebrew who had risen so high and fallen so far. I heard that some of the priests believed this marked the end of the prophecy that many had feared. In taking the overseer's life, I had elevated a Hebrew and brought an Egyptian low, but not in the way they had originally feared. I saw faces I recognized, a few sympathetic, but most were hostile. And at the front sat the overseer's family, their faces hard with grief and anger.

"Ramses sat upon the elevated throne, wearing his formal regalia. He looked every bit the Pharaoh that day, not my friend. The proceedings were formal, ritualized. The charges were read: I, Moses, advisor to Pharaoh, had unlawfully taken the life of an Egyptian overseer named Bakari while defending a Hebrew slave.

"Witnesses were called. The two Hebrews testified that they had found me with the body half-buried in the sand. When they challenged me, I had not denied killing the overseer. The Hebrew who was being beaten when I intervened testified that I had left, but the overseer had angrily pursued me.

"Then the overseer who had recognized me testified. He explained that I claimed it was an accident, that I had only meant to push Bakari away after being accosted, but that Bakari had tripped and fallen against my chariot wheel, striking his head. He testified that I had tried to leave, that Bakari pursued and pushed me first, suggesting this was self-defense. He was doing his best to help me.

"However, the prosecution then presented evidence I hadn't expected. They produced records from years ago—the report of my trial of the charioteer who had killed the Hebrew supply driver. They read my judgment aloud, using my own words about how killing in anger could not be forgiven, that violence resulting in

164

death, even accidental, deserved the harshest punishment. I condemned myself out of my own mouth.

"When all the witnesses had spoken, the council began its deliberations. The debate went on for hours. Some argued for execution. Others argued for exile. A few argued for leniency given my service to Egypt. The weight of opinion was clear. I had killed an Egyptian in anger. The law and my own words demanded death.

"Finally, Ramses stood. The chamber went silent. He spoke of my service to Egypt, of the campaigns I had led, of the victories I had won in honor of the Two Lands. He reminded them of Kadesh, of how I had saved his life at great risk to my own. And then he invoked something I hadn't anticipated."

Moses looked at his sons. "He invoked his blood debt. It's an ancient custom that is rarely used. When someone saves the life of Pharaoh in battle, Pharaoh owes them a blood debt—a life for a life. Ramses declared that he was now paying that debt. Instead of execution, I would be exiled to the desert without food, water, or weapons. My survival would be left to the judgment of the gods. With this, his blood debt would be paid.

"The chamber erupted. Some shouted in approval, others in outrage. But Ramses' word was final. He was Pharaoh, and he was within the law.

"I was given three days to settle my affairs. Then I would be taken east to the western edge of the desert and released. If the gods favored me, I would survive. If not..." Moses shrugged. "Then I would die in the wilderness, and that would be the end of it. The council had no choice but to accept Ramses' judgment. He had saved my life, but he had also ended it. I could never return to Egypt. I was to be exiled into the desert to face whatever the Most High had decided."

Help in the Desert

"So, what happened then?" Gershom asked.

"Members of Ramses' personal guard escorted me back to the Great Estate, mostly for my own protection. Ramses had made it clear that he expected me to show up for my exile in three days. I assured him I would come as required. Asati, Nazim, and Miriam were waiting for my return. Word of the verdict and my exile had already reached them. Before I could speak, Asati said, 'We have a plan to help you.'

"I had already resigned myself to my fate, so I told them there was nothing they could do to help. Asati grew angry. She reminded me that Amun-Ra's committed agents would use this opportunity to kill me. It was their last chance, and they would not waste it. Nazim added that they could place a cache of weapons, food, and water at a reasonable distance from where I would be released into exile, someplace hidden but marked by a flag. Too far for anyone to notice, but close enough for me to reach within an hour or two. At least that would give me a fighting chance.

"I started to refuse, to say they shouldn't risk themselves. But Miriam cut me off. She said, 'Moses, this isn't about what you deserve or don't deserve. This is about survival. And whether you want to admit it or not, you're still my brother.'

"That stopped me. Asati looked surprised—she hadn't known Miriam was my sister. But she didn't ask any questions. She just nodded and pushed forward, 'Then we have three days. We need to move quickly.'

"The first day was spent planning and gathering the necessary items. Nazim had connections from his years with the Ne'arin. He knew where the best weapons were stored, including captured

Hittite equipment that had been sitting in armories for years. He said he could acquire what I needed without raising too many questions."

"What kind of weapons?" Gershom asked.

"He gave me a short iron sword he had captured at Kadesh years earlier—one of the finest Hittite blades he'd ever seen, sharp enough to cut through bronze armor. Two spears with iron tips: a long one for throwing and a shorter one for close combat. A small shield with an iron facing. A composite bow with fifty iron-tipped arrows was the most important weapon. It allowed me to attack from a distance. Nazim said the iron arrows would pierce anything I might face. Finally, a sturdy walking and fighting staff. It was the same one that Semri and I had trained with. In the right hands, it was as deadly as any blade.

"Beyond weapons, he gathered field supplies including yarrow salve to stop bleeding, flint, and tinder for fire. He knew what it took to survive in harsh conditions. He had lived through enough campaigns to understand what I would face."

"What about food and water?" Eliezer asked.

"That was Miriam's responsibility. She gathered dried meat, hard bread, and dried dates. She only chose foods that wouldn't spoil in the desert heat. Miriam and Nazim loaded as many water skins as the cart could carry. She said water was more important than anything else. A man could go days without food, but in the desert, without water, I could die within two days.

"Nazim and the estate carpenter converted a one-man chariot into a cart. The chariot's wheels would roll more easily than a regular cart, allowing me to carry more water. They moved the axle to the center for balance—when loaded properly, all my energy would go into forward movement rather than lifting weight. It ultimately made the difference.

"While they worked on the second day, preparing the cart to hold the cache, I spent time with Asati. We sat in her courtyard, and I tried to tell her things I should have said years before. I thanked her for saving me as a child, for raising me, and for protecting me all these years. I told her I was sorry for the pain I had caused her, for the danger my actions had brought to her household."

"What did she say?" Eliezer asked quietly.

"She looked me straight in the eye and said, 'Stop apologizing. I knew from the moment I pulled you from the Nile that neither of our lives would be simple. I knew that there was something different about you. I watched you struggle between two worlds, and it broke my heart because I couldn't help you.' Then she asked me if I was truly Hebrew and had never really been Egyptian. She asked, 'Is that the secret you had been keeping all these years?'

"I told her yes. I told her about my mother, about Miriam, and my brother Aaron, and how I had spent my life trying to hide who I was, trying to fit into a world that would never fully accept me. She listened, and when I finished, she embraced me. She said, 'You are my son. That will never change, no matter what blood runs in your veins.'

"We moved on to practical matters. I arranged for everything I owned to be sold and for the gold and silver to be transferred to her. She said she didn't need my money, but I insisted she use it to help Miriam and my family, however she could. She agreed and promised she would do what she could without drawing undue attention. It was getting late. She embraced me, not wanting to let go. Finally, she pulled away and left for her quarters."

168

He paused, his voice growing rougher. "That was the last time I got to share any real time with her. Everything after that was preparation for leaving."

"Late on the second day, Nazim and Miriam prepared to transport the cache. They had to do it carefully, without drawing attention. Nazim created a removable brush that could be attached to the cart's rear. They used it while positioning the cart to hide their path into the desert. Later, I could drag it behind the cart to hide my tracks from any pursuers."

"How did they get it out there without being seen?" Gershom asked.

"They left that evening. Miriam brought a trusted Hebrew worker who knew the desert and could navigate even in the darkness. They dressed as merchants and loaded some trading goods atop the cart to complete the disguise. Nazim later told me they went first to the exile point, several hours east of Memphis, by chariot. From there, they traveled another hour eastward toward Midian, far enough that my escorts wouldn't see the cache, but close enough for me to reach it within an hour or two if I knew where to look."

Moses shifted his weight. "They chose the location carefully. They found a rock formation far enough from the release point to be invisible to my escorts, but distinctive enough for me to find if I knew what to look for. They placed the cart behind the rocks and erected a pole with a red cloth tied to the top. The flag would be visible once I knew where to search."

"While they were gone, I walked the training grounds one last time, visited the rooms where my daughters had lived, and sat on Nashwa's side of our bed, holding things that had been hers.

"That night, I prayed. I went to my room and prayed more

earnestly than I had in many years. I asked the Most High for forgiveness for all the years I had ignored Him, for the denial of who I was. I didn't ask to survive the desert, only that if I died out there, He would grant me peace. Then I tried to sleep. I needed my strength for what lay ahead.

"The third day was the hardest. Nazim and Miriam returned before dawn. They looked exhausted but said everything was in place. Nazim drew me a map in the dirt, showed me exactly how far to walk, what landmarks to watch for, and where the flag would be visible. He made me repeat it back to him three times until he was satisfied I wouldn't forget.

"Miriam gave me the directions again, differently, using the sun's position and the shape of the dunes. She said if I got disoriented, I should wait until evening and use the stars."

Moses paused. "Then she looked at me and said something I hadn't expected. She said, 'Moses, I don't know if we'll ever see each other again. But I want you to know—Mother forgave you. For not being at Father's or her burial, for all those years of distance. She loved you until her last breath and forgave you. And so do I.'

"I couldn't speak. I just nodded. She embraced me quickly, then left before I could respond."

He shifted his position, stretching his stiffening back. "I spent the morning preparing myself. I ate well, drank plenty of water, and rested as much as I could. Nazim came to my room, and we talked about what I might face—not just the desert, but also the possibility of pursuit. He said Amun-Ra's agents would likely wait a day or two before following, to make it look like the desert had killed me rather than an assassination. That would give me time to find the cache and prepare."

"Did he think you would survive?" Gershom asked.

"He said if I found the cache, if I rationed the water carefully, if I avoided their pursuit or found a good place for an ambush, the bow gave me a chance. But he was honest about the odds. The desert kills most men who enter it unprepared. And while I would be entering it as prepared as they could make me, I had a long distance to travel and had to do that with multiple pursuers tracking me.

"Then he asked me, 'When was the last time you shot a bow?'

"'A long time,' I replied. 'At the end, Semri and I mostly practiced our close combat skills.'

"We went out to the area where Semri and I used to practice, and for over an hour, we worked at regaining my skills with the composite bow of Egypt. Nazim was surprised at how fast my body remembered, and soon my movements became smooth and accurate enough to be lethal at about one hundred cubits. My muscles began to rebel at the long-forgotten exertion, and Nazim said, 'You are good enough if you plan your ambush well.' We returned to the house."

Moses looked at his sons. "Late that afternoon, Asati came to my room. She brought me a cloak and a hat. They were made from simple, undyed linen, nothing that would mark me as Egyptian or Hebrew. She said it would protect me from the sun during the day and help keep me warm at night. Then she gave me something else. She said Miriam had helped her obtain it. It was a small pendant on a cord, inscribed with the Hebrew name of the Most High. She said, 'He has protected you all these years. I do not think He will abandon you now. I believe He still has important things for you to do. Never forget that.' Then she put it around my neck and kissed my forehead.

"We stood there for a moment in silence. Then she said, 'Moses, whatever happens in the desert, know that I have always loved you. You were my son in every way that mattered. And I'm proud of the man you became, even with all your recent struggles. Even with all your mistakes.'

"I told her I loved her, too. That she had given me a life when I should have died in the river, and I was grateful for every moment of it, even the painful ones. Then I left. Any longer and I might lose my resolve.

"Nazim was waiting with the chariot. Ramses' guards were already outside the estate. They were formal, respectful, but there was no question that I was their prisoner. It was time. I climbed into the chariot, and we rode out of the Great Estate to the first ferry that crossed into Memphis. I didn't look back. I couldn't."

He fell silent, staring into the fire. "Everything was in place. All that remained was to see if I would survive long enough to find it."

Exile

"When we arrived, Ramses was waiting. I spent the night at the palace. Nazim stepped forward and asked permission to accompany us to the place of exile. Ramses looked at him for a long moment, then nodded. 'You may come. Moses deserves at least one friendly face at the end.'

"Ramses had a good meal prepared for me that night and told me to rest well. I would need all the strength I could muster. We sat over the evening meal, talking about better days. Ramses said, 'I prefer to remember only the good times we shared. Let the rest disappear into the night, not to be remembered.'

"Nazim and I went to the room that had been prepared for me.

Two guards escorted us and stood outside. Nazim urged me to get to sleep as soon as possible and produced some herbs, poured them into a cup of water, and insisted I drink. I don't know what they were, but the next thing I knew, Nazim was waking me, and the morning light was just breaking through. It took me a few moments to wake fully, but I felt rested and ready.

"We washed up and knocked on the door. It opened, and the two guards escorted us to my final meal: bread, fruit, plenty to drink, nothing heavy. Then we left for the palace courtyard. Ramses was already waiting with his royal guard. He wore his full regalia: the double crown, the ceremonial armor, and the crook and flail. He looked every bit the Pharaoh, not the friend I had known for so many years.

"Nazim and I climbed into the waiting chariot. We traveled in a formal procession. Ramses in the lead chariot, Nazim and I in the second, followed by Pharaoh's personal guard. At the back were two chariots with members of Pharaoh's council as witnesses to the exile. We moved through the city as the sun rose, and people stopped to watch. Some knew who I was, what was happening. Others just saw a condemned man being taken to his fate.

"The journey took most of the morning. We traveled east, away from the Nile, toward the edge of the desert where cultivation ended, and the sand began. No one spoke during the ride. There was nothing left to say.

"When we reached the designated place, Ramses raised his hand, and the procession stopped. He climbed down from his chariot and walked toward me. The guards stepped back, giving us space. Ramses gestured for me to follow him a short distance away."

"What did he say?" Eliezer asked quietly.

"He looked at me, and for the first time that morning, I saw not Pharaoh but my friend. Ramses' voice was low, meant only for me. He said, 'Moses, I wish this could have ended differently. You have been like a brother to me. What we went through at Kadesh, the campaigns that followed, what we built together with the Ne'arin, and the treaty with the Hittites. Those things mattered. They still matter.'

"I told him I knew. That I was grateful for all the years we shared, for all the protection he had given me. He shook his head. 'I'm sending you into the desert to die. That's what this is. Don't pretend otherwise. The blood debt allows me to claim I've honored our bond while still satisfying those who want you dead. But we both know the desert has no mercy. It will kill you.'

"I told him I understood, that I didn't blame him. That he had done more for me than I had any right to expect. He asked, 'Do you think your God will save you?' I looked out at the vast emptiness of sand. 'It is all in the Most High's hands. If He wills that I survive, I will survive. If not, then I will die, and perhaps that is what I deserve.'

"Ramses stared at me, then said, 'I hope He is merciful, Moses. I hope you survive this. And if you do—if you somehow find your way to a life beyond this desert—know that in another world, we would still be brothers.'

"He put his hand on my shoulder and said, 'Goodbye.' Then he stepped back, his face hardening into Pharaoh's mask again. He said loudly, for all to hear, 'Moses, son of the Nile, you have been judged and found guilty of taking the life of an Egyptian. By right, you should die. But I have invoked the blood debt owed from Kadesh. You are hereby exiled into the desert. You go without food, water, or weapons. Your fate rests with the gods. If they favor you, you will live. If not, the desert will claim you.'

"Two guards came forward and searched me thoroughly, examining my robes, sandals, and body. I had no hidden knife, no water skin, no food. When they were satisfied, they stepped back and reported to Ramses that I had nothing.

"Ramses nodded. 'It is done. Moses, you are released into exile. You may not return to Egypt on pain of immediate death. Go!'

"I turned toward the desert. The sand stretched endlessly before me, empty and brutal under the morning sun. I took a step, then another. Behind me, I heard Nazim's voice. 'Wait.'

"I stopped. Nazim was walking toward me. The guards looked at Ramses, uncertain whether to stop him. Ramses nodded permission. Nazim came to me and embraced me tightly. He held me for a long moment, then leaned close to my ear. He whispered, 'East. An hour. A rocky outcropping with a red flag. The Most High be with you.'

"As he released me, he turned me slightly north of where I had been facing. My original direction would have led me to the Red Sea, leaving me stranded without the cache. He gave me a hard shove, sending me stumbling forward into the sand. He said loudly, so all could hear, 'Goodbye, my lord. May the gods judge you fairly.'

"I didn't look back. I couldn't. I walked forward into the sand, each step taking me farther from everything I had known. Behind me, I heard the chariots turning, the horses moving away. Quickly, the sound faded. They were gone, and I was alone."

"What did you do then?" Eliezer asked.

"The sun beat down on me. The sand was featureless and hostile. I had no water, no food, no weapon, no shelter. I had only the direction Nazim had given me—east, an hour, a rocky outcropping, and a red flag—and the faint hope that I would survive long enough to find it."

He looked at his sons. "I began to walk. The sand was soft in some places, making those steps an effort. The heat was already building, and I could feel the sun through the linen cloak and hat on my head. I was grateful for them, but the sun beat through anyway. I tried to conserve my strength, to move steadily without exhausting myself. The morning meal sustained me, but I had to reach the cache before the worst heat drained my strength. Nazim had said an hour, but in this heat, through this sand, it would take longer. Thirst was already building. I drew on all those years of training, of Semri pushing me past exhaustion, never allowing me to give in, and kept moving.

"I was truly alone now, a single man in an endless desert. I continued to look east in the direction Nazim had sent me, trying to see any sign of the rock formation he had described. The desert made it hard to judge distance. In the shimmering heat, everything looked the same."

"How did you find the cache?" Gershom asked.

"It took a while. First, I had to deal with the fear that hit me as I walked. Not fear of dying. I had accepted that possibility. But I feared that I would die without ever getting an answer to my questions. Why had the Most High let everything fall apart? Why had my family been taken? Why had I been allowed to rise so high only to fall so far? Why, if there was a purpose to my life, did it seem to have ended in exile and shame? Standing there in the sand, alone and empty, I prayed one more time.

'Most High, I do not know if You will hear me or if You care. But if there is a reason for all of this, let me find the cache. Let

me survive long enough to understand. And if I'm meant to die here, grant me a quick death.'

"However, I knew that if I did not find the cache, my pursuers might grant me the quick death I had asked for, or they might torture me for days before killing me.

"Then I started walking again. Slightly north of east, using Nazim's directions. His route would take me just north of the Red Sea, toward whatever fate was waiting for me in the desert. I focused only on the next step, then the next, drawing on the determination that had carried me through countless training sessions. After what felt like hours, I saw the outcropping, and, as I drew closer, I saw the red flag. I stumbled forward, reached the cart, and grabbed one of the water bags hanging off the side. I fell down in the sand, uncorked the spout and drank deeply, then poured water over my face and neck."

Preparing for the Amun-Ra Assassins

"That must have felt so good," Gershom said.

"It did. I moved into the narrow shade provided by the outcropping and slowly began to recover. Over the next half hour or so, I drank the entire waterskin. I found a small bag of salt tied to its neck. Several times, I put a pinch in my mouth and drank it down with water, hoping the salt would help with the cramps that had begun in my legs.

"I had not eaten anything since early this morning. I waited for the salt to take effect, and the cramps slowly subsided. I carefully got up, not wanting the spasms to start again. I went to the cart, untied the cover, and found a bag of dried beef. Taking that and another waterskin to the shade, I began chewing the beef, using just enough water in my mouth to soften it and make it easier to chew. I ate half the bag. Yes, more than I should have, but these first few days would determine whether I lived or died. I needed my strength. I had to figure out a strategy to deal with the assassins.

"Much depended on whether they would come in chariots or on foot. I suspected chariots. I hoped they would not be real charioteers but priestly assassins with minimal training, expecting an easy target.

"I knew I needed rest more than anything. The sun was setting, and the desert cold would come soon. I pulled the cover from the cart and wrapped it around myself. It wasn't much, but it would keep the worst of the cold away.

"The night was brutal in a different way than the day. The temperature dropped fast once the sun disappeared. I lay there in the darkness, wrapped in the cover, listening to the silence of the desert. No sounds of the city, no voices, no animals. Just the wind moving across the sand and the occasional crack of the rocks as they cooled. I welcomed the wind, despite the chill. It would obscure my tracks, making it far more difficult for them to follow.

"Despite everything—the cold, the uncertainty, the knowledge that assassins would soon be tracking me—I slept. My body demanded it, and I had learned long ago to sleep when I could. A soldier who can't sleep before a fight wouldn't survive many battles.

"I woke before dawn. The cold was still biting, but I could see the first gray light on the horizon. I finished the bag of dried beef, drank more water, and considered my options. I needed to find defensible ground before the assassins caught up to me. But more than that, I needed a long-term plan for survival."

"Which direction did you go?" Gershom asked.

"East, toward Sinai and eventually Midian. It was the only sensible choice. North along the Palestinian coast was impossible, as that route was dotted with Egyptian forts and military regiments protecting Egypt's northern border. If I were recognized at any of those outposts, escape would be difficult, if not impossible. The soldiers there would have heard about my exile from Egypt, and I would be hunted down within days.

"South was nothing but a deeper desert with no destination, still within Egypt's reach. West was back toward Egypt. That left east. I had to cross the northern edge of the Red Sea, travel through the Sinai desert, and eventually across the Gulf of Aqaba into Midian. It was a land of isolated shepherds with only small cities and no Egyptian presence. I knew from court trade reports that many of the Midianites were followers of the Most High. It was the perfect place to disappear.

"But first, I had to survive the assassins. The terrain immediately east provided possibilities. The desert landscape was not all sand. There were rocky outcroppings, wadis, and narrow passages. These were places where a single man with the right weapons, especially a bow with iron-headed arrows, could hold off multiple attackers, if he chose his ground carefully. I loaded the cart and checked the weapons Nazim had provided, making sure my bow and arrows were readily accessible. I positioned the brush Nazim had included so that it would drag behind, wiping away my tracks. Before the sun had risen, I started pulling it eastward.

"I was looking for specific terrain. Not open sand where chariots could maneuver freely, but somewhere with rocks, elevation, and natural barriers. Somewhere I could see them coming long before they could see me. That way I could assess their strengths and weaknesses and make them fight on my terms, not theirs."

The Final Attempt of Amun-Ra

"So, you began to remember the Moses who had trained the Ne'arin and fought at Kadesh," Gershom said.

"I did. Everything started to come back to me, almost as if I had never left it. For the first time in years, I had a real purpose, something I could understand and plan for. I have to admit, it energized me. For the rest of that day, I traveled eastward. The cart worked better than I had hoped. I settled into an easy pace, carefully navigating the best path through the irregular terrain. I made good time. I had perhaps one day before they caught up. Even with chariots, they couldn't be sure where I had gone, so they would have to split up—going north, south, and east—searching for footprints in the sand or any sign that would reveal my direction of travel. They would have no idea I was so well provisioned. I suspected one of them had been in the group that accompanied Ramses to my exile. They would expect me to be thirsty and ragged by now. They just had to find me, but I could spot their dust cloud long before they could see me.

"I pressed on through the heat, stopping at regular intervals to search behind me for any sign of pursuit. I saw none. About midday, I took a break. Taking the cart cover and my two spears, I made a shade tent and sat down facing west, watching for pursuit. I ate part of another bag of dried beef, several dates, and finished my second waterskin. After an hour's rest, I stowed everything and resumed my journey.

"By mid-afternoon, I found what I was looking for. A wadi with high rocky sides, narrow enough that chariots would have to slow down, with good elevation on both sides, and rocks to hide behind. I circled around to the wadi's northern side and began the difficult climb, pulling the cart behind me. It took almost an hour to reach the top. I positioned the cart behind several rocks where it couldn't be seen from below. I removed my weapons, then draped the cover over the cart and threw sand over it to hide it from anyone passing through the wadi below.

"I was just finishing my preparations when, perhaps two hours before sunset, I saw the dust. Two chariots, single riders, coming from the west. They were moving cautiously, scanning the ground for tracks. I took out my bow and several arrows. When they entered the wadi, they had to slow down even more to navigate the rocky ground."

"They came right into your trap?" Gershom asked.

"Yes. I let them pass my position. When they were perhaps fifty cubits beyond me, their backs exposed, still moving forward, I stood, drew the bow, and loosed the first arrow.

"The first man went down instantly. The arrow took him in the back, between the shoulder blades. He fell from his chariot without a sound. The second chariot was only a few lengths ahead. The driver heard his companion fall and started to turn. I had already nocked the second arrow, which I loosed before he could react. The second arrow struck him in the side, below the ribs. Not as clean as the first. He fell from his chariot but didn't die immediately. Both chariots, now without drivers, continued a short distance before the horses stopped, their reins dragging on the ground.

"I climbed down from my position, bow still ready, arrow nocked, and approached. The first man was dead. The second was on his back in the sand, blood spreading from the wound. He saw me coming and tried to get up to reach for a weapon. But he couldn't. The arrow had done too much damage."

"What did he say?" Eliezer asked quietly.

"He stared at me like he was seeing a ghost. His voice was weak, disbelieving. He said, 'How? How do you have weapons? Where did you get a bow? You should be dying of thirst by now. I saw Pharaoh's guards search you. You had nothing!'

"I recognized him then. He had been one of the council members who attended my exile. He had watched me searched, watched me sent into the desert with nothing. He couldn't understand how I was standing over him, armed and healthy, while he was dying.

"I looked down at him and said, 'Did you believe I had no one willing to help me? They left a cache for me in the desert. I am well prepared.' He tried to speak, but coughed up blood. Then he said, 'You're still a dead man. More are coming. They will find you. They will kill you.'

"I looked down at him and said, 'Not by your hand, or theirs either.'

"He tried to curse me, to say something else, but the coughing took him. Within moments, he was gone.

"I stood there between the two bodies, holding the bow, and felt...not guilt, not satisfaction. Just the cold certainty that this wouldn't be the last. The man had said more were coming. And I would have to kill them too, or die. But something had changed. My warrior's heart had revived. Gone was the indecision and emptiness, replaced by the surety Semri had drilled into me."

"What did you do with the bodies?" Gershom asked.

"I removed the arrows so their cause of death would not be immediately obvious from a distance. Up close, the wounds would tell the story, but I hoped that even if they were cautious about approaching, they would not be concerned about an archer, which would hurt my chances at a second trap. I left them where they died, one behind the other in the narrow wadi. Whoever came next would have to stop to investigate, and in this confined space, they'd be just as vulnerable as these two had been. In tomorrow's heat, the bodies would swell, and it wouldn't take long for the bodies to begin to stink. Altogether, it would create the perfect ambush.

"I went to their chariots and searched them for anything useful. I took my time. I was sure the earliest anyone else could arrive would be tomorrow, but more likely the day after. I collected everything into one chariot. I took their weapons, food, water, medicine pouches, bedrolls, and rope. The other chariot I drove out of the wadi and left it where it couldn't be seen. I unhitched its horse, removed the bridle and harness, and gave it as much water as it wanted. After it had drunk its fill, I slapped its rump hard, sending it away. Someone would find it eventually.

"The remaining chariot, loaded with supplies, I led around the wadi. I didn't need all of their weapons, but I did want the better of the two bows, their arrows, and the four spears. I could use those spears with my cart cover to create better shade while I waited, which might take days. The chariot could not climb all the way to my position, so I found a place below where I could hobble the horse again, keeping it out of sight of anyone approaching the wadi. It was my backup in case I had to flee. I took some of the water and slowly gave it to the horse. It drank desperately. They had not taken care of their mounts."

"It appears they were not prepared for such a long pursuit," Gershom noted.

"That is a good observation. I took the weapons up to my hideout first, then went back with the cover cloth and loaded up everything else. I now had food and water for three or four more days. I bundled the other items in the cloth and carried them up to my position on the ridge above the wadi. After setting up my sun cover, I ate some of their food. Miriam had given me survival food. They had brought comfort food, including bread and pastries. I decided to treat myself while I had the chance. I was surprised when one of the waterskins turned out to be wine. I set that aside. I knew what that would do to me, and with the rest of my pursuers still out there, I needed a clear head and sharp reflexes.

"I got comfortable and began wondering what I would do if any of my attackers surrendered. I couldn't execute prisoners who surrendered. But I couldn't let them return to guide others to me either. I decided I would send them back on foot with one waterskin. They might survive. They might not. But at least I wouldn't have killed them in cold blood.

"With that decided, I lay down, using their bedrolls, facing west, watching for any sign of the others. No one appeared for the rest of that day, and as night fell, I knew they would stop and set up camp. I could finally get the rest I needed."

"When did the others finally come?" Gershom asked.

"Late the next day. There were four of them. They stopped before the wadi, debating how to go through, when one of them spotted a vulture taking off from the two bodies at the other end of the wadi. They couldn't be sure it was their two companions, but it made them extremely cautious."

Both Gershom and Eliezer leaned forward expectantly.

"They argued about what to do for several minutes. While I waited, I drove ten arrows into the sand in front of me. I nocked one arrow on the string, ready to shoot, and held another against the bow for a fast second shot. The other bow I had taken from them was within reach to my rear, should I lose my bowstring.

"They finally decided one of them would go down the wadi to check the bodies, while the other three waited at the entrance to the wadi. It was a good tactical decision. They drew lots to see who would go.

"I couldn't attack while they remained at the wadi entrance, so I just waited. The loser of the lot rode through the wadi, stopping a few cubits from the bodies. The stench must have been overwhelming. He pulled out a cloth and placed it over his nose and mouth. He waved them forward, but they refused and waved him back. He gave up and rode back to them.

"I could just make out their discussion. 'What did you see?' his companions asked. He replied, 'It is hard to tell how they died. The stench kept me from getting close enough to know for sure. I can see two chariot tracks leading out from the wadi, but I have no idea where they go. The only way to find out is to overcome the smell, examine the bodies, and then follow the tracks to see where they lead.'

'What is your best guess?'

'If it was Moses who had killed them, he probably took their chariots and ran, keeping one in reserve. He has their weapons and supplies now, which probably means he is long gone, with a full day's head start.'

"They debated for several more minutes. Finally, they decided they needed to know how their companions had died and which direction I had gone. But they weren't foolish. They agreed to stay spread out. Two would approach the bodies on foot while the other two held back about twenty cubits, mounted and ready to flee if there was trouble.

"It was a good plan. It would have worked against most threats. But not against an archer positioned above them and to their rear.

"The two dismounted and hobbled their horses. They began walking toward the bodies, slowly, khopeshes drawn. The other two stayed back, watching, their horses restless.

"I waited until the two on foot were committed, too far from their horses to get back quickly. Then I stood and drew.

"I shot the mounted ones first. They were the ones who could escape, carry word back. Their backs were to me. The first arrow took the rider on the left through his spine, between the shoulder blades. He fell from his chariot before his companion even registered what had happened. I had already nocked the second arrow. As I released the second arrow, he started to turn, trying to register what had happened. The arrow caught him just under the armpit, driving deep into his side. He went down hard.

"Less than five heartbeats. Both were down."

Eliezer's eyes were wide. "And the other two?"

"The ones on foot heard the impacts, heard the bodies fall. They turned and saw their companions down. I had already grabbed two fresh arrows from the sand, nocking one. The quicker of the two started to run back toward his horse. Before he had taken two steps, I loosed. It caught him flush in the chest mid-step. He went down face-first in the sand.

"The last one understood immediately. He didn't run. He threw his weapon aside and threw himself to the ground, flat on his face. He started yelling over and over, 'I surrender! I surrender! Don't shoot! I yield! Please!'

"He tried to see me as he kept yelling, but I was too high on the ridge. I had an arrow nocked, aimed at his back. I could have killed him easily. But he had surrendered. And I had already decided how I would deal with someone who surrendered."

"What did you do?" Gershom asked.

"I picked up the rope, strapped on my iron sword, took my bow and two arrows, and walked down the ridge to the wadi. I approached cautiously. The man lay face down, trembling.

"First, I secured the horses. I hobbled the two from the mounted men I'd shot. I couldn't let them wander. Then I approached the survivor.

"'Stand up slowly,' I told him. 'Hands where I can see them.'

"He obeyed, shaking. Young, maybe twenty. Terrified. I took a section of the rope and bound it around his knees, tight enough that he could shuffle and move, but not run. I left his hands free.

"'You're going to work for your life,' I told him. 'Do exactly what I say, and you might survive this. Understand?'

"He nodded frantically.

"'Collect all their gear, weapons, food, and water, everything. Make a pile here.'

"He shuffled from body to body, from chariot to chariot, gathering everything while I watched. It took him the better part of an hour.

"When he finished, I had him drag the five bodies, one by one, and load them into the sturdiest chariot. The last two he dragged were hard work. He had avoided them as long as possible. They had been dead two days and were badly reeking. He vomited twice. I didn't help him.

"'Cover them,' I said, pointing to a bedroll.

"He did.

"'Now water the other three horses. Give them all they want. When that is done, unhobble them one by one and lead them out of the wadi and off to the right side. Then unharness them and send them running. They will go far enough that someone will eventually find them.'

"When he had released the horses, I yelled, 'Come back.'

"He shuffled back, exhausted, covered in blood, sand, and sweat.

"I made him sit in front of me while I thought about what to ask him.

"'What are you going to do with me?'

"'You're going back to Memphis. You'll lead this chariot filled with your companions' bodies and report what happened here. But you'll do it on my terms.'

"He stared at me, not understanding.

"'I'll remove all but one rein, and that one I will cut too short to use to drive the chariot. It will be long enough for you to lead the horse, but that is all. I'm also going to use the rest of the rope to tie the bodies down, using enough knots that it would take you a whole day to work them free. By then, you'd be out of water and time. So, you'll lead the horse on foot, walking all the way back. It is getting late, so you will leave at first light tomorrow morning. But first, I have a few questions.'

"He looked at me, willing to do anything that might help him survive. 'What do you want to know?' he asked, sitting down and trying to get comfortable despite his bound knees.

"'After Nephura and Ameny died in the storm, why did the temple continue pursuing me? And the boat that killed my family—did you sabotage it?'

"'You don't understand how it was at Amun-Ra. I was orphaned in my first year and raised in the temple. Everything we knew, everything we were taught, it all came from Nephura and the high priests. They hated you. They made us hate you. It was...it was all we knew.'

"He paused, then added quietly, 'Yes. We sabotaged the boat. The order came from the new high priest himself after Nephura died. The leadership changed, but the mission remained the same. He demanded that their deaths had to look like an accident. I wasn't there, but I heard about it afterward. They celebrated it as a victory.'

"My anger almost got the best of me, but after swallowing my bile, I felt something unexpected—pity. Then he asked something I hadn't expected.

"'Do I have to go back?'

"'What do you mean?' I asked.

"'With everyone dead... with the mission failed...I'm the only one who knows what happened. They'll kill me to keep it quiet. I know too much, and I failed. If I want to live, I can't go back.'

"That put an unexpected twist on my plan."

A Difficult Decision

"What did you do?" Eliezer asked.

"My most serious concern was honoring the Most High and remaining true to my decision not to cross the line into outright murder. I sat down a few cubits away, and we were both quiet for a long time. I was in a quandary. I had never faced such a perplexing dilemma. I realized that what he said was true. The ones in Amun-

Ra still seeking my death could not allow him to stay alive. The failure had to be kept quiet, and he would be the sole remaining witness. But if I released him, would he still pursue me? Would he try to complete the mission to earn glory among his people?

"Then there was the matter of the man himself. He was young, perhaps twenty years of age. He had been trained as a killer, though apparently not very well. I had looked into the eyes of countless soldiers, and I recognized what was missing in his. Every man who takes lives develops an unmistakable hardness. He had not yet become that man. Sitting there, bound and helpless, he no longer looked like an assassin. He looked like what he was: a frightened young man caught between forces larger than himself."

Eliezer leaned forward. "Did he speak again?"

"Not for some time. We sat as the late afternoon sun beat down. I got a water bag and shared it with him. He greedily drank his fill but remained silent.

"I prayed. I asked the Most High what He would have me do. Was mercy in this case wisdom, or merely the postponement of a necessary evil? Would releasing him be an act of faith or an act of foolishness that would cost other lives?"

"And did you receive an answer?" Eliezer asked.

Moses smiled faintly. "Not in the way I hoped. No voice from heaven, no surge of certainty in my chest, as had happened in the past to guide me. But a thought came. It was quiet, yet clear and insistent.

'You did not kill him when you had cause. Do not seek reasons to justify what you have already decided against.'

This time, Gershom spoke first. "So, you let him go?"

"Not immediately. I needed to know his mind first. I asked him his name. He hesitated, then told me: Amuntankh, a name I understood to mean 'Amun lives.' Since he was orphaned as a baby, he had no family other than those who raised him at the temple. I asked him about his training, how he came to be chosen for this task. And as he spoke, I realized something...

"He was not so different from the man I had been when Semri began training me. Young, certain of his purpose, he was willing to kill for what he believed was righteous. The only difference was that the Most High had guided my path and shown me a different way.

"I decided to appeal to his religious beliefs, to use his own theology to show him the truth. 'Are you a true follower of Amun-Ra?'

"He looked me straight in the eye and said with true passion, 'Amun-Ra is my all, my everything.'

"That gave me the opening I needed to help him see clearly what had been hidden from him all these years. Since he was no longer under the influence of Nephura or any of his followers, I asked him the obvious question, 'Do you think your god approves of pursuing me to my death? Of killing my family?'

"What about the goddess Ma'at? Do you know about her requirements?'

"'I know she is the goddess of justice and truth. Why does she matter in this?'

"I could now take that opening and draw on what I had learned at Temple School and what I had witnessed with Ramses at Kadesh to drive the wedge deeper. 'Because she is the foundation of Egypt's greatness. Have you ever wondered what Ma'at has to say about all of this? I don't know what they taught you, but I learned that even the Pharaoh and the gods of Egypt are required to adhere to the demands of Ma'at. What allows the priests of Amun-Ra to violate those dictates?'

"He looked confused and shot back, 'You are trying to trick me.'

"'There is no trick. It is a simple, honest question all the followers of every god of Egypt must ask themselves. But I want to make sure you understand one thing: do you know why the edict was rescinded?'

"'We never discussed the edict, but I was led to believe it was done through trickery, just like you are trying to do now.'

"'That is not true. There were signs throughout the temples of Memphis, and yes, a star did fall and hit the west bank of the Nile, very near the great lock, but they were not the primary reason.'

"'What was it then?'

"'Ma'at. Many were coming to believe that the annihilation of a whole people by the killing, no, let's use Amun-Ra's argument, sacrificing all the male babies to Sobek for the good of Egypt, went against the dictates of Ma'at. Opinion within the council session was already turning against Nephura. That's when Nephura himself invoked the goddess to justify reversing the edict.'

"'That can't be true.'

"'It is. I would tell you to check the public record, but you cannot. You would have to go back to Egypt, and you said you would be killed. So, I will ask you again: Can the priests of Amun-Ra violate Ma'at and still claim they serve their god? Yes or no?'

"I could see he was lost. Everything he had built his life upon, all he had been taught and assumed to be true, came crashing down around him. He slapped his head repeatedly with both hands, as if trying to stop the chaos in his mind. He began to cry, which grew into choking sobs as his whole world came apart. I waited, letting him find his own way. Eventually, he became quiet, his head hanging down. I pressed him again. 'Yes or no?'

"He looked up at me, his eyes red, his decision clear.

"'No,' he said, resignation heavy in his voice. 'I am lost. I no longer know who I am.'

"I had to give him something he could hold onto. 'You are a loyal follower of Amun-Ra who has begun to learn what his god demands of him. No more, no less. For the first time in your life, you are free, free to follow what your god demands, not what others have told you he demands.'

"I could see the shift in him. This was not a deception. He had fundamentally broken with his past."

"So, what did you do?" Eliezer asked.

"I told him I would take him with me until we found a caravan he could join. He looked relieved. For the first time, he believed he had a chance to survive this whole debacle.

"He spent the remaining hours of daylight removing the bodies from the chariot and spreading them out toward the entrance to the wadi. I then told him to clean the chariot thoroughly so he could ride in it. He used some of the extra bedding, but very little water. We needed to save every drop we could.

"I told him he would have to remain bound at his knees for a while, and I would tie his hands while we slept. I looked him directly in the eyes and said, 'I have learned, over many years of dealing with soldiers, that it was one thing to hear someone tell me of his change, but you need to show me that you have truly changed and not just once. Trust is built over time.' He simply replied, 'I understand.'

"I brought my cart and the other chariot down the ridge to the wadi, far enough from the bodies that their stench would not reach us. I hobbled both horses, gave them water and dates, and prepared a meal for us. We ate from the supplies of his former companions. Afterward, I tied his wrists together, leaving enough rope to tie him to the wheel of the chariot he had cleaned. It would keep him far enough away from me if he changed his mind. I helped him with his bedding and then went to my chariot and lay down."

The Journey East Toward Midian

"The next morning, I woke before dawn. Amuntankh was still asleep, tied to his chariot wheel as I had left him. I lay there thinking about the five bodies we'd left in the wadi.

"Eventually, someone would find them—scavengers certainly, perhaps a caravan passing through. They would be impossible to miss, but hopefully by then the desert would have done its work. Unless the temple sent a search party, which seemed unlikely, no one would know who these men were or why they'd died here.

"My real concern was what the temple would think when none of their assassins returned. Would they send more? There was no way to know. I'd never traveled this route. All my campaigns had been north toward Syria, so I had no idea how frequently caravans passed through or who might discover the bodies.

"As to whether I was still being pursued, I decided that those who continued Nephura's work at the temple of Amun-Ra relied on secrecy and deniability to maintain their efforts. Sending searchers might expose the mission. Better to wait and wonder, to let the silence become its own message. The men were either dead or had fled. Either way, it wouldn't take long before they came to the conclusion that their assassins would not return. They would have heard about my exile, that I had gone into the desert with nothing. The logical conclusion: I had perished in the desert, and something unexpected—bandits, a sandstorm, some other misfortune—had intercepted their assassins.

"With my presumed death, what purpose remained for their continued plotting? There were so many unknowns. Maybe my captive would have an opinion about that."

"Did you ask him?" Eliezer asked.

"Not right away. We needed to get started, so I rose and began preparing for the journey. I gave Amuntankh water and loosened his bonds enough for him to relieve himself and wash his face. He was stiff from sleeping bound to the wheel, but he did not complain. I fed the horses, checked the wheels and harnesses, and loaded the captured supplies into my cart. I left nothing behind. I lashed the cart to the rear of Amuntankh's chariot, further restricting his ability to try to flee. It would slow us down, but for now, there was no other choice. After eating some more of the dead men's rations, we prepared to leave.

"I looked back toward the wadi one last time. The bodies were far enough away and spread out enough that I could barely see them, but I knew they were there. The vultures circling above made that obvious. This far into the desert, it would take the jackals a while to find them, but eventually they would join in. Five men who had set out to kill me had found their own deaths instead. I felt no satisfaction in it, only sadness over five needless deaths.

"'Are you ready?' I asked Amuntankh.

"He nodded, and we set out east toward Midian. I kept him bound at the knees, but his hands were free to steer the chariot. He looked at the cart lashed behind him but made no comment. The time passed with hardly any conversation. He seemed lost in his thoughts, and I let him be. I had decided to wait and ask him my questions later as we traveled. It would help break the monotony.

"We stopped for a midday meal, if you could call it that. Just a few dates and water. I was conserving water for the horses. They were our best chance for surviving the rest of our journey.

"As the afternoon wore on, I began asking Amuntankh about what the followers of Nephura would do now that they presumed I was dead. Wouldn't they now just return to their normal routine of serving their god?

"He thought they would find something else to rally around. They had been at this for forty years. Giving up the network they had created, their sense of destiny, and the power that came with it wouldn't be easy. They would find a new purpose for its use.

"That first day, we actually made better time than I had expected, and the night passed quietly. On the second day, as we stopped to water the horses, he spoke. 'The left rear wheel on the chariot is beginning to work loose. I heard it yesterday but said nothing. Today it is worse. We should tighten it before it fails.'

"I examined the wheel. He was right. The wedge pin had shifted. I looked at him. 'Why tell me now and not yesterday?'

"'Yesterday I was still deciding if I wanted you to reach Midian safely. Today, I know I do.'

"I tightened the wheel, and that evening, I told him, 'I will remove the binding from your knees tomorrow. You will be able to stand freely, but I will still bind your hands at night.'

"He nodded. 'I would do the same.'

"As the days passed, he began asking questions. First about the Most High, then about Ma'at, and whether I thought the Egyptian gods were false. I told him I could not answer the last question. I was only sure that the Most High had revealed Himself to me as the one true God. But I also told him that if he served Amun-Ra according to Ma'at, seeking truth and justice, he would be a better man than those who served falsely in the temples. Many priests exploited their gods for personal gain rather than worshiping them sincerely.

"'Can I ever return to Egypt?' he asked one evening.

"'How? What would your story be that would prevent them from killing you to preserve their secret?'

"'Then where do I go?' he asked.

"'That is for you to decide. You are free now, truly free. But freedom means you must choose your own path.'

"On the sixth day, fortune favored us. We saw dust on the horizon. It was a caravan moving across our path, heading toward Syria. Even from a distance, I recognized the lead merchant, a man named Basemeth. He was a big man who always wore brightly colored, distinctive clothing. He traded between southern Midian, Damascus, and sometimes Memphis, where I had seen him numerous times over the years. He was honest, as honest as any merchant could be.

"We sped up to intercept them. I told Amuntankh to wait while I spoke with Basemeth privately. I told the caravan leader that I had a young man who needed passage away from Egypt. He was not a criminal, but he could not return home. Basemeth looked at Amuntankh, then at me.

"'He is fleeing temple politics?' Basemeth asked.

"'Something like that.'

"Basemeth nodded. 'I can take him as far as Damascus. After that, he is on his own.'

"I bent close to him and said, so only he could hear, 'You never saw him or me, is that clear?'

"'Is Amun-Ra still after you?'

"'Yes, but there is more than that. An Egyptian overseer died in an accident I caused, and Ramses exiled me. I need my Amun-Ra enemies to believe I died in the desert.'

"'I never liked those pompous pigs. When Nephura was lost in the sandstorm, I said good riddance. Your secret is safe with me.'

"I thanked him and went back to Amuntankh, telling him that the caravan leader would take him as far as Damascus. It was time for him to decide whether to go with them. This would likely be his best opportunity for a fresh start. I told him he could take his chariot, but he needed to make a decision quickly. We were holding up the caravan.

"He looked at me, sighed, and said, 'There is so much more I wanted to talk with you about, but you are right, this is my best option. I will go with them. Thank you for giving me the chariot. May I take a few days' food and water?'

"'Yes. I will also give you what silver I can spare. You will need to buy food and water for your horse and yourself. It should get you to Damascus with enough left over for a few weeks, if you're careful.'

"He thanked me profusely and said, 'I owe you my life. I will never forget that.'

"I looked him straight in the eyes and said, 'Just remember what you learned. Serve your god faithfully, not as others tell you. And never return to Egypt.'

"He looked at me with an expression I had seen before, in young soldiers who realized their commander had saved their lives. 'I need to ask. Why did you not kill me?'

"'Because the Most High did not require it of me. And because you reminded me of who I once was.'

"He embraced me, something I had not expected. Then he joined the caravan. I watched them move north until the dust settled and they disappeared from view. I never saw him again, but I have often wondered what became of him."

Facing the Desert

"Now that Amuntankh is gone, what happened next?" Eliezer asked.

"I faced the desert alone. My most important consideration was finding water. I should have asked Basemeth, since he knew the area well, where the nearest water was, but I was so concerned about getting Amuntankh into his caravan and making sure he would tell no one I was alive that it never occurred to me. Big mistake."

"What did you do?" Gershom asked.

"I assessed my water supplies and decided that if I was careful, I had up to six or seven days before I ran out of water. Once the water ran out, I might survive another two or three days, but my horse would die, and then I could only take what I could carry, which wouldn't be a lot.

"This route had to have water at some point. I'd seen no sources since leaving the place of exile, but caravans regularly used this route. There had to be at least one oasis ahead, probably more. I needed to find water within six days, or I would never reach Madyan, the small city that lay in the midst of a large oasis marking the transition from desert to fertile land in Midian.

"The area around Madyan's oasis was famous for its mangos, one of the main cargoes of caravans that brought the much-desired fruit to Memphis and southern Egypt. The land further from the city supported many wells used by shepherd families who grazed their flocks on the area's grasslands. Much of the wool traded at Perunifer came from those flocks.

"Those pastures were my real destination, the sparsely populated area that had rolling grasslands and was the domain of shepherds. I knew a little about those shepherds. They were Midianites, sometimes referred to as Cushites, descendants of our father Abraham through Keturah, his wife after the death of Sarah, and followers of the Most High. Among those shepherds was a location where I could hide from my past and be among people who served the same God that I followed, with whom I might forge a future."

"You came to us on purpose, then?" Eliezer asked.

"Yes, I did. But first, I had to find water to get there. I needed to find a way to give myself more time. I stopped to think. I decided that I would last much longer if I traveled at night and slept under my makeshift tent during the day. I could even provide shade for most of my horse if I were careful. I was sure that would stretch our water for at least two or three more days by avoiding the daytime sun and heat. It would force me to travel a little more slowly since road hazards would be harder to see. It would probably lengthen my journey by several days. At this point, anything that stretched my water was worth trying.

"I also had another concern. If I arrived in an Egyptian chariot with iron weapons, it would draw attention to me, which might undo all my efforts. But while I tried to work out a survival scenario, the Most High had other plans."

"What did He do?" Eliezer excitedly asked.

"Patience, my son. We will get there. Switching to night travel worked better than I could have hoped. I never found any water, but I traveled even faster in the cool night air, and my water lasted longer than I expected.

"But, despite all my efforts, my horse and I were on death's door. The horse moved like he was walking through mud, his head hanging low. I had to stop every few hundred cubits to rest, leaning against the cart for support.

"I prayed constantly, sometimes aloud, sometimes just in my mind.

> *'Most High, if this is how I die, at least it will be in freedom, not in Egypt's shadow.'*

"But we kept moving. One step. Then another. Because stopping meant dying, and neither of us was ready to die just yet. That's when I saw the dust on the horizon. A caravan.

"I saw them stop for the night a short distance ahead—a large caravan loaded with wool. Later, I learned they'd left Madyan four days earlier, which meant I was perhaps three days' journey from the city. They would travel slower than my chariot. This was their fourth night on the road.

"I approached them cautiously, leading my horse forward, but barely able to stand. Their guards came out in chariots to confront me, but upon seeing my condition, the man in the lead chariot rushed forward and offered me a water bag. He was surprised when, using my cupped hand, I watered my horse first. Only after I gave him over half the bag did I take some for myself.

"Then the caravan leader came forward to see what his guards had intercepted. He was a grizzled merchant named Berekiah. He looked at my Egyptian chariot and iron weapons with interest, then at my condition with concern. 'You look half-dead, friend. Where are you coming from?'

"'Egypt,' I said simply. 'I need to reach Madyan.'

"He nodded slowly. 'We just left Madyan four days ago. You should have found water before now. There are two small oases with wells along the route you just traveled. One is about five days back the way you came, and another is about fifteen days further west. Did you not see them?'

"My heart sank. 'I traveled by night to conserve water. I must have passed them in the darkness.'

"'They're set back from the road,' Berekiah explained. 'You have to know where to look. The rocky terrain hides them from casual view, and the rough ground means you can only approach them on foot. They are several hundred cubits off the main road. We will stop at the first one to refill our water as we continue west.' He paused, looking at me thoughtfully. 'You're fortunate we came along when we did.'

"'The Most High was watching over me,' I said.

"He gestured toward my chariot. 'That's fine Egyptian work. It's not a military issue, but fine work just the same. You know how to drive a chariot. Are you a soldier?'

"'I used to be,' I said carefully. 'But that life is behind me now. In fact, I was planning to sell this chariot and the weapons I have. My friends gave them to me as a parting gift to help deal with the dangers on the road. I need money to start my new life. I don't suppose you'd be interested in purchasing a chariot and some really fine weapons?'

"His eyes lit up. We both knew how valuable such things were in these lands. 'I might be. Let's discuss it after you've rested, had some food, and had more water. You are in no condition to bargain now, and I am not a thief.'

"That night, over a good meal and much water, I negotiated the sale of my chariot, my iron weapons, and my horse. Berekiah drove a hard bargain, but seeing the iron weapons, his guards stepped into the discussion, begging him to buy them. In the end, he was fair. The gold he gave me would be enough to start a new life in Madyan. I only kept an iron knife and my heavy walking staff. Everything else was sold.

"I purchased enough food and water from their supplies for ten days. Once I'd rested and regained my strength, I would continue to Madyan on foot, pulling my cart. That way, I was just another traveler, not an Egyptian fugitive.

"The next morning, the caravan prepared to continue its journey westward. As they formed up to leave, I watched one of Berekiah's guards climb into my former chariot, clearly pleased with his new assignment. He noticed me watching and raised his hand in salute, a gesture of respect I had not expected. I returned it, then watched as the caravan moved out, the dust of their passing slowly settling in the morning air."

"You were right when you said the Most High had other plans," Eliezer said.

"Indeed. I remained under my makeshift tent for another full day. As I rested, I found myself thinking about everything that had brought me to this moment. Five years ago, I had been an advisor to Pharaoh, living in luxury, respected at court, with a beautiful family. Now I was a fugitive pulling a cart through the desert, and everything I owned of value had been sold for gold to start over.

"But strangely, I felt no regret. The weight I'd carried for so long—the secrets, the dual identity, the constant vigilance—was gone. For the first time in my life, I could simply be who I was: a Hebrew, a follower of the Most High, heading toward people who I hoped would accept me without questions or suspicions.

"Nashwa and my daughters would never see this freedom. That grief would never leave me. But perhaps their deaths had purchased this liberty for me, however unwillingly. I could honor them by living fully in this new life, no longer hiding my ancestry.

"I ate well, drank freely from my newly purchased supplies, and felt life returning to my body. As the sun set that evening, I packed my cart and set out eastward toward Madyan. Traveling in the coolness of night made pulling the cart far less demanding than it would have been in the brutal heat of day. I moved slowly but steadily, and with each passing hour, I felt stronger."

"After five nights of travel, I reached the outskirts of Madyan just as the sun was rising. The grasslands were greener than I had imagined, dotted with small orchards and grazing flocks in the distance. It was so different from Egypt. No massive monuments declaring the glory of Pharaoh. No teeming cities with their noise and crowds. Just an oasis and a small city, open land, scattered camps, and shepherds moving quietly with their flocks.

"The people I passed greeted me openly, without suspicion. In Egypt, a stranger with a cart would have been questioned, assessed for threat or opportunity. Here, several people simply called out greetings as I passed, asking if I needed directions or water. One family even offered me dates from their evening meal.

"I felt something I hadn't felt in years: the simple comfort of being among people who weren't judging my bloodline, who didn't care about court politics or ancient prophecies. Just shepherds, living their lives, following the Most High in peace.

"I traveled during the daytime now. As I walked along, pulling my cart, I encountered a group of men heading home from their work in the mango orchards, carrying some of the fruit they had been tending.

"I stopped them and asked, 'Friends, I'm looking for work as a shepherd. I have some experience with flocks and am hoping to find an honest clan to work with, perhaps eventually starting my own small flock. Can you recommend anyone?'

"They looked at each other, and one of them, an older man with a weathered face, spoke up. 'There are several shepherds in the area, but if you want my advice, there's only one man you should trust. His name is Jethro. He is both a shepherd and a priest of Midian. He is honest and treats his workers fairly.'

"'A priest?' I asked, interested.

"'Yes, a priest of the Most High. And you're in luck,' another worker added with a grin. 'He only has one son, but the rest are daughters, seven of them. He's always looking for good men to help with his flocks. Work hard and prove yourself, and who knows? Maybe he'll marry one of them off to you!'

"The others laughed good-naturedly at this, but I could see they were serious about Jethro's character. 'Where can I find him?' I asked.

"'His grazing lands are to the south, about a day and a half's walk from here. There's a well where his daughters water the flocks most evenings. You'll find them there, or you can follow the main path to his camp. Anyone can point you in the right direction.'

"I thanked them, and they continued on their way, leaving me standing at the edge of my new life."

The Confrontation at the Well of Jethro

"So that's how you came to our grandfather's well and saved mother and her sisters," Gershom said.

"Yes. I have always believed that the chance meeting with the orchard workers was planned by the Most High to both save your mother and bring me to your grandfather's household.

"I approached the well late on my second day of travel. I heard shouting before I saw anything. Women's voices, raised in anger and fear, and men's laughter. Grabbing my staff, I quickened my pace, leaving my cart behind, and came over a small rise to see the well below.

"What I saw made my blood run cold. There were seven men, all rough-looking, armed with clubs and two short swords. They were in the process of binding a group of young women. Six were already tied, their hands behind their backs, sitting on the ground. The seventh was still fighting, kicking at one of the men as two others tried to hold her still.

"I recognized immediately what I was seeing. These weren't local shepherds disputing water rights. They were slavers.

"Although there were seven of them, my staff would be sufficient. I doubted they had any real fighting training. I moved quickly down the slope. The men were so focused on subduing the last woman that they didn't notice me until I was nearly upon them. The first man I reached was tying a rope to a seated woman, binding her to the others so they could be led away. I brought my staff down hard across his arm, and I heard the bone crack. He screamed and fell away.

"The others turned, startled. One reached for his club, but I was faster. I swept his legs out from under him and struck him across the head as he fell. He went down and didn't move.

"'Get away from them!' I shouted.

"Two of the men released the fighting woman and came at me together. I used their momentum against them, stepping aside as they charged by. I used my staff to trip the first one, sending him sprawling face down in the dirt, while striking the other hard in the ribs. He staggered back, gasping for air.

"The one who had staggered back pulled a short sword. He was more cautious now, circling me. I kept my staff ready, watching his eyes while keeping the others in view. The remaining men hung back, unwilling to engage while their companion still fought. When he lunged, I sidestepped and brought my staff down on his wrist. I heard the bone crack as his sword fell from his hand. He screamed and immediately retreated.

"Five were still standing, though one had a broken arm and another a fractured wrist. They looked at each other, then at their fallen companions, then at me. They had no desire to continue this fight. Without a word, they all turned and fled, leaving behind the two unconscious ones.

"I turned to the women. They were staring at me with wide eyes, breathing hard. The one who had been fighting was now free, and she immediately began untying her sisters.

"'Are you hurt?' I asked.

"The one doing the untying, who I would later learn was Zipporah, your mother, shook her head. 'Bruises, nothing more. You came just in time. Any longer and they would have had us all tied up, ready for travel.'

"As she helped her sisters free themselves, one of the unconscious men suddenly got to his feet and, without looking back, ran off. I went to the other slaver. He was breathing, but still unconscious. I dragged him away from the well. After getting the rope they had tried to use on Zipporah, I tied his hands in front of him and bound his feet together. I asked for a cup of water, which I threw on his face. He sputtered, tried to get up, but fell back down. He rolled over into a sitting position and looked at me defiantly.

"'You're not going anywhere unless I let you,' I told him. He looked at my staff, then me, and decided I had the advantage. He was sullen at first, but when I reminded him that I could easily turn him over to the local authorities or to Jethro himself for fatherly justice, he decided to talk.

"He told me they had heard about Jethro's daughters coming to the well each evening to water their flocks. Seven young women, alone, seemed like easy targets for capture and sale in the slave markets to the north. They had been watching for several days, waiting for the right moment.

"'We thought they'd be helpless,' he said bitterly. 'But these women fought like wildcats. One nearly broke my nose before we got them tied up. Then you showed up.' He rubbed the knot on his head.

"'You picked the wrong women to target,' I told him. 'And the wrong day to do it.' I untied his hands and told him to untie his feet himself. As he stood up, still a little dizzy, I said, 'Get out of here before I change my mind about letting you go.'

"He stumbled away, rubbing his aching head, and I turned back to the well where Jethro's daughters had finished untying themselves."

Eliezer and Gershom were silent for a moment, absorbing what they'd just heard.

"That's incredible!" Gershom finally said, his eyes wide. "You really taught them a lesson. I bet they never came back."

"We never saw them again, so yes, they learned a harsh lesson, but they still had their lives.

"With the slavers gone, I turned to Zipporah and her sisters. They were remarkably composed for what they'd just been through. Your mother, in particular, showed no fear, only anger at what had nearly happened.

"She was the first to approach me properly. 'I am Zipporah,' she said, extending her hand in the manner of greeting among equals. 'These are my sisters.' She introduced them one by one, and I noticed how the others deferred to her, though I would later learn she was not the eldest.

"Zipporah stood out from her sisters. She had dark hair, strong features, and eyes that missed nothing. But what struck me most was the way she carried herself. She moved with the confidence of someone accustomed to handling difficult situations.

"'What's your name?' she asked directly.

"'Moses,' I said. 'I'm a traveler, newly arrived in the area. I was told there might be work with the flocks.'

"'Well, Moses,' she said with the smallest hint of a smile, 'you've certainly made a strong introduction. My father will want to meet the man who scattered seven slavers with nothing but a staff.' She glanced at her sisters, who nodded in agreement. 'You must come back to our home. Father needs to hear what happened here, and we owe you proper thanks for what you did.'

"I hesitated. 'I don't want to impose.'

"'It's not an imposition,' she said firmly. 'It's hospitality. My father is Jethro, a priest of Midian, and he has one of the largest flocks in the area. He's always looking for good men to help with the sheep, if you are interested. He will need help now more than ever.' She gestured at her sisters. 'After today, he'll want capable men around even more.'

"I agreed to go with them and went to retrieve my cart, which I'd left just past the rise above the well. When I returned, the women had finished watering their flocks and were preparing to drive them home. I fell in beside them, pulling my cart, and we made our way toward their compound as the setting sun touched the horizon.

"The sisters talked among themselves as we walked, glancing at me with curiosity. Zipporah walked at the front, leading the way, occasionally calling out instructions to her sisters about managing the flocks. I could see she was the natural leader among them, the one they looked to when decisions needed to be made.

"When we arrived at their home—a substantial compound with

stone walls and several buildings—Zipporah told me to wait in the courtyard while she went to find her father. I stood there with my cart, suddenly aware of how travel-worn I must look, how out of place.

"Moments later, she emerged with a man I immediately recognized as someone of substance. Your grandfather was perhaps forty-five years old, with a long beard just beginning to show touches of gray. He wore the simple robes of a shepherd-priest. His gaze was steady and direct, his eyes sharp and intelligent. He stood tall and strong, exuding quiet authority.

"Zipporah quickly told him what had happened at the well—the slavers, the attack, how I had intervened. She didn't exaggerate or dramatize; she simply told the facts. But even in her plain telling, I could see your grandfather's expression grow more serious.

"When she finished, he turned to me and studied my face for a long moment. Then he smiled. 'Moses, is it? You have done my family a great service today. I am Jethro, priest of Midian and father to these troublesome daughters.' He said the last part with obvious affection, and the sisters laughed.

"'I only did what anyone should do,' I said.

"'But most would not,' he replied. 'Come, you must stay for our evening meal. We have much to discuss: the attack, your journey here, and perhaps this work you're seeking.' He gestured toward the main house. 'Please, be welcome in my home.'

"'I am grateful for your hospitality,' I said as I followed him inside, while several of his daughters giggled behind us.

"You should know it took almost six months before your grandfather suggested to your mother that we should marry. He wanted to verify my trustworthiness. It was one thing to save his daughters; another to become part of the family. And you all know the rest of the story. You have heard it many times."

Preparing to Leave

"Thank you, father," Eliezer said. Gershom nodded, adding his thanks also. Eliezer continued, "We understand why you kept your previous life a secret. You were ensuring that nothing about you would get back to Egypt and that the life you were building wouldn't be destroyed. I am sure I speak for Gershom also when I say, you have given us reason to love and respect you even more."

"I agree," Gershom said.

"You are fine sons. Thank you. It will be morning in a few hours," Moses said. "We need to get as much rest as we can. We start a long trek down the mountain and back home."

Gershom put out the campfire and then went to his bedroll. Eliezer and Moses crawled into theirs and quickly fell asleep.

Moses woke at the first streaks of dawn, as he always did. For a moment, he lay there, listening to the sound of his sons' breathing. Last night, he had told them everything. Every secret he had carried for decades, every truth he had hidden to protect this life they had built together.

He briefly wondered if he had made the right choice. Would they see him differently now? Not just as their father, the shepherd and husband, but as the man who had killed, who had commanded armies, who had lived a life of violence and court intrigue before finding peace here?

But Eliezer's words echoed in his mind: "You have given us reason to love and respect you even more." Perhaps he had underestimated them. Perhaps they understood better than he had hoped. They now knew that a man's past need not define his present, that the Most High could redeem even the most broken life and make it new.

The sun would rise soon. It was time to go home.

Moses roused his two sons, and they began their morning tasks. Gershom started cooking breakfast as Eliezer began putting the last of their equipment into their cart. Over the years, their father had built several of these carts using his original as the starting point. The chariot-style axle and wheels were the most important part, since they made pulling the cart easy. When Nazim made the first cart, he placed the axle in the center, so that when loaded properly, the cart was balanced and all your energy went into pulling it. Almost no energy was needed to lift it. All the family's carts followed that design.

They quickly ate their morning meal, then finished loading the last of the supplies.

Gershom and Eliezer went to the flock and started moving them down the mountainside. Eliezer took the lead sheep to the front, and the rest began to follow her slowly down the trail.

Gershom came back and began pulling the cart at the rear of the flock. Every once in a while, he would have to park the cart and drive a few wandering strays back into the group with a hard knock of his staff. That eventually discouraged the worst wanderers.

Moses did his best to keep up.

As they descended, he watched his sons work the flock. They moved with practiced ease, anticipating the sheep's movements, working together without needing words. Gershom caught his father's eye once and smiled. It was not his usual casual smile, but something deeper. Understanding, perhaps. Or pride in knowing where he came from.

That evening, as they ate their simple meal, Eliezer asked quietly, "Father, do you ever miss it? Egypt, I mean. The power, the court, the..." he trailed off.

Moses considered the question carefully. "I miss nothing of Egypt except the people I lost there. Your grandmother Asati, who saved my life. Nari, my teacher and confidant. Miriam, who never stopped believing I could be better than I was. Nashwa and your sisters, who deserved a longer life. And Semri. Dear Semri, without whom I wouldn't be here. His training saved your mother and me."

He looked at both his sons. "But I do not miss the man I was. That man became lost, divided, never truly at peace. Here, with your mother, with you, with the flocks under the sky, is where I belong. This is the life the Most High meant for me."

Gershom nodded slowly. "And yet, you still remember how to fight. How to lead. Those skills haven't left you."

"No," Moses admitted. "They haven't. I have prayed that I would never need them. But if the Most High calls me to use them in His service, if my body will cooperate, I will be ready."

They were bringing the flock down the west side of the mountain. It was about a six-day journey east from their home, just past Horeb, the mountain of God. No one else came this far, so they had good grazing all summer and no contention with other shepherds. It was worth the extra effort.

By late afternoon, they were close to the base of the mountain and stopped to set up camp for the night. They were all tired from the night before, and as soon as Gershom found a suitable place, they stopped.

They set up a simple traveling camp, with a simple meal, no tents, and split up their sleeping positions to surround the flock. Tonight, the stars were their covering.

His sons rose early, prepared another simple meal, packed their bedding, and within a couple of hours, they reached the plain below. Turning the flock west, they headed toward Horeb and home. The journey would take them six days, possibly longer, as they walked slowly enough for their father to keep up.

By the third day, Moses' legs were protesting. At eighty years old, climbing down mountains was harder than it used to be. There was a time when he could have made this journey in half the time, barely breaking a sweat. Now, each step reminded him that his body had accumulated decades of hard use: battles, desert marches, and years of labor with the flocks.

But he didn't complain. Gershom and Eliezer were patient, never pushing the pace beyond what he could keep up with. They knew their father was struggling, though he tried to hide it. They were good sons.

As Moses watched Gershom pull the cart, he thought of Nazim. He had saved his life with that design: the chariot-style axle, the balanced load, and the brush attachment that had hidden his tracks in the desert.

Moses had built numerous carts over the years, each one slightly improving on Nazim's original design. Every time he built one, he thought of his driver and of the friendship they had shared. The risks Nazim had taken to give Moses a chance at survival saved his life. These carts were more than tools. They were a memorial to a man who had shown him kindness when he could have looked the other way. Moses wondered sometimes what had become of him. Had he thrived during his final years helping Asati? Had he thought of his Hebrew friend, wondering if he had survived?

Moses' hands, calloused from years of holding a shepherd's staff, still remembered what it felt like to grip a sword, to hold a bow, to command from a chariot. Muscle memory doesn't fade completely, even when muscles do. He wondered sometimes if the Most High had preserved those memories, those skills, for some purpose yet to be revealed.

As they traveled across the plain toward Horeb, Moses found himself seeing the landscape differently than he had for forty years. Before, he had seen it as a shepherd. Good grazing here, water sources there, or shelter from storms in those rocks. Now, having told his sons everything, he saw it through both sets of eyes: the shepherd's and the soldier's.

Those ridges would make excellent defensive positions. That wadi could hide an ambush. That open ground would favor chariots. Moses shook his head, trying to push away those thoughts. He was now an old shepherd, no longer a warrior. He had left that life behind in the desert sand forty years ago.

And yet, he couldn't quite silence the newly aroused part of himself that thought tactically, that assessed terrain for threats and opportunities. Perhaps some things, once learned, could never be fully unlearned.

The Burning Bush

After several more days of travel, they were a short distance from Horeb, the mountain of God. As they approached, Eliezer, who was still leading the flock with his trained leader, called out. "Father, there is an odd sight on the mountain of God."

Gershom called back, somewhat irritated, "This is no time for

216

joking, Eliezer."

"I am not joking. Look about five hundred cubits up the west edge of the mountain. You can see something glowing. It looks like fire, but it's not spreading."

Moses' eyes were still sharp. Following his son's directions, he could see a bush on the western edge of the mountain that appeared to be on fire. He yelled up to Eliezer to stop. Then, as they stood there and watched, it continued to burn, but the fire didn't consume the bush. The three of them stood transfixed, unable to look away. None of them had ever seen anything like it.

Moses yelled to Eliezer to move the flock just past the mountain. That would give them a better view. The longer Moses watched the fire burn without consuming the bush, the more certain he became that this had to be a message from the Most High. It meant he would have to go up the mountain.

Moses told Gershom and Eliezer to stop and said, "I have to go up there. I believe this is a message from the Most High."

"Are you sure?" Eliezer asked.

"It doesn't matter. The only way to be sure is to go there."

"I will go with you," Gershom said. "It is not an easy climb."

"No," Moses replied. "I must do this alone. If the Most High wants to speak with me, He will make a way."

"Please be careful," Eliezer said.

"I will. Wait here for me."

"Don't worry. We'll wait as long as it takes," Gershom said.

Moses slowly moved to the base of the west side of the mountain, and there he found a well-worn path no one had seen from the trail. He began the slow, arduous climb.

Despite his exhaustion from days of travel, despite his aching legs, Moses felt strength flowing into his body with each step. Whether from divine aid or sheer determination, he could not say.

It took Moses almost an hour to get about fifty cubits from the bush. The fire still burned, but the bush remained unburnt. His heart began to pound, though he couldn't say whether it was from the climb or anticipation.

Moses stopped for a few moments to let his heart slow down. When he took another step, a Voice called out from the midst of the bush, as if from an angel, saying, "Moses, Moses!"

Startled, Moses stopped and said, "Here I am."

When the Voice came again, he knew it was God.

God said, "Do not come near; take your sandals off your feet, because the place on which you are standing is holy ground."

Moses immediately stopped and removed his sandals. He waited, and then God said, "I am the God of your fathers, the God of Abraham, the God of Isaac, and the God of Jacob."

Moses was overwhelmed with fear and hid his face. He was afraid to look at God for fear that he would die. Looking down at the ground, Moses asked, "What do You want from me, O Most High?"

The Lord replied, "I have seen the affliction and desolation of My people who are in Egypt. I have heard their cry because of their taskmasters who oppress them, and I can see their pain and suffering. I stopped you because I have come down to rescue them from the power of the Egyptians, and to bring them up from Egypt, the land of captivity, to a land that is good and spacious, to a land overflowing with milk and honey, a land of plenty. I will give them the place of the Canaanite, the Hittite, the Amorite, the Perizzite, the Hivite, and the Jebusite. Behold, I want them to know that the cry of my children, Israel, has come to Me, and I have seen how the Egyptians unfairly oppress them."

"It is time for you to go back. I am sending you to Pharaoh to bring my people, the People of Israel, out of Egypt."

Moses, less fearful of dying, looked up and answered God, "But why me? What makes you think that I could ever go to Pharaoh and lead the children of Israel out of Egypt? I am old and ache with every step, and besides, I am only one man."

And God said, "Know this, I, your Lord God, will be with you, and this shall be the sign that it is I who has sent you: when you have brought the people out of Egypt, you shall travel with your people to this mountain to serve and worship me, your God."

Still unconvinced, Moses said to God, "Suppose I go to the People of Israel and I tell them, 'The God of your fathers sent me to you';

and they ask me, 'What is his name?' What do I tell them?"

God said to Moses, "*I Am Who I Am,*" and then He said, "You shall say this to the Israelites, '*I Am has sent me to you.*' Then you shall tell them this is My Name forever, and this is My memorial name to all generations of My people Israel. Go, gather the tribal leaders of Israel together, and say to them, 'I have seen what's being done to you in Egypt, and I have determined to free you from the affliction of the Egyptians and take you to the land of the Canaanite, the Hittite, the Amorite, the Perizzite, the Hivite, and the Jebusite, a land brimming over with milk and honey.'

"The elders of the tribes will listen to what you say. Then you, along with the elders of Israel, shall go to Pharaoh, the King of Egypt, and you shall say to him, 'God, the God of the Hebrews, has met with us. Let us go on a three-day journey into the wilderness, where we will worship the Lord our God.'

"I know that the King of Egypt won't let you go unless he is forced to. Because of his resistance, I will reach out My hand and strike Egypt with all My wonders so that he will let you go. And I will grant to my people favor and respect in the sight of the Egyptians. So that when you leave your captivity in Egypt, you will not go empty-handed. As you leave, every Hebrew woman shall insist that her neighbor and any woman who lives in her neighbor's house give to her articles of silver, articles of gold, and fine clothing. You shall put these things on your sons and daughters. In this way, you will plunder the Egyptians. You will leave your bondage carrying great possessions that are rightfully yours."

Then Moses answered the Lord and said, "What if they will not believe me or take seriously what I say? They may argue and say, 'The Lord has not appeared to you.'"

And the Lord said to Moses, "What is that in your hand?"

And he said, "My staff."

God said, "Take your staff and throw it on the ground."

So Moses threw his staff to the ground, and it became a living serpent, just like the royal symbol on the front of the crown of Pharaoh. It startled Moses, and he turned to run from it.

But the Lord God said to Moses, "Stop! Reach out your hand and grasp it by the tail."

Only because God commanded it, Moses returned to the snake and cautiously reached down his hand and caught it by its tail. To his great surprise, it became his staff again.

"You shall do this in front of the elders," said the Lord God, "so that all doubt will be removed that I, the Lord, the God of their fathers, the God of Abraham, the God of Isaac, and the God of Jacob, have appeared to you and told you to do this."

Moses was still hesitant and further argued, "What if they still do not believe?"

Then the Lord God said to him, "Put your hand into your robe where it covers your chest and take it out again."

Moses put his free hand into his robe, and when he took it out, his hand was leprous, as white as snow. Seeing his hand, Moses was afraid.

Then God said, "Put your hand into your robe again."

So, Moses obeyed and put his hand back into his robe, and when he took it out again, it was healed and no longer leprous, and Moses marveled at what he had seen.

"If they will not believe you or pay attention to the evidence of the first sign, they will believe the evidence of the second sign. But if they will not believe either of these signs or are unwilling to pay attention to what you say, you are to take some water from the Nile and pour it onto the dry ground. The water that you take out of the river will turn into blood as it falls onto the dry ground."

Moses still tried to find a way to avoid returning to Egypt and to do what the Lord was calling him to do. He could not bear going back to the land of his exile and said, "Please, Lord, You know that I am not a man of eloquent words. You know my speech is not fluent. For many years, I have been this way. You know that if I have to speak in front of a crowd, I will fumble my words and even stutter."

The Lord God said to Moses, "Listen to Me. Who made man's mouth? Who makes a man mute or the deaf, or to see or be blind? I do! I am the Lord your God. Stop complaining and go, and know that I will be with your mouth, and I will teach you what you shall say."

But even with these assurances, Moses continued to complain, to avoid this journey, saying, "Please, my Lord, send Your message of rescue to Israel by someone else. Choose someone else. I am not worthy."

Then the Lord God became angry, and the fire of His anger burned against Moses. Moses felt the heat of God's displeasure and threw himself fully to the ground.

God said, "You know that your brother, Aaron the Levite, is there in Egypt. He speaks fluently. Also, I have spoken to him, and he is coming out to meet you. When he sees you, he will be overjoyed. You must tell him what I have commanded so that he can speak the words I have given you. Know, do not doubt, that I will be with your mouth and with his mouth. Fear not, I will teach you what you are to do. Since you say you cannot speak, your brother shall speak for you; he will act as a mouthpiece for you, and you stand in the place of the Lord your God, telling Aaron what I say to you. You shall take your staff in your hand. You will use this staff to perform the signs and all the miracles that you will use to prove I, the Most High, have sent you."

As those words echoed around him, Moses looked up, and the bush was just an unburnt bush. There was no fire, no angel of the Lord. He was alone. As he got up and went back to his sandals, he realized that this ground would always be holy ground.

He went to retrieve his sandals, and two things became clear to him: First, he was not the man he used to be—strong and confident—and second, he knew he had shamed himself before the Lord. Before putting on his sandals, he went to his knees and repented his failure. As he begged God for forgiveness, he felt the warmth of the Most High sweep over him, coursing through every fiber of his body. When he stood up, he felt different. His aches seemed to fade, overshadowed by a renewed sense of purpose. He stood taller and walked more strongly. Whether this was divine healing or divine calling, he was ready for the task.

Secondly, he knew his time in Midian was over. His sons were waiting below. He would need to tell them everything and then prepare Zipporah for what was to come. He would return to Egypt and complete the task his father Amram had dreamed of. He was back on the path he had been born for, and that destiny awaited him. He raised his hands to heaven and shouted, "Thank you, O Lord Most High!"

Glossary of Gods, People, Places, and Terms

Aakhepesh – General of the Amun corps.

Aaron – Moses' brother, a Levite who remained in Egypt and served as Moses's spokesman on his return due to Moses's speech difficulties. Moses never met him during his first forty years in Egypt. Called by God to meet Moses and assist in the Exodus mission.

Abanoub – General of the Sutekh corps.

Abasi – Moses' chariot driver who was killed in the Hittite ambush.

Abenu – Commander of the Nubian archers in the Ne'arin corps.

Akhenaten – The *"Pharaoh Who is Not Named,"* who tried to convert Egypt's religion from many gods to one god, Aten, represented by the sun. He almost drove Egypt into ruin before his death. He was succeeded by Tutankhamen, who helped Egypt begin the long road to recovery.

Akhuty – Sherden commander of Ramses' twenty-five-man personal chariot group and blood-sworn bodyguard.

Ameny – Young priest of Amun-Ra who becomes part of the intrigue on the day when he gathers information for the temple. He later becomes the First Priest of Amun-Ra in Memphis when Nephura rises to the First Priest of the god in Thebes. He supports Nephura's positions, especially ridding Egypt of Moses, who he considered a Hebrew bastard, a usurper, and an anathema to everything his god stood for. Dies in a sandstorm on the way to Amun-Ra's desert temple.

Amram – Moses' father, who had prophetic dreams about his son saving his people, but died before the battle of Kadesh.

224

Amunen – The Amun-Ra spy captured by the Ne'arin, who is exposed to Ramses Nephura's and Ameny's treachery.

Amun-Ra – The chief god of Egypt with the most powerful priesthood. The god rode the sun as a chariot across the sky, bringing each new day.

Amuntankh – Young temple assassin sent by Nephura's followers to kill Moses in exile. His name means 'Amun lives.' After Moses defeats him and uses Ma'at theology to show him the corruption of his mission, he converts and is sent to Damascus with a caravan. Moses never sees him again.

Apophis – Also known as Apep, this snake god was regarded as the enemy of order and, consequently, the nemesis of Ra and Ma'at. He was the perfect deity for assassins, especially those who preferred using vipers.

Asati – Daughter of Ramses I and sister of Seti, who was married to Prince Amunthura and infertile, despite being dedicated to Satis, goddess of the First Cataract and emblem of fertility. Her husband's death proves providential in the ending of the first book, *Beginnings*, as she takes Moses as a gift from her patron Satis. Semri marries the princess, and together they raise Moses as a Prince of Egypt.

Aten – The sun god, whom Akhenaton tried to establish as the only god over Egypt. In our story, many of the priests of Egypt believed that this new god of the *Pharaoh Not Named* was taken from the God of the Hebrews, and therefore, they blamed these descendants of Israel for the pharaoh's heresy.

Bakari – The Egyptian overseer whose death led to Moses's trial and exile.

Baktari – The head of Semri's chariot group who rescued Moses from the Hittite ambush and was pivotal at the battle of Kadesh.

Basemeth – The wool merchant traveling north from Madyan, whose caravan Moses encounters. He agrees to take Amuntankh to Damascus, giving the converted assassin safe passage away from Egypt.

Bennu – The Chief Scout of Ne'arin Corps, whom Moses sent on the night mission to Kadesh, where he intercepted Ramses' scout, Narmer.

Berekiah – A merchant whose caravan finds Moses near death in the desert. He purchases Moses's Egyptian chariot, iron weapons, and a horse, providing Moses with gold to start his new life and ensuring Moses enters Midian without Egyptian identifiers.

Burning Bush – Taken from Exodus 3:1– 4:17 and is the closing event of this book, where Moses uses every excuse possible to not go back to Egypt, but the Most High overcame all of his objections, commissioning Moses to rescue his people from captivity. I have him repent of his reluctance to return, and instead, he embraces the mission the Most High has given him.

Composite bow – A bow made of wood combined with long sections of bone, glued and wrapped with linen and waxed string to the limbs, which gave their arrows a greater range, easily over 400 cubits (approximately 600 feet), compared to a little more than 300 cubits with wood alone The Egyptians learned this technology from the Hyksos, who had conquered northern Egypt, and it became an integral part of their army's success. Often made with a slight recurve, which added to their power, these bows gave the Egyptian army, especially its chariots, a distinct advantage over its enemies. Used by the most famous archers in the ancient world, the Nubians, who composed companies of 500 strong in each Egyptian corps.

Cubit – 45.72 centimeters (about 18 inches). The average length from the elbow to the tip of the longest finger of a grown man.

Derden – Leader of Moses' Sherden personal bodyguard and chariot group.

Eliezer – Moses' younger son. More intellectually gifted than his brother, he enjoyed reading anything he could get his hands on. He had Moses' gift for languages, which he picked up as needed to read the scrolls he had access to. He was very inquisitive and was constantly asking questions, sometimes to the point of irritation.

Gershom – Moses' eldest son. He was more physically gifted than his brother and enjoyed working with his hands. He was more interested in his father's exploits in war and battle stories.

Greatest of Fifty – Military rank/unit designation.

Hamatarma – Muwatalli's oldest brother, killed in the northern chariot charge at Kadesh by the Ne'arin.

Hapi – A god who was identified with the inundation and sacred water of the Nile itself and, in its divine characterization, was represented by the hippo. He was seen as the source of all fertility, as the Nile itself provided life to Egypt and her people.

Hasani – General of the Ptah corps.

Hattusili – Muwatalli's brother, who survived the chariot charge at Kadesh but was wounded in the retreat. He later became King of Hattiland. Fifteen years after the battle of Kadesh, Ramses and Hattusili signed a treaty that lasted forty years. It was the first such treaty in the ancient world.

Horan – Moses' friend who was killed in the Hittite ambush.

Horeb – The mountain of God where the burning bush encounter occurs.

Jethro – Priest of Midian and shepherd, father of seven daughters, including Zipporah and one son. A follower of the Most High and descendant of Abraham through Keturah, his wife after the death of Sarah. He takes Moses into his household after Moses rescues his daughters from slavers, eventually giving Zipporah to Moses in marriage.

Jochebed – Mother of Moses and wife of Amram, who became a wet nurse to Moses in the household of Asati and prayed fervently for his safety.

Kadesh – The fortress city in southern Syria that sparked the war between Egypt and Hattiland (Hittites), and between Ramses and Muwatalli.

Khay – Ramses' future vizier and the official who delivers Egypt's copy of the Hittite treaty to Hattusili.

Khafre – Chariot commander of the Ne'arin corps.

Khopesh – An Egyptian sickle-like sword made of bronze that could hook and pull, as well as slash and stab. It was a versatile and formidable weapon.

Korum – Moses' friend who was killed in the Hittite ambush.

Labarnas – Commander of the Hittite scout team looking for the Ne'arin.

Ma'at – The Egyptian concept of law, morality, truth, and justice rolled into one, maintaining the proper balance and order of everything. When personified, Ma'at was a goddess who regulated the stars, seasons, and actions of mortals and deities. This feminine stabilizing force drew order out of the roiling chaos from the moment of creation. Everyone, even pharaohs and the gods themselves, was subject to the demands of Ma'at.

Medjay – A specialized group of Nubian mercenaries with long, heavy-duty bronze-tipped spears, about eight cubits in length (almost 14 feet), used to defend against chariots. Every Egyptian corps had a group of Medjay.

Memphis – The city of white walls, the first capital of Egypt, and the current residence of Pharaoh. Its port, Perunifer, was the main port for all of Egypt and contained a thriving international marketplace and trading center.

Merti – The name of Moses' first daughter from his Egyptian wife, Nashwa. Her name means 'beloved,' and she was smart and inquisitive.

Mesniti – The Egyptian blacksmith or metal worker who was an important member of a large estate or the army. He could do everything from fixing a plow to repairing a sword or spear, which was critical if a battle stretched on for days.

Midian – The sparsely populated land Moses settled in after successfully surviving the events after his exile by Ramses. Some, like Jethro (see entry), Moses' father-in-law, were followers of the Most High (Yahweh). Others in Midian followed various pagan deities, including Baal-peor and Ashteroth.

Mioa – The chief counselor and all-around fixer for Nephura, First Priest of Amun-Ra in Memphis.

Miriam – Moses' sister, whose home his mother, Jochebed, was living in in her later years. She constantly challenged him not to abandon his Hebrew heritage.

Muršili – The Hittite Chief Scout, who was a chief counselor to the Hittite king. His name means the King is my Sun.

Muwatalli – The Hittite King, who initiates the Battle of Kadesh with a declaration of war. He arrives first on the battlefield, launching two surprise chariot charges at the Egyptians, a tactic that had defeated all other opponents before, but fails here due to the Egyptians' tactics, mobile chariots, Medjay, and devastating composite bows.

Nashwa – Moses' Egyptian wife and mother of Merti and Sitra. Her name meant happiness and was the great love of Moses' life. She and their daughters were killed when their boat capsized in a storm on the Nile, a loss that haunted Moses throughout his exile.

Nari – Chief maidservant of Princess Asati, whose family had been an important follower of Akhenaton's monotheistic god, Aten. As a result, her family was disgraced and lost its position in Egyptian society. Because she still secretly held the rejected beliefs, she was predisposed to favor the Hebrews.

Narmer – Ramses' night scout sent to find the Ne'arin Corps, who, the night before the battle of Kadesh, met Bennu, where they exchanged important information about Hittite weaknesses.

Nazim – A guard at the Great Estate, he was one of the best bowmen in Egypt. He had served in the army alongside Semri, his closest friend. He replaces Moses' slain driver for the battle of Kadesh and is not concerned over the Hittite prince's challenge to Moses for single combat, knowing how well trained he is.

Ne'arin – A mixed-race corps composed of foreigners, Hebrews, Egyptians, and Nubians, whom no Egyptian general wanted to command. Semri and Moses molded them together into an effective battle force. Their motto became *"We are one army; we fight as one warrior."* They defeated the northern Hittite chariot charge, saving Ramses' rear, and captured an Amun-Ra spy who had facilitated the Hittite ambush in which Moses' friends and driver died.

Nephura – Second Priest of Amun-Ra and First Priest of the god's temple in Memphis, he was a mortal enemy of the Hebrews. He despised their monotheism, which he claimed caused the heresy of the *"Pharaoh Who is Not Named,"* Akhenaton. He sought the Hebrews' complete annihilation, but especially the death of Moses, whom he considered an abomination. He built a secret network within Amun-Ra that continuously sought Moses' death or to hurt him by killing those close to him. He died in the sandstorm that struck their caravan on the way to the Amun-Ra desert temple complex, but his network continued pursuing Moses even into exile.

Nubia – A resource-rich African country that was directly south of Egypt. The source of Egyptian bowmen and the Medjay, as well as most of Egypt's gold.

Nubian bowmen – One of Egypt's most significant military resources. These archers were renowned in the ancient world for their unrivaled accuracy. Using modern distances, it was said they could put your eye out at one hundred yards. They were known as Archers of the Eye for their deadly accuracy, and Nubia was called the "Land of the Bow" by the Egyptians. It was not until the Mongol archers of Genghis Khan that their like was seen again.

Osahar – The Seer Priest of Asati, who Sostris uses to compose prayers and enchantments for Moses and Ramses' safety.

Paphnu – The commander of the Ne'arin spearmen.

Papyrus – A tall reedy plant that grew along the banks of the Nile and its tributaries. Used for everything in Egypt, from boats and baskets to making paper, rope, and string.

Paser – He was Ramses' vizier who carried over his duties from Seti into the first years of the new pharaoh's reign. He was an accomplished soldier who had served under Ramses' father. He was loyal, sharp-witted, and a good tactician.

Perunifer – The port which stood between Memphis and the west bank of the Nile. It was an international trading center, always filled with foreigners and merchants.

Piankh – P'Re's general, who, along with Paser, succeeded in rallying his remaining troops after the devastating Hittite chariot attack. Many of his soldiers, not killed in the initial onslaught, ran, but he skillfully used his remaining men and chariots to counterattack the Hittites. His bowmen attacked on the backs of the enemy chariots as they turned toward Ramses' camp, and when they later attempted to retreat, he unleashed his Nubian archers.

Ptah – The primordial god who called creation into being. His cultic center was in Memphis, where he was revered as the god of craftsmen and reincarnation, hence his ability to bring things back again, such as Queen Tuya's lost dreams in Book One, *Beginnings*.

Ramses II –Son of Seti and the Pharaoh of our story. Asati was his aunt, and Moses was his adopted cousin. He was the most famous Pharaoh in Egyptian history, living into his early 90s. The Battle of Kadesh was the titular moment at the beginning of his long reign. Usually just called Ramses in our story.

River unit – A long unit of measure equal to 20,000 cubits or about 10.5 kilometres.

Saisa – Priest/magician-in-training from the Temple of Satis, who, while getting clean water from the Nile, saw the falling star strike the Nile in front of him. He later became the first priest in the Temple of Satis at Memphis.

Satis – Goddess of the First Cataract and sender of the inundation, who was the patron of Asati. She rose in power alongside the family of Pramesse (Ramses I).

Sau-Priest – Worked protective magic, preparing amulets and potions.

Seer Priest – Interpreter priests; their office was prophetic, since they read signs and portents and interpreted dreams.

 **Sekhmet** – Fierce war goddess whose amulet many Egyptian soldiers wore. She was represented by a lion–headed woman and was called the 'Eye of Ra', representing Ra's vengeful power.

Semri – Chief of the guards at the Great Estate, who was placed in that position by Seti, whom he served under in the army before Seti's ascension to Pharaoh. He was a natural leader, an accomplished close combat fighter, and an exceptional spear thrower. He dealt with the assassins sent to kill Moses the day he was taken out of the Nile. He married Asati after her husband's death and raised and trained Moses into the exceptional warrior he became.

Sephra – Asati's servant and Nari's companion, who dies saving her at the Perunifer market.

Seti – Second Pharaoh of the New Kingdom and father of Ramses, whose recission of the Hebrew edict saved Moses and laid the groundwork for the treachery by Nephura and Ameny and the priesthood of Amun-Ra in our story.

Sirius (Alpha Canis Majoris) – The brightest star in the sky, Canis Major, the Greater Dog, represents Orion's larger hunting dog and is commonly called the "Dog Star." It was only visible for a part of the year from within Egypt. The first glimpse of Sirius in the dawn sky after its absence signaled the expected rising of the Nile and the beginning of the inundation.

Sitra – Moses' younger daughter. She enjoyed physical things, wanted to become a warrior despite her sex, and frequently watched her father and Semri train. She began training as soon as she could lift a sword.

Shu – The Egyptian god of air and wind, who is the son of the first creator god, Atum.

Sobek – The deification of crocodiles, who represented the fertility the Nile brought to the land, and could undo evil and cure ills. He was also the patron of the army, representing Egypt's strength and power. It was to him, to undo the evil Akhenaton had done and reinvigorate Egypt's strength and power, that the Hebrew newborn males were sacrificed.

Sostris – Chief priest of Satis, goddess of the First Cataract of the Nile, who was a patron of Asati. Known first to Asati's father, Ramses I, her brother Seti I also came to rely on his sound judgment. He had recently moved to Memphis, where a new temple to Satis was under construction, initially supported by Ramses and later continued by Seti when he became Pharaoh.

Spetrin – Muwatalli's middle brother, who led the southern chariot charge and was killed after breaching the Amun shield wall.

Thebes – The southern power center and sometimes the capital of Egypt, it was the seat of the priesthood of Amun-Ra. It was often called the city of a hundred gods since each of its one hundred gates was named after a god.

Toilet – Everything it took to get ready to appear in public, especially the intricate makeup worn by both men and women, particularly Egyptian royalty. Everything had to be done perfectly and touched up whenever necessary.

Tuya – Ramses' overly protective mother and wife of Seti, who had a prophetic dream about Moses and Ramses working together.

 **Wedjat Eye** – The most powerful magic symbol in ancient Egypt, it was often formed into amulets and worn for protection.

Worset – A friend of Semri and a powerful swordsman and hand-to-hand fighter, he was part of the guard at the Great Estate. He remained behind to guard the estate and Asati, while Semri, Moses, and Nazim went to war at Kadesh.

Zipporah – Moses' Midianite wife and daughter of Jethro. Strong-willed and capable, she was the natural leader among her seven sisters. Moses rescued her and her sisters from slavers at Jethro's well, leading to their marriage. Mother of Gershom and Eliezer.

Exodus and the Burning Bush passage

The biblical Burning Bush passage is challenging to render in novel form, and simply reading the biblical text can be confusing for many readers. I have compiled a composite of several translations as a paraphrase, staying true to the text's meaning while hopefully making it more readable for the casual reader. This section covers Exodus 3:1–4:17 for those who want to read the original text, using your choice of translation.

www.ingramcontent.com/pod-product-compliance
Lightning Source LLC
Chambersburg PA
CBHW070745180626
46818CB00007B/2989